REQUIEMS
FOR THE
DEPARTED

Published by Morrígan Books
Östra Promenaden 43,
602 29 Norrköping,
Sweden
www.morriganbooks.com

ISBN: 9781451539684

Editors: Gerard Brennan & Mike Stone
Cover art by Reece Notley © 2010

First Published June 2010

Queen of the Hill © Stuart Neville
Hound of Culann © Tony Black
Hats off to Mary © Garry Kilworth
Sliabh Ban © Arlene Hunt
Red Hand of Ulster © Sam Millar
She Wails Through the Fair © Ken Bruen
A Price to Pay © Maxim Jakubowski
Red Milk © T.A. Moore
Bog Man © John McAllister
The Sea is Not Full © Una McCormack
The Druid's Dance © Tony Bailie
Children of Gear © Neville Thompson
Diarmaid and Grainne © Adrian McKinty
The Fortunate Isles © Dave Hutchinson
First to Score © Garbhan Downey
Fisherman's Blues © Brian McGilloway
The Life Business © John Grant

The moral rights of the authors have been asserted.
All those characters in this publication, other than those clearly in the public domain, are fictitious and any resemblance to real persons, living or dead, is purely coincidental.

All rights reserved. No part of this publication may be reproduced or transmitted in any forms by any means, electronic or mechanical including photocopying, recoding or any information retrieval system, without prior permission, in writing, from the publisher.

The book is sold subject to the condition that it shall not, by way of trade or otherwise, be lent, resold, hired out, or otherwise circulated without the publisher's prior consent in any form of binding or cover other than that in which it is published and without a similar condition including this condition being imposed on the subsequent purchaser.

REQUIEMS
FOR THE
DEPARTED

EDITED BY GERARD BRENNAN & MIKE STONE

MORRIGAN BOOKS

Available titles from Morrígan Books

THE EVEN
by T. A. Moore

HOW TO MAKE MONSTERS
by Gary McMahon

VOICES
Edited by Mark S. Deniz & Amanda Pillar

GRANTS PASS
Edited by Amanda Pillar & Jennifer Brozek

DEAD SOULS
Edited by Mark S. Deniz

THE PHANTOM QUEEN AWAKES
Edited by Mark S. Deniz & Amanda Pillar

ACKNOWLEDGMENTS

The editors raise their glasses to toast everyone at Morrigan Books for their enthusiasm and commitment, especially Mark Deniz, Amanda Pillar and Reece Notley.

And *sláinte* also to Mihai Adascilitei, Pete Kempshall, Ruth Merriam and Sharon Ring, who are proofers without peer.

So, what's next, guys?

FOREWORD
GERARD BRENNAN, 2010

Requiems for the Departed first popped into existence as a fledgling thought when Morrígan Books' top boy, Mark Deniz, approached me with the idea of putting together a crime fiction anthology for him. He tentatively suggested an Irish theme as he knew I was working hard on my blog, Crime Scene NI, reviewing Irish crime fiction and interviewing a number of the top authors in the sub-genre. Basically, I'd fooled him into thinking I knew a thing or two. So, I did what any rogue would do, I told him I was the ideal man for the job and he could look forward to the best collection he'd ever read.

Seemed like a good idea at the time.

But then I had to actually deliver the anthology.

However, Mark had brought this to me at the perfect time. My good friend and uber-talented writing contemporary, Mike Stone, was due over to Ireland to visit me and my family soon after Mark's proposal. I figured that if anybody could help me pull this thing together, it was Mike. He'd been my first reader for years and I knew he'd a knack for editing and a brutally straightforward approach to feedback. I could rely on him to keep me honest.

Mike agreed to help me out and with all his usual enthusiasm, got the ball rolling immediately with a lengthy chat or three on the theme of the collection. We were both aware that the mighty Ken Bruen had recently edited an Irish crime fiction anthology titled, *Dublin Noir,* and rumour had it that the equally mighty Colin Bateman was working on a similar offering with a Belfast flavour, so straight crime fiction was out the window.

We batted a few ideas back and forth, deciding on crime fiction with supernatural elements, as a lot of the work coming out of the Morrígan stable was of the dark fantasy and horror genre, and so this would have been a natural transition. However, crime fiction with some supernatural elements seemed a somewhat unfocused genre tag. We needed something with more direction. Of course, the answer was staring us in the face the whole time. After all, the Morrígan, our publisher's namesake, is only one of the most powerful figures in Irish mythology. Why not see if we could find a way to get her and all her friends into the book?

And so, with the theme settled, Mike and I went panhandling through our respective lists of writing contacts and finished up with seventeen bloody marvellous stories that...well, let them speak for themselves.

So flip the page and get stuck in to *Requiems for the Departed*; you won't be disappointed.

MIKE STONE, 2010

The weekend Gerard refers to in his introduction above is one I remember well, in particular, the morning we spent at Quay Point — a spit of coastline located a few hundred yards from the centre of Dundrum village. We went there to teach my daughter to skim stones across the water. Kids have their uses, and giving adults the excuse to indulge in childlike pastimes is one of them.

Gerard was rattling off some of the names he'd thought of inviting to this anthology and, as I listened, my interest grew into excitement, and then kept on climbing, passing right through nervous anticipation and six degrees of trepidation to a state best described as "bricking it". The writers he was so casually bandying around were the very novelists whose names graced the spines on my bookshelves. The sort of names that crop up whenever there's a crime writing award being handed out, usually in the shape of a dagger. Not to be outdone, I mentioned a handful of writers in my address book that could boast a smattering of silverware and bestselling novels.

"Blimey," we said (because my daughter was in earshot). How on earth did we — a couple of young upstarts working for an indie book publisher — think we were going to pull this off? If we didn't watch our step, we'd end up with one of those dagger-shaped awards shoved where the sun don't shine (and I'm not talking about Burnley).

In the event, we needn't have worried. The people whose work you are about to read proved to be a professional, friendly and hard-working lot, giving freely of their time and knowledge, even when the editors were pressing for yet another (probably) needless revision.

You know, I don't think any of 'em twigged that they were dealing with a couple of upstarts. I actually think we got away with it.

But let's keep it between ourselves, eh?

TABLE OF CONTENTS

QUEEN OF THE HILL • STUART NEVILLE _____ 1

HOUND OF CULANN • TONY BLACK _____ 13

HATS OFF TO MARY • GARRY KILWORTH _____ 21

SLIABH BAN • ARLENE HUNT _____ 33

RED HAND OF ULSTER • SAM MILLAR _____ 53

SHE WAILS THROUGH THE FAIR • KEN BRUEN _____ 83

A PRICE TO PAY • MAXIM JAKUBOWSKI _____ 95

RED MILK • T.A. MOORE _____ 105

BOG MAN • JOHN MCALLISTER _____ 127

THE SEA IS NOT FULL • UNA MCCORMACK _____ 141

THE DRUID'S DANCE • TONY BAILIE _____ 161

THE CHILDREN OF GEAR • NEVILLE THOMPSON _____ 179

DIARMAID AND GRAINNE • ADRIAN MCKINTY _____ 185

THE FORTUNATE ISLES • DAVE HUTCHINSON _____ 203

FIRST TO SCORE • GARBHAN DOWNEY _____ 231

FISHERMAN'S BLUES • BRIAN MCGILLOWAY _____ 257

THE LIFE BUSINESS • JOHN GRANT _____ 267

ULSTER

QUEEN OF THE HILL
WRITTEN BY STUART NEVILLE

Queen Macha wasn't a difficult choice for my story. After all, my home town of Armagh is named after her. So Ard Macha, meaning Macha's high place, becomes Queen of the Hill, and she allows me to set a story in my own neck of the woods for the first time. But Macha is a slippery customer, and she could be any one of three mythical figures. Rather than choosing one, my Queen of the Hill takes a little from each. For example, the legend of the race against the king's horses in which she gave birth to twins as she crossed the finish line becomes a game of poker and a ruined pair of shoes.

But one aspect of the legend is universal in all versions: her domination of the men she rules. She is a fearsome warrior, of course, but she also used her sexuality to control those who desired her. In other words, she was that great archetype of noir fiction, the character that drove so many men to their dooms: she was the original *femme fatale.*

Watch out, or she'll be the death of you.

—

Cam the Hun set off from his flat on Victoria Street with fear in his heart and heat in his loins. He pulled his coat tight around him. There'd be no snow for Christmas, but it might manage a frost.

Not that he cared much about Christmas this year. If he

did this awful thing, if he could actually go through with it, he intended drinking every last drop of alcohol in the flat. He'd drink until he passed out, and drink some more when he woke up. With any luck, he'd stay under right through to Boxing Day.

Davy Pollock told Cam the Hun he could come back to Orangefield. The banishment would be lifted, he could return and see his mother, so long as he did as Davy asked. But Cam the Hun knew he wouldn't be able to face her if he did the job, not on Christmas, no matter how badly he wanted to spend the day at her bedside. He'd been put out of the estate seven years ago for "running with the taigs", as Davy put it. Still and all, Davy didn't mind coming to Cam the Hun when he needed supplies from the other side. When Es and blow were thin on the ground in Armagh, just like any other town, the unbridgeable divide between Loyalist and Republican narrowed pretty quickly. Cam the Hun had his uses. He had that much to be grateful for.

He crossed towards Barrack Street, the Mall on his right, the old prison on his left. Christmas lights sprawled across the front of the gaol, ridiculous baubles on such a grim, desperate building. The Church of Ireland cathedral loomed up ahead, glowing at the top of the hill, lit up like a stage set. He couldn't see the Queen's house from here, but it stood just beneath the cathedral. It was an old Georgian place, three storeys, and would've cost a fortune before the property crash.

She didn't pay a penny for it. The Queen of the Hill won her palace in a game of cards.

Anne Mahon and her then-boyfriend had rented a flat on the top floor from Paddy Dolan, a lawyer who laundered cash for the IRA through property investment. She was pregnant, ready to pop at any moment, when Dolan and the boyfriend started a drunken game of poker. When the boyfriend was down to his last ten-pound note, he boasted of Anne's skill, said she could beat any man in the country. Dolan challenged her to a game. She refused, but Dolan wouldn't let it be. He said if she didn't play him, he'd put her and her fuckwit boyfriend out on the street that very night, pregnant or not.

Her water broke just as she laid out the hand that won the house, and Paddy Dolan's shoes were ruined. Not that it mattered in the end. The cops found him at the bottom of Newry Canal, tied to the driver's seat of his 5-Series BMW, nine days after he handed over the deeds. The boyfriend lasted a week longer. A bullet in the gut did for him, but the 'Ra let Anne keep the house. They said they wouldn't evict a young woman with newborn twins. The talk around town was a Sinn Féin councillor was sweet on her and smoothed things over with the balaclava boys.

Anne Mahon knew how to use men in that way. That's what made her Queen of the Hill. Once she got her claws into you, that was that. You were clean fucked.

Like Cam the Hun.

He kept his head down as he passed the shaven-headed men smoking outside the pub on Barrack Street. They knew who he was, knew he ran with the other sort, and glared as he walked by. One of them wore a Santa hat with a Red Hand of Ulster badge pinned to the brim.

As Cam the Hun began the climb up Scotch Street, the warmth in his groin grew with the terror in his stomach. The two sensations butted against each other somewhere beneath his navel. It was almost a year since he'd last seen her. That long night had left him drained and walking like John Wayne. She'd made him earn it, though. Two likely lads had been dealing right on her doorstep, and he'd sorted them out for her.

Back then he'd have done anything for a taste of the Queen, but as she took the last of him, his fingers tangled in her dyed crimson hair, he noticed the blood congealing on his swollen knuckles. The image of the two boys' broken faces swamped his mind, and he swore right then he'd never touch her again. She was poison. Like the goods she distributed from her fortress on the hill, too much would kill you, but there was no such thing as enough.

He walked to the far side of the library on Market Street. Metal fencing portioned off a path up the steep slope. The council was wasting more money renovating the town centre, leaving the area between the library and the closed-down cinema covered in rubble. Christmas Eve revellers puffed on cigarettes outside the theatre, girls draped with tinsel, young men shivering in their shirtsleeves. The sight of them caused dark thoughts to pass behind Cam the Hun's eyes. He seized on the resentment, brought it close to his heart. He'd need all the anger and hate he could muster.

He'd phoned the Queen that afternoon and told her it had been too long. He needed her.

"Tonight," she'd said, "Christmas party at my place."

The house came into view as Cam the Hun climbed the slope past the library. Last house on the terrace to his left, facing the theatre across the square, the cathedral towering over it all. Her palace, her fortress. The fear slammed into his belly, and he stopped dead.

Could he do it? He'd done worse things in his life. She was a cancer in Armagh, feeding off the misery she sowed with her powders and potions. The world would be no poorer without her. She'd offloaded her twin sons on their grandmother and rarely saw them. No one depended on her but the dealers she owned, and they'd have Davy Pollock to turn to when she was gone. No, the air in this town could only be sweeter for her passing. The logic of it was insurmountable. Cam the Hun could and would do this thing.

But he loved her.

The sudden weight of it forced the air from his lungs. He knew it was a foolish notion, a symptom of his weakness and her power over him. But the knowledge went no further than his head. His heart and loins knew different.

One or two of the smokers outside the theatre noticed him, this slight figure with his coat wrapped tight around him. If he stood rooted to the spot much longer, they would remember him. When they heard the news the next day, they would recall his face. Cam the Hun thought of the ten grand the job would pay and started walking.

For a moment he considered veering right into the theatre bar, shouldering his way through the crowd and ordering a pint of Stella and a shot of Black Bush. Instead, he thought of his debts. And there'd be some left over to pay for home-help for his mother, even if it was only for a month or two. He headed left, towards the Queen's house.

His chest strained as he neared the top of the hill, his breath misting around him. He gripped the railing by her door and willed his heart to slow. Jesus, he needed to get more exercise. That would be his New Year's resolution. Get healthy. He rang the doorbell.

The muffled rumble of Black Sabbath's *Supernaut* came from inside. Cam the Hun listened for movement in the hall. When none came, he hit the doorbell twice more. He watched a shadow move against the ceiling through the glass above the front door. Something obscured the point of light at the peephole. He heard a bar move aside and three locks snap open. Warm air ferried the sweet tang of cannabis and perfume out into the night.

"Campbell Hunter," she said. "It's been a while."

She still wore her hair dyed crimson red with a black streak at her left temple. A black corset top revealed a trail from her deep cleavage, along her flat stomach, to the smooth skin above her low-cut jeans. Part of the raven tattoo was just visible above the button fly. He remembered the silken feel against his lips, the scent of her, the firmness of her body. She could afford the best work; the surgeons left little sign of her childbearing, save for the scar that cut the raven in two.

"A year," Cam the Hun said. "Too long."

She stepped back, and he crossed her threshold knowing it would be the last time. She locked the steel-backed door and lowered the bar into place. Neither bullet nor battering ram could break through. He followed her to the living room. Ozzy Osbourne wailed over Tony Iommi's guitar. A black, artificial Christmas tree stood in the corner, small skulls, crows and inverted crosses as ornaments among the red tinsel. Men and women lay about on cushions and blankets, their lids drooping over distant eyes. Spoons and foil wraps, needles and rolled-up money, papers and tobacco, crumbs of resins and wafts of powder.

"Good party," Cam the Hun said, his voice raised above the music.

"You know me," she said as she took a bottle of Gordon's gin and two glasses from the sideboard. "I'm the hostess with mostest. Come on."

As she brushed past him, sparks leaping between their bodies, Cam the Hun caught her perfume through the room's mingled aromas. A white-hot bolt crackled from his brain down to his groin. She headed to the stairs in the hall, stopped, turned on her heel, showed him the maddening undulations of her figure. "Well?" she asked. "What are you waiting for?"

Cam the Hun forced one foot in front of the other and followed her up the stairs. The rhythm of her hips held him spellbound, and he tripped. She looked back over her naked shoulder and smiled down at him. He returned the smile as he thanked God the knife in his coat pocket had a folding blade. He found his feet and stayed behind her as she climbed the second flight to her bedroom on the top floor.

The décor hadn't changed in a year, blacks and reds, silks and satins. Suspended sheets of shimmering fabric formed a canopy over the wrought-iron bedstead. A huge mound of pillows in all shapes and sizes lay at one end. He wondered if she still had the cuffs, or the—

Cam the Hun stamped on that thought. He had to keep his mind behind his eyes and between his ears, not let it creep down to where it could do him no good.

"Take your coat off," she said. She set the glasses on the dressing table and poured three fingers of neat gin into each.

He hung his coat on her bedpost, careful not to let the knife clang against the iron. She handed him a glass. He sat on the edge of the bed and took a sip. He tried not to cough at the stinging juniper taste. He failed.

Somewhere beneath the gin's cloying odour, and the soft sweetness of her perfume, he caught the hint of another smell. Something lower, meaner, like ripe meat. The alcohol reached his belly. He swallowed again to keep it there.

The Queen of the Hill smiled her crooked smile and sat in the chair facing him. She hooked one leg over its arm, her jeans hinting at secrets he already knew. She took a mouthful of gin, washed it around her teeth, and hissed as it went down.

"I'm glad you called," she said.

"Are you?"

"Of course," she said. She winked and let a finger trace the shape of her left breast. "And not just for that."

Cam the Hun tried to quell the stirring in his trousers by studying the black painted floorboards. "Oh?" he said.

"There's trouble coming," she said. "I'll need your help."

He allowed himself a glance at her. "What kind of trouble?"

"The Davy Pollock kind."

His stomach lurched. He took a deeper swig of gin, forced it down. His eyes burned.

"He's been spreading talk about me," she said. "Says he wants me out of the way. Says he wants my business. Says he'll pay good money to anyone who'll do it for him."

"Is that right?" Cam the Hun asked.

"That's right." She let her leg drop from the arm of the chair, her heel like a gunshot on the floor, and sat forward. "But he's got no takers. No one on that side of town wants the fight. They know I've too many friends."

He managed a laugh. "Who'd be that stupid?"

"Exactly," she said.

He drained the glass and coughed. His eyes streamed, and when he sniffed back the scorching tears, he got that ripe meat smell again. His stomach wanted to expel the gin, but he willed it to be quiet.

"So, what do you want me to do?" he asked.

She swallowed the last of her gin and said, "Him."

He dropped his glass. It didn't shatter, but rolled across the floor to stop at her feet. "What?"

"I want you to do him," she said.

He could only blink and open his mouth.

"It'll be all right," she said. "I've cleared it with everyone that matters. His own side have wanted shot of him for years. Davy Pollock is a piece of shit. He steals from his own neighbours, threatens old ladies and children, talks like he's the big man when everyone knows he's an arsewipe. You'd be doing this town a favour."

Cam the Hun shook his head. "I can't," he said.

"Course you can." She smiled at him. "Besides, there's fifteen grand in it for you. And you can go back to Orangefield to see your mother. Picture it. You could have Christmas dinner with your ma tomorrow."

"But I'd have to—"

"Tonight," she said. "That's right."

"But how?"

"How? Sure, everyone knows Cam the Hun's handy with a knife." She drew a line across her throat with her finger. "Just like that. You won't even have to go looking for him. I know where he's resting his pretty wee head right this minute."

"No," he said.

She placed her glass on the floor next to his and rose to her feet, her hands gliding over her thighs, along her body, and up to her hair. Her heels click-clacked on the floorboards as she crossed to him. "Consider it my Christmas present," she said.

He went to stand, but she put a hand on his shoulder.

"But first I'm going to give you yours," she purred. "Do you want it?"

"God," he said.

The Queen of the Hill unlaced her corset top and let it fall away.

"Jesus," he said.

She pulled him to her breasts, let him take in her warmth. He kissed her there while she toyed with his hair. A minute stretched out to eternity before she pushed him back with a gentle hand on his chest. His right mind shrieked in protest as she straddled him, grinding against his body as she got into position, a knee either side of his waist. She leaned forward.

"Close your eyes," she said.

"No," he said, the word dying in his throat before it found his vocal cords.

"Shush," she said. She wiped her hand across his eyelids, sealed out the dim light. Her weight shifted and pillows tumbled around him. Her breasts pressed against his chest, her breath warmed his cheek. Lips met his, an open mouth cold and dry, coarse stubble, a tongue like ripe meat.

Cam the Hun opened one eye and saw a milky white globe an inch from his own, a thick, dark brow above it, pale skin blotched with red.

He screamed.

The Queen of the Hill laughed and pushed Davy Pollock's severed head down, rubbing the dead flesh and stubble against Cam the Hun's face.

Cam the Hun screamed again and threw his arms upward. The heel of his hand connected with her jaw. She tumbled backwards and spilled onto the floor. The head bounced twice and rolled to a halt at her side. She hooted and cackled as she sprawled there, her legs kicking.

He squealed until his voice broke. He wiped his mouth and cheeks with his hands and sleeves until the chill of dead flesh was replaced by raw burning. He rolled on his side and vomited, the gin and foulness soaking her black satin sheets. He retched until his stomach felt like it had turned itself inside-out.

All the time, her laughter tore at him, ripping his sanity away shred by shred.

"Shut up," he wanted to shout, but it came out a thin whine.

"Shut up." He managed a weak croak this time. He reached for his coat, fumbled for the pocket, found the knife. He tried to stand, couldn't, tried again. He grabbed the iron bedpost with his left hand for balance. The blade snapped open in his right.

Her laughter stopped, leaving only the rushing in his ears. She looked up at him, grinning, a trickle of blood running to her chin.

"What are you?" he asked.

She giggled.

"What are you?" A tear rolled down his cheek, leaving a hot trail behind it.

"I'm the Queen of the Hill." Her tongue flicked out, smeared the blood across her lips. "I'm the goddess. I'm the death of you and any man who crosses me."

"No," he said, "not me." He raised the knife and stepped towards her.

She reached for Davy Pollock's head, grabbed it by the hair.

Cam the Hun took another step and opened his mouth to roar. He held the knife high, ready to bring it down on her exposed heart.

He saw it coming, but it was too late. Davy Pollock's cranium shattered Cam the Hun's nose, and he fell into feathery darkness.

He awoke choking on his own blood and bile. He coughed and spat. A deep, searing pain radiated from beneath his eyes to encompass the entire world. The Queen of the Hill cradled his head in her lap. He went to speak, but could only gargle and sputter.

"Shush, now," she said.

He tried to raise himself up, pushing with the last of his strength. She clucked and gathered him to her bosom. He stained her breasts red.

"We could've been good together, you and me," she said.

His mouth opened and closed, but the words couldn't force their way past the coppery warm liquid. He wanted to weep, but the pain blocked his tears.

"You could've been my king," she said. She rocked him and kissed his forehead. "This could've been our palace on the hill. But that's all gone. Now there's only this."

She brought the knife into his vision, the blade so bright and pretty. "Close your eyes," she said.

He did as he was told. Her fingers were warm and soft as she loosened his collar and pulled the fabric away from his throat.

The cathedral bells rang out. He counted the chimes, just like he'd done as a child, listening to his mother's old clock as he waited for Santa Claus. Twelve and it would be Christmas.

It didn't hurt for long.

HOUND OF CULANN
WRITTEN BY **TONY BLACK**

I first heard about Cuchulainn growing up in Galway in the 1980s and the tales have stayed with me to this day; that's why I chose to write about him. That and the fact that I like getting dogs into stories — dogs in crime fiction rule!

—

He was your typical 'Troubles are over, my arse' Ulsterman. Tats. Sovereign rings. A swagger you could dry clothes on and a number-one to the nut. I'd have sent him packing with a brick up his hole but the well-used Webley in his waistband said he meant business.

I knew right off what he was here for.

I knew right off I didn't have it.

There was a crowd of say, eight, nine people between us. Good ol' boys sucking back stout, stocking up for a shot at the local hoors. None that would move to pull a greasy stick out of a dog's arse, or a lit firework for that matter.

"Any service going, mate? Murder a...beer," I shouted out. Stood up to meet the barman as he rose, slapped the local rag down on the bar-top, spoke: "Beer?"

"Yeah, two...one for me and..."

He lifted a hand, I thought he was flagging me shut-the-fuck-up, "Kind?"

"Come again?"

"Look, lad, I've got beers and beers."

The hard-nut was two yards off, homing in on me, "Right, right, eh...the Harp'll do."

The barman softened. Ironed out his creased brow, said "Good choice."

I watched him slide off, caught sight of two scab-cracked elbows poking through his flannel. The fuck was I doing here? I had Marie now, waiting. I'd promised her.

A sovereign-ringed hand pounded the bar.

※

Culann had said take it easy, but take it. I remembered the words because I'd followed them to the letter.

"Time and place is all I need," I said.

"You'll get a call. Don't miss it. Don't question it. Don't even respond. You got it?"

"Sure mate, no need to boil up yer piss."

Culann had the appearance of what he was, a parasite. A fat fuck. A lazy, loose-moralled — scrub that — amoral, piece of shit. He let his heavy lids hang on his bloodshot eyes for a moment or two then he flashed his tongue like a lizard, "You straight?"

"Mate, you know I am...I fuck up you go medieval on my arse, Culann, that's not happening."

I had him. The eyes sunk back in his fat head. Face played that moronic expression he wore most days. Only this wasn't most days for him...or for me.

※

I felt a tap on my shoulder. Not gentle, but a lot less than I was expecting. These big guys, all talk and no trousers. It's the size, the sheer scale that usually excuses them from any kind of conflict. Pound to a pail of shite, the jaw's never been tested. I mean really tested. As I turned, suddenly, I wasn't for trying the theory.

"Quinn."

"Who's asking?"

The knuckle-dragger removed his hand from the bar. Put his dark eyes on me, "That wasn't a question." From the pocket of his cheapo leather he produced a picture of me, dropped it on the bar. I could hardly look, I was with Culann; I'd never wanted out the life more.

"Looks like you got me."

A nod. No change on his face though, that ancient Irish wisdom thing going on. I tried a smile. Nothing.

The barman arrived with the Harps, "Get them down ye!"

"Cheers, mate." I picked up the beers, offered one to the big fella.

"Don't touch alcohol."

Knew at first sight of him that he was probably pumping his arse with steroids, so should have sussed he wasn't gonna touch the cold stuff.

Barman, appalled "That's a feckin good lager you're turning up, boy!"

"No worries, won't go to waste," I told him.

The pug disagreed, said "Oh, I think it might." He picked up the pint glass, snatched mine with his other hand, then smashed them both together, right in front of my face. Shards and beer splashed over the floor.

The place fell silent.

Then, "Get your fucken arse out to the car, Quinn."

※

The call came at two-twenty in the morning.

I took the details and climbed out of bed. I had an old Golf GTi, never failed me, purred into action first turn of the key.

The streets were quiet heading out through Salthill. I'd

rented a bungalow in the Tirelean to keep everything as low-key as possible. Was ready to cut and run after a couple of days but stuck it out to get the job done. Right down to the 9-5 appearance, suit from Roaches, the lot.

The call dropped me the details of a coastal gaff, out near Connemara. I needed to push the Golf to make the time, but I'd been cruising the suburbs so long, figured the burn would do it good.

When I pulled in there was a set of pimped-up 4X4s in the road outside, Toyotas with the full chrome roll-bar kits. My instructions were simple, take the crate from the local boyos, one marked Galway Airport, bring it back to Culann.

In and out.

Pass GO and collect 2,000 euro.

If only it was so simple.

"So, that's the crate?" I asked the homeboy, Nike cap on backwards, barely a tooth in his gob.

"Yeah, mate...that's Culann's fecken beast!"

"You what?"

"In there. The dog!" He seemed confused, a look that said he'd just been anally-probed. Something told me he preferred doing the probing himself.

"You're shitting me, yeah? No-one said a thing about a dog."

"Mate, why do you think there's so much interest...it's a fecken champion in the pit!"

I put a torch on the crate. Sure enough there was a livestock stamp and clearance papers attached.

"Well, fuck me..."

The two shit-heads laughed, started to slap each other on the back, then, "Fella...yon hound's a fecken killer."

I pulled the top layer of the paper covering the crate and steadied the torch. There was a little movement inside. Then two yellow eyes flashed for a second and the dog threw itself at me, snarling and barking. The fucker went ape.

"You sure about this?"

"Fecken right!" said the mouthy one, he took off his cap and scratched his head, then "Look, I got the word on this coming through from Americkay — I work the airport, greased its arse ye might say."

"But...it's a fighting dog." Culann had pulled some shit, but bringing in beasts like this was a new low, even for him.

"Mate, tis the fecken fight of the century Culann has on!"

"So why haven't I heard about it?"

"'Cos if you had, maybe some mad bastard would get the idea of stealing the fecker..."

The pair of them laughed themselves stupid. It didn't take long. I couldn't watch. The 2,000 euro seemed like small potatoes now.

"Fellas...you have a point."

The laughter stopped flat. "What?"

The pair looked like I'd just torched the 4X4s sitting behind us. I guessed there'd be plenty more opportunities for them to make a killing cherry-picking the cargo bays, but this deal, I decided, wasn't paying them.

"On the road..."

"Y'what—?"

I took the shooter from my belt, "There's been a change of plan..."

⁂

"So, how do I know you're who you say you are?"

The pug didn't even blink, in a flash he had me pressed against the driver's door of the Golf, an armlock so tight you could jack-up the car with it.

"I didn't come here to be fucked over, there's a time factor and not to mention the limits of my patience."

I'd been hardballed before, "There's also the fact that I'm

the one with all the cards here. Now, get your fucken mitts off me or there's gonna be one thirsty, hungry dog gnawing at the confines of a crate 'til it keels."

He twisted harder, said, "Anything happens to Culann's dog—"

"You'll what, break my arm?" I let him get the taste of that for a while, then, "What you think it is out today, four-below...fucken cold for sure. Beast'll be lucky to survive the night."

"Okay, what d'ye want?" said Culann's lump.

"What we agreed."

He loosened off his hold. Stepped back. I could tell he thought I was making a mistake. That I'd be lucky to see the week out. But my conscience was clear. I was doing the right thing; Marie would agree. I'd already queered the deal for Culann, put my arse in a sling, was no way back now — I needed reassurances.

The pug pulled down on his collar, looked out to the horizon. "Culann's losing patience..."

"You know what I want."

"Quinn. You're out. No bastard will work with ye now. Just don't get any ideas about a challenge, that would be fatal." He dropped his chin, laughed. "I'd be going far, far away — I hear Tasmania's nice."

"And the cash?"

He pulled a Jiffy-bag from inside his leather, "You're paid up."

I ripped open the seal. All sound.

It was getting colder. I shielded my eyes from the wind, brushed a layer of muck from the top of the Golf, "Come here," I said.

He followed me round to the front of the car. I wet a finger on my tongue, started to draw a map in the bonnet's grime, "The dog's tucked up in an old barn about three miles from here..."

He left so quickly, looked so gladdened, I never had time to utter the words "Sorry I broke the cunt's neck." But, fair play, it had went for me.

HATS OFF TO MARY
WRITTEN BY GARRY KILWORTH

The Irish goddess Macha once agreed to marry a farmer whose first wife had recently died. The farmer took Macha to a horse race and there fell into the trap of bragging that his new wife could run faster than the king's horses. The king was furious and ordered Macha to race against his thoroughbreds, even though Macha was heavily pregnant. The goddess did so, beat the horses, and gave birth to twins on the finish line. As a punishment for the men who had used her thus, Macha cursed them to suffer labour pains at a time in the future when they most needed to be fit and strong.

The moral is age-old. A wronged woman will seek revenge. There is something of Macha in all women. **Hats Off to Mary** *contains men who use women for their own ends, a bunch of racehorses and a lass whose reprisal for being scorned is equal to that of any vengeful goddess.*

—

Sean Casey loved the horses. Oh yes, he loved the girls too, but he loved the horses more. This was his *raison d'être*, being out here on the green turf, watching the horses thunder by. All his weekends were spent at the track, and some of his weekdays too, when he could fool the boss at the car showrooms. Sometimes he'd take potential customers out for a spin in this or that new model and then persuade them to go with him to the races. Not all of them went, of course, but one or two did. Those who were hooked on gambling like himself. One man once complained to Sean's boss that he'd lost all the money he had saved for a new car on a horse named Lightning Bolt. Sean later said the nag should have been called Light Precipitation.

But this was Saturday, and here was Sean, his head bobbing amongst all the St Patrick's Day bowlers. Suddenly his heart began beating a tattoo as his latest big bet went into the lead. Sean had his binoculars to his eyes and was yelling, "Come on High Stepper, you can do it girl, you can do it—" when he suddenly developed a severe headache. Such was his obsession with the horses he couldn't take the binoculars from his eyes, even when he felt something warm and sticky trickling down his forehead, into his eyebrows. "Come on, you little darlin'—" he gasped out the last words he would ever speak. A moment later, Sean Casey's skull imploded. He let out a final terrible scream of agony, which was lost amongst a high chorus of other excited screams, as his horse danced past the post to win by two lengths.

The binoculars dropped to the turf, his St Patrick's Day bowler fell and rolled. Sean lay there amongst a group of startled punters, staring up at the sky with dead eyes.

Colleagues at the station called Detective Sergeant Frank O'Grady 'The Leprechaun', not because he was small and wore a green cap, but because he only wore one shoe. Frank had lost a foot in the Middle East and it had been replaced by a false one. Since the metal foot was adequate for walking on, Frank did not see the need to wear a shoe. It would have *looked* better, of course, but Frank was not into looks. He was a bulky, raw-boned man with a heavy nose and a lumbering walk. His wife, big Eileen, loved him, but she was one of a kind too, and it's doubtful either would have found a partner if God had not seen fit to send them to the same bakery one Saturday morning, both intent on buying the last cream slice. Frank let the girl have the slice and she showed her gratitude by saying yes when a fortnight later the giant leprechaun asked big Eileen to tie the knot.

Leprechaun has something to do with *one-shoe* in Gaelic.

The naked body of Sean Casey lay on the slab at the morgue, the head tapering at the top to a bloody mess of bone fragments and brains.

"Pretty ugly, eh, Sergeant?" said Detective Connor, wrinkling his nose.

"Why am I here?" asked Frank, ignoring his detective and speaking instead to the pathologist. "A man's head caves in on him. So why call me?"

"It's very unusual," replied the doctor, shrugging. "It may be a natural thing, but I've never heard of it, so I called you just in case you might want to investigate. I found no missile entry, no indication of a blow from a blunt instrument, no evidence of any force being applied to any single part of the skull. From what I can deduce — though I could be wrong — it seems the man's cranium simply collapsed in on itself."

"Nothing like it in medical science, eh?"

"Never seen it before, never heard of it, never read of it."

Frank nodded. "Beg pardon, Doc, but Ballybunnion is hardly the centre of the universe. If we lived in New York..."

"I still keep up with the latest medical knowledge," interrupted the pathologist testily. "We do have the internet here, you know. I'm telling you, Frank, this is not usual. This is something out of nowhere."

"Aliens," said Connor, grinning. "Aliens did it with a death ray."

"Detective," said Frank, eyeing his assistant lazily, "levity is a wonderful thing when a man's not lying dead on a slab of marble with his head in shards." He took another look at the shattered head-bone. "In more pieces than a Greek urn dug up by a cack-handed archaeologist."

"Yes, Sergeant," said Connor, his mouth still twitching. Then he added, "Is that not levity too, Sergeant? The cack-handed digger?"

"No, it's dry wit, which is an entirely different thing. Yours was a cliché, Connor, not an original observation. Now, I know we ran a check on the victim, if I can call him that, before we left the station. What came up?"

"Well, there's no widow, Sergeant, so we have no worries about the jokes, good or bad. He wasn't married. He's — he *was* — a forty-seven year old bachelor. He worked at the local car sales office. He lives with his mother in a house down at the east end of Ballybunnion."

Frank nodded. "Well done, Connor. Now, Doc, where's his stuff? Presumably he was wearing something more than he's got on now?"

The pathologist pointed to a table in the corner of the room.

Frank went to the table and found a suit, shirt, tie, socks, shoes, underpants. The collars of the jacket and shirt were covered in dried black blood, the rest of the gear spattered with it. There was also a bowler hat and a pair of binoculars. Frank picked up the binoculars and began fiddling with the focus wheel. Nothing happened. Nothing startling that is. He'd once seen a horror film where a woman put binoculars to her eyes and turned the focus wheel, which triggered a mechanism that drove two spikes through her eyeballs.

"*Museum of Horrors*," Frank mused to himself, pleased he could remember the title. "I think it was that. Anyway," he sighed, "he didn't get spiked; he had his skull crushed by unknown forces."

What a pity, Frank thought, that for once things couldn't

be simple and straightforward.

He picked up the bowler and saw that the inner band and the brim were also covered in dry blood and bone fragments.

"Well, he certainly made a mess of himself."

Connor was then at his shoulder, holding a bowl full of objects. There was a wallet, a cheap wristwatch, a filthy handkerchief, some coins, a set of keys and a rabbit's foot on a silver chain.

"Shame. He had the winner too." Connor held up a betting ticket. "High Stepper in the third race of the day."

"And you know that because...?"

Connor replied. "Because my money was on Golden Flash II, which was beaten by two lengths, and no — I didn't have a place bet, Sergeant. Only to win."

"Pity. The pints would have been on you."

Connor murmured so the pathologist could not hear, "Of course, we could collect, sir." Connor flicked the ticket with his thumb and forefinger. "There's a fiver on it at twenty-to-one."

"A hundred euros?"

"Yep."

"Collect it, Detective."

Connor grinned. "Yes, Sergeant!"

"And we'll give it to his mother."

Connor's face dropped. "Oh bugger."

Connor left then, to collect the money from the local betting shop. Frank clinked his way back to his car. It sounded as if he had a milk bottle on the end of his leg. Actually, the foot was no trouble, really. Yes, the stump, which was just below the knee, hurt occasionally. There was an ache in it that bothered him somewhat. But it was usually when he was concerned by something else, something that was stressing him out. Most of the time Frank hardly noticed that his foot had gone. And no, Frank emphatically told people at parties, he *never* got an itch between non-existent toes. The bloody foot was gone, it felt gone, and he was now perfectly fine with that. He couldn't play hurley any more, but that was a young man's game anyway. He'd exchanged his hurley stick for a golf club and that suited him fine.

Later, sitting in front of his computer, he hoped to find some sort of answer to the puzzle. Either Sean Casey's skull had been very weak and had collapsed in on itself through age or usage, or it had been subjected to an unseen pressure. He first looked at bone weaknesses brought on by bad genes or disease. Nothing much there. Then he put *Pressure* and *Gravity* into a search engine and came up with one or two texts full of nomenclature that defied reading let alone understanding.

One site in particular interested him for a while. It was entitled *Effect of Pressure and Gravity on the Human Body*. Very quickly though, his eyes began to glaze over as he went from *The human body is subject to enormous pressure from gravitational forces*...which seemed promising, to...*the differentiation of gravity in terms of hypogravity (~0g) and hypergravity (~2g) were studied in a 30 degrees head-down tilted supine body position during tidal breathing and full forced expirations in fifty subjects resulting in electrical impedance tomography in the ventral transverse cross-section*...a statement which left him as bewildered and confused as the musk ox who went into a drug-induced sleep in the Arctic and woke up in a Dublin zoo.

He left the computer and went back to the photographs of the dead body *in situ*, along with the plans of the race course. He noticed that Sean Casey had died within a few yards of a bookie's stand. A phone call established the name of the bookie. He then rang the man's mobile. The bookie was naturally quite wary at first when he knew he was talking to the Garda, but he eventually opened up.

"He just sort of spun like a top, I'm tellin' ye, Sergeant, and then he went down loike a felled tree. Nobody near him, so far as I could see."

Frank thanked the bookie then put the phone down.

Well, that was that. Where else was there to go? The coroner would no doubt call it *death by unknown causes* or something of that nature and it would go down in the annals of mystery deaths. At some time it would be researched by a hack writer wanting to make a few euros on a cheap reference book entitled something like *Cases of Spontaneous Combustion and Other Strange Phenomena*, under a chapter heading which might read *The Unique Case of the Imploding Skull*. Frank's name would not appear of course, for which he was grateful.

"Time to tell the parent," he said to himself.

It was a job he hated, of course. No person with any feelings likes to be the bearer of such news to a parent who has outlived her child, even if that child had been stepping into near middle age. He could make a phone call, or even send a message, but Frank didn't work like that, not since he'd lost his brother in a car accident, a death he had learned of by email. Connor brought him the money from the bet and Frank went to the address found in the victim's wallet.

Once seated in the woman's front room, which was spotlessly clean and probably only used for guests, he gratefully accepted a cup of tea. First he expressed interest in a pair of cowrie shells that decorated the mantelpiece, not because he wanted to know about them, but because he could not go in cold with such terrible news. After talking about the shells and admiring a wooden statuette from someplace in Africa, Frank quietly informed the mother that her son was dead.

She sobbed. He spoke comforting words. The same sort of words he'd used when one of his soldiers had been killed in the Middle East. They were meaningless words, but they had to be said, and the mere tone and feeling of the words helped both him and the bereaved parent. She was not elderly. She was in her late sixties, fit and healthy, and as sharp mentally as any twenty-year-old. Maybe sharper.

"I'm sorry," he said, his hand on her trembling shoulder. "I'm very, very sorry."

"Can I see him?" she asked, lifting her tear-stained face. "He was a bit of a tearaway, but he was my son, and I loved him."

"Of course you can see him. In fact, I'm afraid you have to identify the—" he almost said 'corpse' which would have been a bit insensitive "—him. Would you mind doing that?"

"No, no — shall I come now?"

"I'll take you in my car. By the way, I have some money here, which belonged to your son. It's yours now."

He gave her an envelope containing a hundred euros, but she hardly looked at it, putting it on the coffee table.

He stood up and she looked down at his alloy foot.

"Did you lose your shoe?"

"I never wear one. I'm a bit lazy like that. I lost the foot in an accident. Does it bother you? I'm sorry. I usually deal with criminals and I couldn't care less what *they* think."

"No, it doesn't bother me."

She fetched her coat. But when they left the house it had started to rain, so she went back for an umbrella. Once in the car she was quite calm and seemed to have recovered from the shock. She was talking all the time though and Frank wondered if this was a reaction to the bad news, or her normal mode of operation. Some people rattled on, shock or not, simply because it was in their make-up. As he drove through the wet streets, he heard her say, "...I wonder if I should tell her?"

"Tell who?" he asked as he tried to concentrate on the now-slick surface of the road.

"His ex-fiancée, Mary. Mary would want to know, I'm sure, even after what he put her through."

Another car shot out from a side turning and Frank snarled *Fucking idiot*, but not out loud.

"Through what?"

"Well, he did an awful thing. He left Mary at the altar, you know. Jilted her. She cried like there was no tomorrow, poor lass. It was a bad thing to do. Poor dear Mary. Well, I'm sure she has no love left for my son now, but she'd want to know, wouldn't she?'

Frank said, "What does she do, this Mary?"

"Oh, she's a nurse. Lovely lass. Beautiful complexion. Big brown eyes. But that made no difference to my Sean. He took another girl, to London I think, on the day the wedding was supposed to take place."

Again, in his head, *Sounds like a right bastard to me.*

Out loud, "I suppose he had his reasons?"

Mrs Casey replied, "Yes — he liked sex with different girls."

Frank nearly swallowed his tongue at that one.

A bit later, he said, "A nurse, eh? Not a doctor, or anything?"

"Oh no. She's only just, actually. Passed her exams just two months ago. I'd better tell her about Sean."

Mrs Casey took out a mobile phone, but acting on instinct Frank placed his hand over the instrument.

"No, not yet. Not until you've identified the body."

"Oh yes, of course." She put the phone back in her handbag.

They drove in silence for a while and soon the building which housed the morgue came into view. It was sheeting it down now. They got out of the car and stepped into puddles. Frank's metal foot chinked on the steps going up. They walked down several dreary corridors until they finally reached the morgue. Before going in he tried to steel her for what she was going to see, the virtually headless cadaver now lying in a morgue tray. It still shocked her into silence for many minutes. Then she was shown a mole on the body's right shoulder, a rather large oval-shaped one, and she nodded and wept again. The coroner gave her a bundle of Sean Casey's effects and clothes.

"Yes," she said, walking down the corridor, still weeping, "that was Sean — but oh, how horrible. How horrible. I wish I knew what had caused such a terrible thing to happen to him."

"We all do, Mrs Casey," said Frank.

On the way back in the car she hardly spoke a word. When they got to the house she got out without waiting for him to open the door for her, so Frank stayed in the car. He wound down the window to say goodbye. In the unrelenting downpour, she said, "I'll call Mary now. She lives with her father down by the golf course. He's an inventor, you know. Not a very successful one, unfortunately."

"Really?" Frank replied, not at all impressed by failure. He started to wind up the window. "An inventor?"

"This rain — I wish it would stop," she said through gritted teeth. Then, "Oh yes — Professor Michael Mahoney. He invented a hat which would fit anyone who put it on. It had this gizmo-thing with it. When you pressed a button, the hat adjusted its size."

A firefly suddenly danced across Frank's brain.

He said, very slowly, "So, it went big, or small, according to the wearer's head size?"

Mrs Casey leaned over, putting her head inside the car, out of the rain. "Well, yes, you expanded the hat or you — what's opposite of expanding? It's slipped my mind for the moment."

"Contracting."

"Yes, you could contract the hat to the size of your head. So it was always a perfect fit, no matter who put it on. But it was too expensive. Mary told me the unit cost was too high. Her father tried several firms, even in America, but no one would take it. Shame. Dreadful shame. It should have made him wealthy. Sean thought it would make Professor Mahoney rich when he first heard about it, but then it seemed quite obvious it wasn't going to get beyond the drawing board."

"There was a prototype though?"

"Oh yes, a bowler it was. Here — it's here in this bag the man gave me. Mary sent it to Sean just the other day. She said it was a gift to show there were no hard feelings anymore."

She took out Sean's bowler hat, then searched inside the bag again, saying eventually, "But I can't show you how it works. There's no gizmo-thing here."

"Never mind. May I borrow the hat for a while?"

"Oh yes, sergeant — you've been so kind."

Frank took the blood-blackened bowler.

"Thank you — but you're getting soaked," said Frank, suddenly concerned. "Off you go, Mrs Casey. Have you any relatives or neighbours you can call?"

"My sister, Sarah."

"Call her. But don't call Mary. I'll call her myself. Do you know where she lives? Her phone number?"

"She lives at 17 Corke Street. Wait a minute, I'll tell you her phone number..."

She fiddled with her mobile phone and then told Frank the number. He wrote it on the back of his hand.

Mrs Casey then added, "Such a nice girl. You'll tell her gently, won't you? She's a very sensitive creature, despite being a nurse."

"You can be sure of that, Mrs Casey."

Frank drove away, feeling the inside of the bowler hat with the fingers of his left hand as he steered the car with his right. There was velvet in there, covering something a lot tougher, probably a metal band. It felt metallic anyway, and Frank guessed it would be steel. A steel band that could be expanded, or shrunk, using a remote.

For some reason Frank felt very pleased with himself. Everyone likes to finish a crossword puzzle, even if they've been given the last clue by someone else.

The 'gizmo' was probably at the bottom of a deep lough by now.

"Mary Mahoney," he murmured with sigh, "what am I going to do with you?"

SLIABH BAN
WRITTEN BY ARLENE HUNT

Was there ever a more misunderstood woman than poor Queen Maeve, Queen of Connacht? All she wanted was a loan of The Brown Bull of Cooley for one measly year so that she could be equal in stature to that of her boastful husband, King Ailell, who owned the renowned White-Horned Bull. Hardly much of a request for a Queen to make, one would think. Then all because some drunken mouthpiece couldn't hold his liquor, she was refused and humiliated by Daire Mac Fiachniu of Ulster, the brown bull's owner.

What choice had she but to wage war on Ulster and take what should have been offered freely? It's the principle of the thing. One man's bull is another woman's equal footing in the marital home.

What greater fun is there than to play with the story of a lusty, bawdy, proud woman who will not take no for an answer? Part Xena Warrior princess, part Aphrodite, part Brunhilde and absolutely no part Peig Sayers; Queen Maeve was a whirlwind of passions and headstrong capabilities. I was greatly enthralled with her as a child when I read about her escapades first. I loved her chariot of war, her willingness to do battle at the drop of an insult. She is an Irish icon.

-

The sun rose slowly from behind the stables and washed over the frost-covered meadow.

Pretty, Magda King thought, leaning her forehead against her drawing room window. From here she could see tiny icicles hanging from the barn shed, twinkling like diamonds.

Though chilled, she remained standing, watching the shadows retreat and the workers begin to arrive. She heard the horses strike their hooves against the stable doors, anticipating their morning feed.

Magda had been awake since four. She had not slept a full night since Allen had left her. Five months of wakefulness. Of counting time in the darkness, reaching out, feeling nothing but the emptiness on his side of the bed.

It was, she knew, time to accept it was over, time to move on. So why could she not let go of the rage that all but consumed her?

They said time healed, so where was her scab? It still scorched her to think of that woman. It had been five months since the agonising showdown with her husband, five months since he had left her and shacked up with his floozy, the dopey bovine girl with frizzy split ends and droopy eyes. Five months since he had made a mockery of their vows and a laughing stock of her. Five months of whispering staff and awkward glances, of stilted silences and fake jovial tones.

But she wouldn't give them the satisfaction of seeing her crumble. Magda had held her head high and she had endured. At forty she was a handsome woman, her dark red hair held no traces of silver. Her figure remained graceful and lithe. She knew men desired her, even if Allen was too stupid or blinded by familiarity to understand what he'd had with her.

Magda glanced at the large glass cabinet which stood against the far wall of the living room. It was filled with trophies and medals and rosettes shaded from deep vermillion to faded salmon pink. The wall above it was covered in photos and framed newspaper articles. The largest one, dated two years previous, named her and Allen, "King and Queen of the Track".

Magda picked up the last evening's newspaper from the window seat and re-read the story that she had read eight times already. It hadn't changed. No dawn magic had retold it and the same print met her eyes.

There he was, the great peacock, standing in the winner's circle, with a stupid grin etched across his face, his hussy by his side. Sliabh Ban, her horse, *her horse*, standing sweat-soaked and triumphant between them. The article said Allen was preparing to retire Sliabh Ban; "Going out on the crest of a wave".

Magda hurled the newspaper away with a scream and stalked across the room, yanked up the phone and dialled a number she knew by heart. The number rang and rang, finally clicking on to an answering machine.

"You rotten bastard, you haven't even the balls to answer your phone now? Well fuck you. You think you can rub my nose in it and I'm going to sit back and take it? You and your bloody whore, you'll be sorry. I'll fight you on this, Allen, I'm telling you now. If it takes me every drop of blood in this body, I'll fight you on this."

She hung the phone up and went back to the window.

Behind her, Bess, her collie, sighed.

Later that morning Magda, dressed in jeans and a wax jacket, strode across the yard to talk to her trainer, Fergus.

She found him issuing the staff riders their orders outside the tack room. It never ceased to amaze her how someone as tall as Fergus ever thought he'd make it as a jockey. He looked like Gulliver in amongst the Lilliputians.

"Morning, missus," Fergus said, his dark eyes searching her face. "Be right with you."

"Morning, Fergus. Please, take your time."

Fergus turned back to his crew.

"Right you lot, get tacked up. Shelly, put brushing boots on that filly."

"Yes, sir," one of the identikit munchkins replied.

"Jack, you keep a close eye on your lad, make sure he's reined in. Keep him to a steady canter the whole way round. See if you notice whether he's still dropping that shoulder or not. If you need to use a flash, stick it on before you head out on the gallops."

"Yes, sir."

"Right, get on with it."

Magda watched Fergus as the jockeys skirted past her mumbling their hellos. Magda had a lot of *grá* for Fergus. He was a loyal worker and a dear friend, having been with the stable for nearly ten years now. She knew her husband had offered him a lot of money to leave with him. She wasn't sure which pleased her more: that Fergus had refused or that it had humiliated her husband to be turned down.

"How are we getting on? Will Sea Scape be ready for Saturday?"

Fergus stuck his hands into the sleeveless green jacket he seemed to live in. "I suppose if the going's not too soft he'll have as good a chance as any."

"What's the weather forecast for Friday?"

"Rain."

"Damn it."

"You never know, it might hold off."

Magda struggled to keep her voice casual. "I suppose you saw the papers."

"I did."

"He wants to retire Sliabh Ban, put him out to stud. My horse, the money-making machine. Who the hell does he think he is? He didn't even consult me."

Fergus looked embarrassed. Magda took a deep breath and unclenched her fists.

"Belle's foal looks to be doing well," he said. "I had a look at her yesterday out in the paddock."

"She ready to be weaned, do you think?"

"Another few weeks or so and she's good to go."

"She's the last of Sliabh Ban's line." Magda kicked a stone across the cobbles. "We need new blood, Fergus. New stock."

"We can breed them. You still have some fine mares. There's plenty of good stud stallions around if—"

"Nothing compared to Sliabh Ban."

Fergus lit a cigarette and blew grey smoke through his nostrils. "Aye, he is a hard act to follow."

"It's her you know. She's behind it. She's got him twisted around her finger." Magda jerked away, looking across the lawn to the house, her jaw bunched with contained emotion.

"Missus, I—"

"How are we for feed?"

Fergus looked down at his feet. "We could do with a few more sacks of nuts. Maybe order up a few more round bales while you're at it."

Magda strode off without a goodbye. She couldn't stand the look of sympathy in Fergus' eye. It sickened her.

Sliabh Ban had been her horse. Allen had bought him for her when he was only a yearling. She had watched over that horse as he grew from awkward colt to seventeen hands of sheer magnificence. She had walked him through bouts of colic. Held and soothed him before race meets, clipped him by hand. She had been there every day when Fergus backed him and started him on. He was her pride and joy, a mammoth in the field. No other horse could match him for speed and strength. She had turned down interest from Sheiks and syndicates, ignoring their flashy chequebooks and their crude offers. He was not for sale, not him. She had been content to watch her stallion run for the love of running, his great flanks streaked with foam and sweat as he tore away from the field, his nostrils red and flared, heading for the post, always to the fore. What price could anyone put on such majesty?

The weeks passed. The snow melted on the hilltops and snowdrops pushed their way free of the warming soil. Everywhere signs of spring and rebirth appeared. The shadows lifted for everyone.

Everyone, it seemed, but Magda.

She attended sales and auctions, travelled the length and breadth of the country, watched countless animals trotted before her and yet nothing, not a single beast caught her eye. *Inferior*, she thought. Like she felt now. *Inferior*.

The final day of the Ballydonnell sales found her depressed and half cut, downing one drink after another in the breeders' tent. She had gone to the sale with Fergus having picked up wind that there was quality to be had. If there was, she hadn't noticed. She made her way to the bar and was ordering up another when she overheard an interesting conversation.

"Never saw anything like him. French lines they say. Gallic. Part Arab I'm thinking from the way Brendan Breen described him. He's got a smallish kind of head. Brendan said he'd never seen a horse move as fast in all his born days."

"I heard he near took the arm off the last fella that tried to shoe him."

"Be Jaysus and he was lucky so. I heard he kicked a vet clean out over the top of the stable door, and sure that was after it took four men and a couple of dogs to catch him."

"Out all year, Tom has him."

"Must be, he has a mane on him you'd see on a lion. But

'clare to God, I've never seen anything like the foals. I'm telling you now, there's no bating the blood."

"As true a word was never spoken."

"Isn't it gas, Tom won't breed him unless he's personally happy with the mare and the bloodline? I heard he turned down astronomical fees altogether."

"Go 'wan."

"True as God, Tom Daire's a quare sort of old lad anyway. Sure, his own colts are half-wild and he won't sell them. Will you have another pint?"

"Deed and I might as well."

Magda pushed off the bar a little unsteadily and slipped from the tent to go find Fergus. She found him leaning across a fence, admiring a pair of Irish draft pulling a plough.

"Fergus! There you are." She stumbled against him. Fergus tried to steady her but she shook his hands off. "Bloody heels."

"Aye. You need to be careful in this mud."

"Do you know a man called Tom Daire?"

Fergus furrowed his brow. "I know of him."

"Why don't I know him? What does he do? Is he involved in racing?"

"I don't think so. He's a breeder up in Cooley, last I heard anyway. He's a bit of an oddball."

"Right, let's go then."

"Where?"

"Cooley."

"Are you okay, missus?"

"Look at them, Fergus."

Fergus looked around.

"You see the way they look at me?" Magda glanced across the bedraggled crowd and tossed her plastic glass over her shoulder. "I do, but I'll show him. I'll show all of them."

Fergus put out his hand. "Missus, if you don't mind, I

think I'll drive us."

Magda fumbled around in her purse, located her keys and slapped them into his hand. "Cooley."

"Shouldn't we try calling him first?"

"Let's go."

She lurched towards the car park. Fergus sighed and followed in her wake.

※

They drove North, neither talking much. By the time they'd reached the tiny village of Cooley dusk was fast approaching. A slanting rain was falling and the temperature had dropped a couple of degrees. They took a right hand turn at a fork in the road just after the village. The small road was not much more than a track. Grass grew in the centre and as they climbed, the rain turned to sleet and the surrounding terrain became rougher and more barren.

"If this stallion is anything like what I've been hearing about, we could create a new bloodline. Imagine Fergus, imagine what we could achieve."

"If he's what they say," Fergus said.

"Why are you saying that? In *that* way?"

"I just don't want you to get your hopes up."

"My hopes?" Magda laughed. She looked out window at the rain. "Oh Fergus, you needn't worry about *that*."

※

Tom Daire's home was a crumbling two-storey farmhouse with a number of outhouses attached. It looked derelict and an air of desolation hung over the place.

Fergus parked the jeep and climbed out. A nondescript mongrel crept out from under a long-abandoned van set up on blocks and barked at them.

"Hello?" he called out as the wind whipped him and the

sleet bounced off his skin like gravel. "Anybody home?"

"Try the house," Magda said, rolling down her window.

Fergus did as he was asked. He hammered on the door but no one answered.

"We can come back another day."

Magda rolled her eyes and climbed out of the jeep. The dog took one look at her and decided to high tail it around the back of the house.

"Let's go."

They found Tom Daire dunking hay nets into a rain barrel, whistling as he worked.

He looked like a tiny troll in wellies. He wore a filthy jacket tied around the waist with baler twine and a cloth cap so dirty is was impossible to make out the colour, if it ever had one.

"Hello there!" Magda called. "Mr Daire!"

"Whist, will you," he said. "Naw need to be shouting. What do you want?"

Magda forced a smile and squelched her way through the thick mud towards him. "We're here about your horses, Mr Daire. I'm told you have some fine-looking animals."

"Oh aye?"

"My name is Magda King."

"Oh aye?"

Magda offered her hand and after a moment's hesitation Daire took it. When Magda reclaimed it she noticed a streak of dirt now lined her sleeve.

"I'm sorry we arrived unannounced, we couldn't find a number for you —"

"Naw, don't have one."

"Right, well, terrific...location you have here."

The old man looked at her as though she was doo-lally. Magda racked her smile up another notch.

"I hear you've got some exceptional colts."

"Aye."

"I'd love to see them."

He looked down at her shoes and grinned. "Come on up to the back pasture and take a gander so."

They trooped out of the yard and down a short path. At the end of the path, Daire shouldered open a six-bar gate and gave a roar that made Magda flinch.

Within seconds an answering whinny was heard across the air, and following that a small group of horses galloped over the crest of the hill and thundered towards them.

There were seven horses in all, Daire explained, three mares and four younger animals ranging from that year's foals to a two-year-old colt. Magda recognised the quality of the colt immediately as he charged down the hill, kicking up his heels with excitement and delight.

He was deep chestnut in colouring, with elegant proportions. He outran the small herd and came skidding to a halt inches from where Daire stood.

"He is a fine looking colt," Magda said. "A fine looking animal, indeed."

"That's his dam there to the rear. Her first foal is the best point-to-pointer this county has ever seen. I tell you she'd jump the moon that one, and when this fellow come of age, with his speed, there'll be no match, I tell you that."

"He's wonderful."

"He's nawtin' compared to the big lad."

"The big lad?" Magda glanced at Fergus.

Tom Daire smiled toothlessly. "I know ye didn't come all this way for guessing games. Come on."

※

It would be fair to say Magda King was rarely speechless. "It was," she told Fergus later that same day, "like discovering a diamond in a shit." But speechless she was when Tom Daire led her and Fergus to a stone shed at the back of the property that housed two stables. The first stable contained three shaggy-haired calves and a startled cockerel, the second, the most perfect equine specimen Magda King had ever laid eyes on.

He stood over seventeen hands high, bay with two white socks and a crooked blaze that looked like a lightning strike. His mane was wild and uncared for, but his head was small and finely boned, his eyes alert and intelligent. Old Tom opened the door and threw a head collar on him. As he danced out, his hooves rung off the mossy stones like musical bells. When he moved, his neck arched and his flanks rippled with muscle. He reared once, pawing the air with his front hooves, snorting at the foreign scent of the interlopers.

"This is Cooley Cove."

Magda stared. Fergus said, "Be the hokey."

Tom trotted the stallion up and down the yard, moving in a sprightly fashion for a man of his advanced years. The horse's action was high and light, his gait finely balanced. He moved as though the air itself acted as a cushion against the natural world.

Finally Magda managed to find some words.

"How much?"

Tom pulled up in front of them. The stallion tossed his head, and whinnied.

"Naw, he's not for sale."

"What about breeding then? I have some of the finest brood mares you'll—"

"Naw. He has bred twice this year already. I only breed him twice a year."

"Twice a year?" Magda's smile wilted. "What do you mean, *twice a year?*"

Tom put the horse back into the stable and removed the head collar. "I have two horses lined up for next year too, but sure if one of them cancels I can stick you in."

Magda looked at Fergus, then at Tom Daire. She began to laugh. "Mr Daire, are you pulling my leg?"

"Naw."

"I can offer you substantial money for, well, your quite frankly unproven stallion."

"Unproven? What proof do I need, sure I'm looking at him, aren't I?"

"Are you honestly telling me to wait, what, one maybe two years?"

Tom closed the door and leaned against it. "Aye, that's about the size of it."

"But that's ridiculous. If it's an issue of security I can bring the mares here to be covered."

"I told you, I only breed him twice a year."

※

"He's mad. One slice short of a full loaf," Magda said, later back at the stud. She threw ice into two glasses with such force half of the cubes bounced back out. She poured liberal splashes of Knob Creek over the ice and shunted one glass over the table to Fergus.

Fergus took the glass and had a sip. "So now what?"

"He's being unreasonable."

"He's within his rights to refuse."

"Why is everyone against me?" Magda sank into a wingback chair. She began to cry. "I need to work, Fergus, I need to restore this yard to what it was before that bastard and his floozy destroyed it all."

"I know, missus," Fergus said softly. He put down his glass, reached across the space and laid his hand on hers. "I know you do."

"He made a laughing stock of me. A mockery of everything we built together. He lied and he cheated and who gets left to pick up the pieces? Me, the fool that I am."

"He never made a fool out of you, missus, only out of himself. No one laughs at you."

Magda glanced at Fergus, the ghost of a smile playing on her lips. She put down her glass and cupped Fergus' face in her hands.

"You're a good friend Fergus. You'll help me, won't you?"

Fergus swallowed. "I, well, sure."

"I mean, I appreciate everything you've ever done for me. You'll help me, won't you, Fergus? I can't do it all alone."

"Missus — I'd do anything for you, you know that."

She kissed him on the mouth. Her tongue slipped in behind his teeth. And later that night as she lay staring at the ceiling, her legs intertwined with his, she knew he was telling the truth about that.

Magda called twice to Cooley to apologise. She even offered Old Tom one of her mares, but the old man was not for turning and each entreaty was met with a furious dismissal.

Enraged, Magda took to parking across from his land, spying on the great horse as he grazed. After a few weeks she knew the horse better than she knew her own.

"I want that animal," she said to Fergus, pacing up and down the kitchen, Bess trailing after her.

"You need to give him time to cool his heels."

"Damn him and his heels," Magda cried. "If you won't help me what good are you? Go on, get the hell out."

Fergus picked up his cap and set it on his head. "Magda please, don't be like this."

Magda ignored him until he left.

Obsessive, compulsive, seething and unable to rest, Magda brooded long and hard the following few weeks. She took less and less interest in the day-to-day running of the yard, and were it not for Fergus and his management skills, it would have suffered a great deal. Not that he received any thanks for his troubles.

The Cheltenham races came and went. A five-year old gelding, a son of Sliabh Ban, won the main race. Allen was photographed congratulating the owner of the gelding, his face beaming with pride. The newspaper praised his "contribution" to racing and his continued success in the "oft difficult skill of breeding".

Magda drank a bottle of Knob Creek and retired to her bed for two days.

When she arose that Friday, everyone who saw her said she looked different, haunted. At noon she crossed the lawn to the yard and ordered everyone off her property.

Fergus, who had been out mending fences, found Magda seated by the fire, her slender hands resting on the first rosette Sliabh Ban had ever won

"You sent everyone home?"

"What's the point of having them here?" Magda stared into the orange flames. "I am undone."

"Missus." Fergus dropped to his knees beside her chair and laid his hands on her lap. "Come on now, it will be all right."

"I have nothing. Everything I put together he has torn asunder."

"There are other stallions. We can—"

"We?" She laughed bitterly and pushed his hands away. "There is nothing like him, except Cooley Cove."

"You'll come through this." Fergus grabbed her hand in his again. "You're a strong woman."

"Sometimes Fergus, strength is not enough."

The logs crackled in the hearth. Fergus stared at the flames, thinking. Magda stood up and walked out of the room, letting the rosette fall to the floor.

That night Magda could not sleep. She had spent most of the evening looking through the old photo albums, swilling glass after glass of bourbon. At eleven she went to bed but tossed and turned until finally she kicked free of her sheets in a sweaty drunken temper. She went to the window to look across the lawn to the yard.

Twenty years she had given Allen, twenty of her best years. She had given him her youth, her vitality, and this was her reward?

She thought of his new woman, the flaccid limp drip he had left her for. Were they lying together now? Making love?

Magda veered away from the window and crossed the floor. She yanked open the wardrobes and pulled out the case containing her father's antique shotgun.

Bess, who had been sleeping at the foot of the bed, whined.

"Don't worry, Bess," she said upending cartridges onto the floor. "I won't kill him. I'll just get what is rightfully mine."

Magda grabbed up a handful of extra cartridges, snapped the shotgun shut and rushed downstairs. She pulled her wax jacket on over her nightgown and slipped her feet into her boots. Then she raced across the yard and climbed into the truck used to transport horses to the sales.

"Fuck you, Allen!" she screamed, putting her foot to the floor and careening out of the drive onto the road. "You can keep your fucking cow, but I'm coming for my horse and you better not stand in my god-damned way."

It took Magda exactly one hour and forty minutes to reach the farm Allen now rented. The lights were off and the main gate was locked.

Magda curled her lip and backed the truck up. She revved the engine and floored it.

The wooden gates sprang apart as though she'd hit them with a wrecking ball.

"*Woo hooo!*" Magda screamed, bouncing about the cab as she struggled to keep control.

She raced up the lane and around the back of the building to where she knew the stables were.

Lights came on in the house.

Magda leaped out of the truck and lowered the ramp. With the shotgun cradled over her arm she ran down the stables, calling to her horse.

A short startled whinny came from the last stable on the left. She saw a flash of silver, and then heard another whinny.

Magda grinned. She snatched up a lead rope from a stable door and raced along the cobbles.

"There you are. It's me. Whoa now, easy my darling, it's me."

She patted the neck of the great silver stallion, allowing him time to absorb her scent. He knew her well, but all stallions could be unpredictable when alarmed.

"Come on, my boy, come on now."

She threw back the bolts and grabbed a hold of his head collar. Sliabh Ban threw his head up in surprise, almost lifting her off the ground, but she held on and seconds later he allowed her to lead him out of the stable and towards the truck.

She hurtled up the ramp with him before he created a fuss and closed the doors. As she was putting her shoulder under the ramp the floodlights came on.

"You crazy bitch."

She snapped the last lock into place and whirled around. She snatched up the shotgun from where she had left it resting by the back wheels.

"Hello, Allen."

"Jesus Christ Magda, have you lost your mind?"

"No, in fact I think I've just come to my senses."

Sliabh Ban began to kick the sides of the truck. Allen shook his head, disgusted.

"Mary-Ann wanted to call the police. I told her I'd talk to you."

"Big of you." Magda backed towards the driver's door, keeping the gun trained on her husband.

"Have you been drinking?" He took a step towards her.

"Repeatedly," Magda said. She was almost to the door.

"Put the gun down."

"I don't think so."

"You can't get away with this."

"He's my horse, Allen. You bought him for me."

"That's not what the law says."

Magda bared her teeth, "How much credence do you think I'm going to give the law this night?"

"Magda—"

"One more step, Allen, and I swear to Christ I'll blow you clean out of those fancy slippers."

He stopped moving. "You're going to be sorry."

"I'm already sorry. Sorry I wasted as many years as I did on you."

She climbed into the cab, slammed the door and drove away.

She knew she didn't have much time. She planned to get back to her farm, release Sliabh Ban into the paddocks behind the house where she hoped he'd gather his mares to him and do what God and nature had created him to do.

She half expected the cops to show up any second as she drove across the cattle grate at the bottom of her driveway, but the house remained in darkness and there was no sign of anyone following her.

The bastard probably didn't want to cause a fuss, she thought, it wouldn't suit his image to have his shiny new personal life pored over in the papers.

Magda laughed out loud. She felt slightly crazy, as though she had been away to war. She drove the truck into the yard and parked up. She leaned across the driver's wheel breathing heavily, after a while her shoulders began to shake, and then finally the laughter came. She laughed until her sides ached and her breath caught in her chest.

She climbed out and opened the rear doors.

"Welcome home, my darling!" she said as the grey stallion pranced down the ramp, snorting and blowing. He threw back his head and whinnied. Magda was thrilled.

"That's right, you're home. You're back where you belong. And don't worry, I—"

An answering whinny split the night air, angry and urgent.

Sliabh Ban danced around Magda in a circle, his ears twitching this way and that. He rolled his lips back over his teeth, testing the air for scent. Magda tried to hold on to him, but he was no longer even remotely interested in her.

He whinnied. Again it was answered.

"Easy now, easy."

Sliabh Ban jerked free of Magda and cantered up and down the yard. Suddenly his head came up sharp, and before Magda could stop him, he galloped off behind the stables.

"*Sliabh Ban!*" Magda rushed after him. But he was too quick. Before she could stop him he leaped the paddock fence and galloped along the railings. Magda was stunned to see another horse come hurtling across the moonlit grass.

It was Cooley Cove.

Seconds later, before Magda's horrified eyes, the two animals attacked each other.

The stallions fought a running battle, Sliabh Ban, older and more wily, used his bulk to knock Cooley Cove time and time again, but Cooley Cove was fast and cunning; he latched on to Sliabh Ban's neck, ripped his flesh and turned and kicked his ribs with unerring accuracy. They thundered up and down the paddock, gnashing and screaming and pawing and striking. Battered and bloodied they saw nothing and no-one. Their blood was up and, evenly matched as they were, they were determined to fight on.

Magda climbed the fence and tried to reach them, screaming her pleas, trying desperately to get their attention. But their blood lust was too great. All she could do was stand hopelessly as Sliabh Ban stumbled and went down. Cooley Cove reared high and with a piercing scream brought his hooves down on the older horse's neck and head.

Sliabh Ban tried to rise, but blood gushed from his eyes and nostrils and after one last gallant effort he stumbled onto his knees and rose no more.

"Oh no." Magda sank to her knees.

Wild with blood, Cooley Cove tore across the paddock and tried to leap the wall that lead to the road and so to home. He was not to know there was a drainage ditch on the other side of the wall. He saw it too late, and was too exhausted and weak from his battle to clear it to the bank.

He slipped, scrabbled once and toppled backwards into the icy water, his mighty back broken, his death agonising but quick.

Magda made her way slowly back to the house, her hands covered in her Sliabh Ban's blood. She was bereft, confused. How had this happened?

As she reached the side of her house she heard a soft cough. She stopped dead.

"Who's there?"

"It's me, missus."

"Fergus?" Magda rounded the corner. Fergus was sitting at the top of her stone steps, smoking a cigarette.

"I got him, missus, I got him for you."

"You did that? You brought Cooley Cove here?" Magda stepped over him and flung open the door of the porch. "He killed Sliabh Ban, he killed my fucking horse. You should have told me what you were planning. You bloody idiot, Fergus. Now I..."

She put on the porch light and swung round to yell some more. That's when she noticed the blood.

"Oh, Jesus..." Magda knelt down. "Fergus, what's happened? What have you done to yourself?"

Fergus pitched his cigarette away. Even that move caused the blood to bubble from the massive wound in his chest. "I suppose he had a right...to protect his animal. He had a right."

"Stay here, I'll go get help."

She tried to rise but Fergus gripped her wrist hard and pulled her down.

"I did it for you," he said softly "I did it to see you smile again."

"Oh, Fergus." Magda wept. She leaned her face against his shoulder and after a while Fergus was no more.

RED HAND OF ULSTER
A KARL KANE MYSTERY
WRITTEN BY SAM MILLAR

Of all the bloody scenes in Ireland's past, none was as personal as The Red Hand of Ulster when the High King, O'Neill, and a man named Dermott, both wished to be king of that coveted piece of Ireland. The High King suggested a horse race, and first to touch the land would become the winner and sole owner of Ulster. As the two came in sight of the ending point, it seemed that Dermott would win, so O'Neill cut his hand off and threw it. It reached the goal ahead of Dermott's horse, winning for O'Neill the crown of Ulster.

For me, this was the perfect background for Belfast PI, Karl Kane, when he went in search of the elusive Red Hand of Ulster serial killer. I enjoyed the story so much I decided to expand it into a full length novel in the Karl Kane series, due for 2011.

—

Disposing of early morning rubbish, Karl Kane was clad in nothing but a small pink bathrobe when he discovered the severed hand in the back alley of his Belfast office/apartment. He shivered as the cold wind skimming off the River Lagan whistled up his canyon.

Tightening the belt on the bathrobe he bent on one knee to scrutinise the hand. The little finger was missing, but unlike the crisp severance of the wrist stump, the finger had been gnawed off.

Something between columns of uncollected bins caught Karl's attention; a mangy rib-protruding cat with the missing finger clamped between fangs in a bloody mouth. The sight gave him the willies. Never a lover of cats since his ex-wife threw one in his face four years ago, this emaciated creature only compounded his loathing.

"Shitty kitty!" Karl took a wild kick and slipped unceremoniously onto his arse. Regaining his composure he went indoors to call the cops. "I just knew in my piss that this was going to be one of those bloody days," he mumbled.

❧

Two hours later in Karl's living room, Detective Mullan asked, "Any idea why someone would leave a severed hand in your alleyway?" *Downtown Radio* was playing in the background.

"It's not my alleyway," Karl said. "It's shared by twenty other businesses and every drunken bastard taking a shit in the night. Anyway, this isn't the first time a hand's been found in bins. Probably dumped there by that nutcase, the Red Hand of Ulster."

Mullan's face reddened. "The police don't believe there is a serial killer."

"Are you on fucking Mars? Oh, wait, I get it. This is all down to the police trying to calm the public, isn't it? But seriously, two hands — three including this morning's — found in the last two months, and there isn't a serial killer? Thank fuck it's not the Red Cock of Ulster."

"Please tone your language down, Mr Kane. I'm just doing my job as—"

"How long have you been *just* doing your job?"

"I..."

"Well?"

Mullan looked uncomfortable. "Six weeks."

"Six weeks? No wonder you're making such ridiculous—"

"I really need you to focus on the questions, rather than—"

"Where's McKinley? I usually deal with him."

"Detective McKinley is out sick. I'm his replacement until he gets back."

"Well, tell your boss, Wilson — my ex brother-in-law, for your information — to send someone capable of—"

"Coffee, Detective Mullan?" Naomi entered carrying a tray crowned with steaming coffee and biscuits.

"I...yes, thank you." Mullan looked relieved.

Karl glared at his part-time secretary and full-time lover. "Since when did we start running a café?"

"Just ignore him, Detective Mullan," she soothed, placing the tray on top of a table. "He's always cranky in the morning. Hasn't had his *Weetabix*, yet."

Karl waited until Naomi left the room before addressing Mullan: "The hand was obviously dumped in the bin. The cat probably took it out, dropping it because of the weight. Just my bad luck it happened to land close to my door."

"Cat?" Mullan's face knotted. "What cat?"

"The one chewing on the hand's finger. The bastard disappeared with it down the street."

"You should have mentioned that at the beginning," Mullan said irritably, scribbling on the notepad. "That wasn't smart, leaving that out."

Karl's face reddened. "When you arrived on the scene, *you* examined the hand. Yet you didn't bother to query about the missing finger? *That* wasn't smart."

Forty minutes later, a frustrated Mullan exited.

"You could have been a bit more sociable with that young detective, Karl," Naomi said.

"If I'd been any more sociable, I'd have needed a condom. What? What's wrong?"

"Nothing…"

"When you say nothing, with a cliffhanger voice and *that* look, it's always something. What?"

"The hand. It's unnerved me."

"Unnerved *you*? I almost shit my pants — if I'd been wearing any under your bathrobe."

"For once, can you please be serious instead of flippant?"

"I am flippant serious. Can't you tell by—"

Breaking news, stated a voice on the radio. *Sources say a shocked member of the public discovered a severed hand in the City Centre early this morning.*

"Shocked? I wasn't shocked," said Karl. "The bastards better not release my name, otherwise my business will go down the shitter. Who the hell would hire a PI shocked at a hand?"

"You're not going to get involved, are you? I've a bad feeling about this."

"Give me one good reason why I'd want to get involved in one of your bad feelings?"

Other news. An anonymous businessman has said the killings in the City are becoming detrimental for future investments…

"Give the man a cigar," said Karl.

…and has offered a twenty thousand pounds reward for information leading to the arrest of those involved in these heinous crimes.

"Karl? What's wrong?"

"Nothing…"

"When you say nothing, with a cliffhanger voice and *that* look, it's always something. What?"

"Nothing," repeated Karl, thinking *I've just been given twenty thousand reasons to get involved.*

🕸

"Hello, Tom," Karl said, standing in the office doorway of

friend and forensic pathologist, Tom Hicks.

"What the hell are you doing here?" Hicks said, glancing up from a computer.

"Lovely greeting. That's what I get for coming to visit you down in this dungeon."

Hicks made a grunting sound. "Wouldn't have anything to do with severed hands and twenty thousand pounds?"

"Ouch."

"Coffee?" Hicks approached a battered percolator.

"I wouldn't say no."

Karl took a seat while Hicks filled two mugs.

"Enjoy," Hicks said, handing a mug to Karl.

"You could tar and feather some poor bastard with this." Karl took a suspicious sip and made a face. "Ghastly."

"You've ten minutes," Hicks replied. "I've a hand to examine."

"The bloody hand was left on my doorstep."

Hicks almost spat a mouthful of coffee. "You winding me up?"

"My severed hand to God."

"That's some coincidence."

"In my line of work, coincidences can sometimes be deliberate. What theories is the big lad upstairs coming out with?"

"Wilson? He thinks the culprit is in the medical profession, because the cuts are so specialised and precise."

"Wouldn't have to be a brain surgeon to figure that out. A doctor?"

"Or a medical student."

"A doctor — *or student* — by the name of Dermott, perhaps?"

"What?"

"It could well be the descendants of Dermott, out for revenge against the descendants of O'Neill. This could be the oldest and longest grudge in history."

"What are you rambling about?"

"The Red Hand of Ulster myth. O'Neill and Dermott both wished to be King of Ulster. The High King of Ireland suggested a horse race across the land, and the first to touch a certain spot on the land could claim it. As the two came in sight of the ending point, it seemed that Dermott would win, so the mad fucker O'Neill cuts his hand off and throws it, touching the land first."

"Time up. I don't have all day to listen to your nonsense." Hicks placed his mug down before walking back to the computer.

"Fingerprints?"

"They're working on them upstairs."

"What about the faded numbers?"

"What faded numbers?"

"Come on, Tom. I scrutinised the hand before the police arrived." Karl smiled. "Saddled between the index finger and thumb. A blue eighty-eight. Amateurish. Looked like a prison tat. Surely you noticed them?"

"I haven't fully examined the hand," Hicks said, somewhat evasively.

"They *are* minuscule. Probably more by chance that I discovered them," Karl admitted. "A bit like Christopher Columbus."

"Time for you to go."

"Bodies? Any of them turn up, yet?"

"Not yet."

"You'd think someone would've come across a body by now."

"If I hear anything, you'll be the first person I contact," Hicks said, ushering Karl out. "Unfortunately, knowing you, you'll probably discover something before I do."

"Karl?" Naomi said, popping her head into the office. "There's a woman wishing to see you."

"Does she have an appointment?" Karl was scanning the horseracing pages for tomorrow's potential winners. So far this week he had four under his belt. Unfortunately, his ten also-rans devoured the tidy profit made by the gallant steeds.

"No. I told her she needed to make one but she's insistent."

"Okay. Send her in," Karl said, hiding the newspaper in a drawer of his desk.

Seconds later, a woman appeared at the door, shoulder bag dangling. She had large, doe-like eyes and prominent lips.

"I didn't know I had to make an appointment," the woman said, extending a gloved hand. Only now did Karl notice the deep scarring on the left side of her face, not quite camouflaged by make-up.

He shook the gloved hand. "Won't you sit down, Miss...?"

"Martin," she said, sitting down. "Judy Martin. Please, forgive the gloves. This weather has an adverse effect on my skin."

"What can I do for you, Miss Martin?"

"It's my uncle. Benjamin Martin. He's been missing for a few years. My family have been trying to track him down. My father — his brother — wants to get in contact with him before...well, my father is extremely sick, Mr Kane."

"I'm sorry to hear that."

"I really need someone to find Uncle Benjamin, before it's too late."

"I see."

"You'll probably think this sounds awfully stupid, but something guided me to you."

"Really?"

Judy nodded. "I was heading home from my business at

Victoria Square, when my new car just refused to go. An engine malfunction, apparently. Something about the chip in the car's computer, according to the garage attendant."

"The only chips my car knows is the ones I bring home on Saturday nights," Karl said with a smile. "Along with fish."

"The attendant is working on the car right now, so I took a walk while I waited. That was when I saw your business cards attached to a telephone box in Royal Avenue." Judy produced one of Karl's business cards from her pocket.

"I wonder how they got there?" Karl said, feeling his face redden.

"*Kane's Able*," Judy said, reading the maxim on the card. "I thought that brilliant."

"Yes, one of my sharper moments," Karl replied. "When or where was the last time your uncle was seen?"

"According to my father, about six years ago. They had one of those family arguments, over the family business. My uncle left and hasn't been seen since."

"Nothing like a family to destroy a family business. Any photos of him?"

Judy removed a small pouch from her bag. "These are about the best. My uncle hated his photo being taken. I think my father has one or two others. I'll get them to you as soon as I can."

Karl gave the photos a quick once-over. "Mind if I hold on to these?"

"Not at all," she said, rummaging in the bag. "Your fee. We haven't discussed it."

"We can sort that out later, if I decide to take the—"

"Do you take cash or must it be a cheque?"

"Cash is sound. But look, I still don't know if I'm going to take the case."

"I only have two hundred with me," Judy said, thrusting the money into Karl's ever-weakening hands. "I can stop by and pay the rest. Would that be satisfactory?"

"Look...okay. For now though, let me do a bit of investigating. We can talk about the bill afterwards."

"Here's my business card," she said, standing.

"I have to be up front with you, concerning missing persons, Judy. Luck plays a major part of finding the person sought — especially if that person doesn't want to be found. Understand? I just don't want you getting your hopes too high."

"I understand, Karl." They shook hands and Judy disappeared out of the office.

"*We can talk about the bill, later,*" mimicked Naomi, entering the room.

"You were eavesdropping — *again.*"

"Since when did we begin running a charity shop? Miss Judy Wudy looked as if she could afford our *special client* fee, never mind a nominal two hundred."

"I'll ask for it later."

"Tell that to the landlord next week when he comes for his money. Guarantee he won't be saying *we can talk about the bill, later.*"

"Come on. Let's head over to *Nick's Warehouse*," Karl, said holding up the ten twenties in surrender. "I'll buy you a lovely evening meal. I'll even have some expensive candlelight thrown in."

"Most of this will go in the kitty for the landlord," Naomi said, snatching the money from his hands. "Forty pounds should do for a good meal."

※

Karl tried ignoring the incessant screeching of his mobile resting on the bedside table, but the more he ignored it, the more the migraine headache drilled its way into his skull.

"Hello?" he asked in an injured tone.

"Karl? Tom."

"Tom...? Oh, my fucking head."

"You okay?"

"Went out for a meal last night with Naomi. I think she spiked my drink. She'll do anything to get me into bed."

An elbow shot into his ribs.

"*Oh!* That hurt. I thought you were sleeping."

"*Keep me out of your conversation,*" Naomi hissed.

"Go ahead, Tom."

"I've some news on the hand."

"Oh?"

"You were right. It's the number eighty-eight. I didn't want to tell you yesterday, but the other severed hands..."

"They all have eighty-eight etched into them?"

"Yes."

"Could be a cult of some sort. Witchcraft, perhaps."

"Don't be ridiculous. I doubt very much we have a coven of witches running about Belfast."

"You wouldn't be saying that if you'd seen some of the women I went out with," Karl said. "Could be bingo aficionados."

"What?"

"Eighty-eight. Two fat ladies. Those bingo fanatics would kill for a thrill."

"I've got to go," Hicks said, tiring of Karl's puerile prattle.

"Could you do me a big favour, Tom?"

Silence at the other end.

"Tom? I know you're there. I can hear your sexy, heavy breathing."

"What is it?"

"I need you to check the records for a Benjamin Martin. He's missing, but could be dead."

Karl could hear Hicks scribbling something.

"Okay, but that's you favoured-out for the rest of the

month. If I discover anything, I'll let you know. Give my regards to Naomi."

Turning the phone off, Karl squeezed in closer to Naomi's deliciously warm body. She growled a protest at the coldness of his touch.

Disregarding the warning, he snuggled in tighter, inhaling her early morning, womanly smell.

"Leave me alone." She edged away, offering up the emptiness of her back.

Her early-morning hoarseness was titillating. He felt an erection stirring.

"Don't be like that, Naomi."

"Get your roaming hands off my bum," she replied, but he could tell she was smiling.

He pressed hard against her arse, his erection adding an exclamation mark between her buttocks.

She groaned softly, while Karl whispered into her ear. "What do you say we stay in bed all day and do nothing but dirty things to each other?"

"What kind of dirty things, good sir?"

The mobile screeched on the bedside table.

Karl ignored it.

Naomi whispered, "Shouldn't you answer that?" Her hands cupped his balls as if weighing them.

"Answer what? I don't hear a thing except the sound of someone playing *Tubular Bells* on my balls."

"Could be important."

"What's more important than early morning sex with the woman I love?" Karl murmured, ice-skating his nails over her left breast and nipple.

"Business." Naomi swatted his hand away and reached for the phone. "Hello? Oh...yes, one second, please." Making a face, Naomi held her hand over the phone and mouthed, *Miss Judy Wudy.*

Taking the phone, Karl said, "Hello? Yes, Judy. No, you didn't catch me at a bad time."

Less than a minute later, Karl clicked the phone off.

"She has a few more photos of her uncle for me."

"Why didn't you ask for the increase in fees?"

"I will."

"I have to pee," Naomi said, getting out of bed.

"Be quick, my dearest."

"Get stuffed," she replied, walking towards the bathroom, breasts bouncing seductively, small buttocks seesawing mischievously.

"Hurry, my dearest."

She mumbled something nasty before scurrying into the bathroom. The door slammed. Karl heard the toilet seat falling, followed by familiar tinkling sounds.

"I have something for you," he sang out.

"Really? Well, until you get more money from *Judy Wudy*, you can put your tiny dick back in its matchbox," Naomi shouted from the bathroom. "It's not lighting my fire any time soon."

※

The next day Karl was guiding his car into a wasteland of grey buildings and mangled steel frames. "Listen, Tom," he said into his mobile, "I think all those cop mutts are barking up the wrong tree."

"Really? And what tree should they be barking up?"

"The tree I'm heading to right at this moment. The abattoir."

"The abattoir?"

"A good butcher is as skilled at slicing meat as any surgeon, and seeing that this is the only abattoir in Belfast, I've nothing to lose by asking a few questions."

"I've got some news on the fingerprints on one of the

hands — though not the one on your doorstep. His name is — or *was*, assuming he's dead, of course — Billy Browne. A very bad boy indeed according to police and prison records."

"Oh? For what did Bad Boy Billy Browne do time?"

"You name it, he's done it. Rape, arson, attempted murder."

"A record as long as Gerry Adams' face. Anything else?"

"He was a member of the neo-Nazi BNP."

"The British National Front?"

"He's wanted in England for the attempted murder of a young black man in the London Underground four years ago. Been on the run ever since, and was apparently hiding over here, sheltered by loyalist paramilitaries in Limavady and Bangor."

"As if we haven't enough locally grown scumbags, we're now importing them. Perhaps someone within the paramilitaries killed him because he was bringing too much heat?"

"We'll never know unless we find the body — if there is a body."

"I've got to go. I'm at the abattoir now."

"Watch yourself."

"I didn't know you cared." Karl blew a kiss down the phone.

The abattoir was located near Duncrue Street, a desolated, industrial area of the city. Exiting the car, Karl could see that hookers had been busy plying their trade. Used condoms were splattered everywhere.

Outside the abattoir's perimeter gate, he gazed over the building and surrounding land. There was something eerily unsettling and intimidating about the place.

"What the hell are you doing here?" he mumbled to himself.

A sign directed him to an office housing a table, two

battered chairs and a couple of metal cabinets.

"Yes?" asked a middle-aged man, stationed on one of the chairs.

"You the owner?"

"Manager. John Talbot. The owner is Geordie Goodman. And you are...?

"Kane. Karl Kane." He extended a hand and smiled.

"How can I help you?" Talbot asked, shaking Karl's hand.

"I'm a film scout looking for a good location for Channel Four. They're making a zombie horror movie. I hope you're not insulted, but this place looks perfect."

"Zombies? You've come to the right place." Talbot released a howl of laughter. "Most of the so-called workers in here *are* zombies!"

"That's a cracker, John."

"You'd have to see the boss for the final say, of course, but I can give you a quick tour of the place."

"That'd be great."

"Here. Put this on." Talbot handed Karl a battered hardhat before walking towards the door. "You better have a strong stomach. It can be a bloody horrible sight."

"A bit like my ex-wife?"

A quick bark of a laugh burst through Talbot's nose. "Come on. Over beside those two doors."

The two enormous steel doors opened automatically.

The skull-rattling noise of machinery filled a space massive and breathtakingly horrible, like the Sistine Chapel blooded by barbarians. Men and women, saturated in blood and distinguishable only by the tiny whiteness of their eyes packed meat into containers.

"Those are the labourers. Cheap as chops," Talbot said dismissively, pushing through another set of doors. "In here are the real masters."

Inside the large room, butchers were performing an opera

of death with knives flowing fluently like conductors' batons, cutting sinew and meaty parts. Karl wondered which of them wouldn't think twice about slicing and dicing a human being.

"You okay?" Talbot asked. "You look pale."

"I'm fine…I think I've seen enough."

"Okay." Talbot smiled. "Actually, you lasted longer than most people do when they—"

"What on earth is that contraption?" Karl pointed to an enormous metal container stationed at the far side of the room. The device had all the appearances of a medieval torture chamber, with leather straps and numerous levers and buttons protruding from it. To Karl it resembled something out of an Edgar Allan Poe nightmare.

"Oh, the ceremonial chamber. That's where the Jewish butchers do their kosher cleansing. Shechita they call it."

"Shechita?"

"The ritual slaughter of animals according to Jewish dietary laws. Once the animal goes into the ceremonial chamber, it's clamped in tightly, before being inverted by the turning mechanism inside the chamber. Then the animal's upside-down head pops out, exposing the lengthy neck." Talbot stretched out his own neck and made a slicing motion across it. "That's when the deed is done, slicing through to the jugular vein."

Karl thought Talbot was relishing the details a little too much. "Sounds dreadful," he said.

"You have to see it to believe it, Karl."

"I'd rather not."

"Some tea?"

"Coffee, if you have it," Karl said, wondering if his stomach would hold it down.

※

Ten minutes later, Karl watched Talbot rummaging through a

battered cupboard.

"I know I had some," Talbot mumbled, pushing items out of the way.

"Don't trouble yourself, John."

"One of the bastards has sneaked in when they saw me on the floor and nicked my coffee. Back in a tick." Talbot exited the office.

Never one to allow a golden opportunity to slip by, Karl stood and slid open the top drawer of the cabinet marked Employees Payroll. He began scanning the folders for something — anything — to jump out at him.

Unfortunately, it was Karl doing the jumping.

"What the hell do you think you're doing?"

Karl almost slammed the metal drawer on his fingers.

A young, plain-looking woman, walking-cane in hand, glared at him from the doorway. Karl couldn't help but notice the steel braces looping the outside of her legs.

"You better have a damn good reason for rummaging through private property," she said. "Just who the hell are you?"

"Who the hell are *you?*" Karl said, shaken, but brave-facing it with a bluff.

"If that's the way you want it, let the police do all the questioning." Producing a mobile from her pocket, she hit a few numbers before placing it to her ear. "Hello? Yes, can I speak to—?"

"Let's not be too hasty, Miss...?"

"One second, please." She looked straight into Karl's eyes.

"Okay. I'm a private investigator," Karl said, removing one of his business cards and holding it out.

"Place it on the table."

"The way you're talking, you'd think that was a gun in your hand instead of a cane."

Lifting Karl's card from the table, the woman scrutinised it before speaking into the mobile again. "Sorry. False alarm. No, everything is okay. Thank you." She pocketed the phone.

"I guess that means you believe me?"

"Luckily for you, I remember the name *and* face. I saw you on TV, not so long ago. Something to do with finding a kidnapped girl. A university student, wasn't it?"

"My daughter, Katie."

"Oh. She's okay?"

"As well as can be expected, considering what she went through, Miss...?"

"Goodman. Georgina Goodman. Everyone calls me Geordie." She approached the table and sat down.

"*You're* the boss?"

"You look shocked. Don't think women can handle being bosses?"

"No, nothing like that. It's just...this abattoir. Not the most glamorous of places for a young woman."

"It belonged to my father. But that, as they say, is another story. Now, what exactly are you doing here? And no bullshitting."

"No, I'm sure you get enough of that in the pens," Karl said, forcing a smile but receiving only a stony stare from Geordie. "Look, I know a bit of history about this place, the killings which took place a few years back."

Geordie stiffened. "If you're here to blackmail, you're wasting your time. It's all public knowledge, what went on here."

"No, nothing like that, I can assure you. You're aware of the severed hands discovered in the city?"

"Of course."

"The cops think it could be a doctor, but I think—"

"It could be someone working here? I doubt very much that we've a serial killer running about the place. The people working here may look frightening with all that blood on their faces and hands, but it actually washes off at the end of a hard working day."

"I didn't mean to insult the workers, but this is the only abattoir we have in Belfast."

Geordie sighed. "What exactly *do* you want?"

"Have you noticed any unusual behaviour from anyone working here? Someone keeping odd hours; out-of-the-normal absenteeism?"

"I'd have to go through all the files, and I'm afraid that would be time-consuming. We've only recently begun to computerise. My father wasn't a great believer in technology."

"Got some!" Talbot smiled, entering the room. "If I get my hands on the thieving bastard...oh, Geordie. Didn't see you there. You've met Mr Kane? He's a scout for Channel Four."

Karl's face reddened.

Geordie smiled wryly. "Yes, Mr Kane has been explaining his line of work in great detail."

"Anything about the guard dogs?" Talbot asked.

"No, not yet," Geordie said with a shake of the head. "Of course, everyone denies feeding them. I've warned all the workers that if I find the culprit I'll personally slice his balls off."

"Uh, John, I don't think I can stop for that coffee, after all," Karl said, his face tightening.

"Oh, you're going?" Talbot looked disappointed. "Sorry I took so long."

"You will keep me informed, Miss Goodman?" Karl said.

"Good evening, Mr Kane," said Geordie, noncommittally. "Be careful on the way out. The lighting isn't great."

※

The next week, Karl called over to Victoria Square shopping centre to have a word with Judy Martin. The address on her business card guided him to a jewellery store situated in the centre of the impressive shopping complex.

"I probably should have called," Karl said, seeing the look of surprise on Judy's face as he entered the shop.

"No, not at all," she replied, looking flustered. "We can go for a coffee. Let me get my coat and we'll head over to Costa Coffee. I don't want any of my employees knowing my business."

"Of course," Karl said, easing back out of the shop.

"You've got some information on my uncle?" she asked, two minutes later while they waited for coffee.

"Yes, but I don't know if it's what you want to hear."

"He— he's not dead?"

"How well do you know your uncle?"

"Not very well. To be honest, if not for my father, I probably wouldn't be searching."

"He's been in jail, though he's out now."

"Jail? Are you certain?"

"I have contacts in the police. They confirmed it."

"What was he in for?"

"Mostly burglaries in wealthy homes."

"Burglaries? Are you certain?" Judy smiled nervously. "For the love of me, I can't picture Uncle Benjamin as a burglar."

"You'd be surprised what people get up to," Karl said, "in the privacy of *other* people's homes."

"Wait until my family hears this."

"What will you do?"

"I don't honestly know. My family will be ashamed."

"Here's the last known address of your uncle." Karl handed her a note. "At least you know where he is if you want to make contact with him."

"Thank you for all you've done, Karl." She stood and glanced at her watch. "My goodness! Is that the time?"

"It always flies when you're having fun," Karl replied, shaking her hand. "Any more problems, you know where to find me. Take care."

"You too, Karl. Good day."

His mobile began buzzing just as Judy walked away.

"Hello?"

"Mr Kane?"

"Yes."

"Georgina Goodman. I've a bit of information. Don't know if it's relevant to what we discussed last week, but if you want to drop by today sometime, you can decide for yourself."

"I'll be there within the hour." Karl disconnected the call, feeling the hairs on the back of his neck prickle.

✥

"There's been nothing out of the ordinary in any of the workers' time schedules, other than a few sickness notes," Geordie explained, showing Karl a collection of folders. "But on further examination I discovered a few irregularities in the logging-in of a businessman, a Mr Tev Cohen, one of the Jewish butchers."

"How so?"

"He comes here about two in the morning, twice a month, to do his slaughtering."

"Why so late at night?"

"The place is basically empty then, with only a few maintenance men. This gives him privacy. No curious bystanders to witness the slaughter ritual."

"Have you met Cohen?"

"A couple of times. Keeps himself to himself..."

"But...?"

Geordie seemed reluctant to proceed. "He's been here *six* times in each of the last two months. I just found out from one of the night security that Cohen's been bringing in whiskey for the main security guard, asking for a blind eye to be turned by not logging-in every visit."

"Why would Cohen not want the log-ins recorded?"

"He's charged each time he uses the facilities. It can all add up, I suppose—"

"You're supposing something else, though, aren't you?"

"We've never had a problem with his bills. Payments always on time. I just...I don't know."

"You think his nocturnal activity has something to do with the hands?"

"I just want to make sure that there's nothing dodgy being done in my business. I had to fight tooth and nail with the Council to keep this place, after what went on here." Geordie's face tightened. "I'm not going to allow it to be closed — for *anything*. Especially something I know nothing about."

"You want me to do you a favour by making sure that everything really is *kosher* with Cohen." Karl smiled, "Is that it?"

"I thought I was the one doing you the favour."

"Let's just call it *quid pro quo*."

※

Overcoat wrapped to the ears, Karl sat huddled in his car watching slabs of rain batter the windows. The inside of the car was fast becoming as cold as the abattoir when he had visited Geordie three days ago, discussing the information she'd uncovered about Cohen. This was the third night of sitting in the darkness, watching for Cohen, and each night seemed to be stretching longer than the one before. Worse, there was no guarantee that Cohen would show; no guarantee of his involvement.

Unscrewing a thermal flask, Karl poured his fourth coffee of the night. He sipped it for the warmth. It tasted like ink.

A loud tapping at the window startled him. Coffee slopped onto his crotch. "Fuck!"

A face stared in at him.

"What the hell!" Karl shouted winding the window down.

"Haven't seen you about here before, *big* fella," a hooker said with a broad smile. Rain ran off a battered umbrella. "I'm Joanie. You looking for a bit of warmth on this ball-freezing night?"

"Thanks...Joanie, but my balls are quite warm with spilt coffee."

"Want me to rub your magic lamp?" she continued, undeterred. "See what we can conjure *up?*"

"My genie's nice and snug," Karl said, noticing that Joanie was more of a Johnny, with facial features muscularly chiselled by over-use of steroids. The voice didn't help either: it sounded like Humphrey Bogart on acid.

"*Cum* on. Don't be like that. How can I get you to change your mind?"

"Joanie, you aren't wealthy enough and I'm not desperate enough."

"Fuck you!"

"No, thanks." Karl wound the window up while Joanie sauntered across the waste ground like John Wayne suffering from haemorrhoids.

Seconds later, chalky headlights momentarily lit up the interior of the car. A blue Audi halted at the security gate. The barriers eased upwards, permitting entry.

Karl got out and ran to a steel door set into the abattoir perimeter. Geordie had supplied him with a key.

"Faggoty-arsed faggot!" Joanie hissed somewhere behind him.

"Come on," Karl mumbled at the key. Cold and nerves were making heavy weather of the lock.

"If that was your boyfriend's hairy hole you'd have no

problem sticking it in!"

Without warning Karl was cracked across the head. "What the fuck!" He turned just in time to see Joanie bringing the umbrella down again. It landed across the bridge of his nose, staggering him back against the door.

"Dick prick!" Joanie hoisted the umbrella like a spear and thrust it violently towards his face.

Karl barely managed to dodge the jab. He replied with a balled fist to Joanie's chin. The nocturnal he/she went staggering into a pile of discarded cardboard boxes stuffed with damaged fruit.

Down but not out, Joanie launched a spine-shattering kick to Karl's balls. "*Ohhhhh, fuck...*" He slumped to the ground.

Eager fingers began rummaging through his trouser pockets. "That'll teach you!"

Joanie's clicking high heels faded into the distance like dying gunshots.

Karl climbed to his feet, warding off vertigo with deep gulps of air. He felt lighter and knew his wallet was gone.

"Bastard," he hissed, unlocking and opening the side entrance.

Inside the abattoir grounds, guard dogs barked in the distance. Karl's stomach performed involuntary flip-flops. Geordie had assured him the dogs were primarily trained *not* to attack, only to frighten off would-be intruders. Karl had a problem with the word *primarily*. It was too ambiguous. Too grey.

He sneaked across a large expanse of tarmac, a tired moon silhouetting the buildings. "What a fucking place," he mumbled, resisting the urge to use the tiny torch in his pocket.

The tension in his spine was unbearable. He kept hearing Naomi's voice questioning his actions. *And what about Geordie? What if she's setting a trap? You read the newspaper archives about her and her insane sister and father. What they all did. I have a bad feeling about this.* Naomi's dire forecast — coupled with the uncertainty of whatever lay ahead — wasn't helping. Every nerve in his body tingled with adrenaline.

A crafty wind carried with it a medley of nauseating animal stench. Karl could taste it in his mouth. It gave off a vibration like a tuning fork.

He reached the main door of the abattoir building and slipped inside.

Which way?

A noise to his left alerted him. It sounded like a groan. He moved cautiously, using the shadows as cover. The groaning was coming from a closed room to his right.

The groaning became louder, more urgent. Had someone hurt themselves on one of the machines? Debating on whether to remain hidden or call out to the injured, Karl realised he had no alternative.

"Hello!" he shouted, inching his way forward.

"*Ohhhhhhhhhh...*" The voice quivered, threatening to quit altogether.

"Hello!"

Silence.

Outside the door, Karl spotted a red runnel of pooling, thick liquid. The hairs on the back of his neck spiked. Something wasn't right, and he was standing right in the middle of that something.

"Oh, fuck," he muttered, seconds before the lights went out in his head.

※

Karl awoke in a dimly-lit room. A fractured mirror on the wall revealed bloodshot eyes. He looked like shit and felt as weak as a dead man's piss. His head hummed as if it had been cleaved open. He reached to touch it, only to discover that he was bound to a chair, naked with a bloody rag gagging his mouth. A large wall clock told him he had been out cold for at least twenty minutes.

Pieces of hacked meat sat on a metal counter in the centre of the room. Three large machines spewed tubes of slippery-looking sausages. Then Karl noticed the mutilated corpse several feet away. Only its head and torso remained. *Well, Geordie, I can now tell you who's been feeding your dogs, but you're not going to believe with what.*

Two men in blood-soaked overalls stood a small distance away, mingling in the shadows.

"We're going to take the rag from your mouth and ask some questions," said the younger of the two, a bloody serrated knife in his hand. "If you try and scream, I will remove a finger. Lie, and I will remove something a lot more personal. Nod if you understand."

The stench of the bloody rag was burrowing all the way down to Karl's stomach. He wanted to throw up. He nodded.

"Good," the man said, removing the rag.

Karl immediately began sucking in great gulps of air, almost choking on its beautiful taste.

"Why have you no ID?" The man rested the knife on Karl's nose.

There was something about him, his features and his manner, that caused a feeling of *déjà vu* to flow over Karl.

"It was stolen from me, by a man — I mean a woman."

"Very original." The man disappeared behind Karl and grabbed his fingers.

"No! It's the truth!" Karl tried desperately to ball his fingers into a protective shell. "Outside the abattoir, I was accosted by a prostitute and—"

"How many others have you brought with you?"

"There are no others. I came alone."

"Liar!"

"I'm a private investigator, for fuck's sake!" Karl felt the coldness of the knife on his index finger.

"Wait." The older man emerged from the shadow. "What's your name?"

"Karl Kane."

"Kane?" Recognition flickered in the older man's eyes. "How do we know you're telling the truth?"

"Why would I lie about that? My car's parked in the wasteland. Take my keys. Go and check the glove compartment. You'll find a load of my business cards and other scraps of ID."

"Take his keys," the older man commanded. "See what you can find."

Seconds later, Karl and the older man were alone.

"I suppose you're Tev Cohen?" Karl asked, trying not to look at what remained of the corpse.

Cohen ignored the question. "Luckily for you, we found no tattoos on your skin."

"You mean eighty-eight?"

"What do you know about that?"

"Nothing, other than the fact they've been on the hands of victims discovered in and around the city."

"I wouldn't use the word *victims*. Now, I need you to remain quiet, until we find out a little bit more about you."

It was twenty minutes before the younger man returned.

"I found these," he said, handing them to Cohen. "Numerous unpaid parking tickets and crumpled-up betting dockets. Other than that, *nothing.*"

Cohen whispered into the younger man's ear. The younger man produced a mobile, took a photo of Karl's face and then pressed send.

A minute later, the mobile beeped.

Cohen glanced at the screen.

"Why exactly are you here, Mr Kane?" asked Cohen.

Karl let out a sigh of relief. "As I said, I'm investigating the hands."

"Blood money," the younger man spat. "You're after the twenty thousand pounds offered by that dog, Harkin. Is that your worth?"

Karl looked directly at Cohen. "What is the significance of eighty-eight?"

"The eights stand for the eighth letter of the alphabet, H. Coupled together, HH stands for *Heil Hitler.*" Cohen said the words as if he had tasted poison.

"You're *Nazi* hunters?" It sounded ridiculous.

"Justice seekers."

The younger man exploded. "Why are we explaining this to *him*?"

"Go back and finish our work, Joseph," Cohen said, his voice gentle but imposing. "We haven't much time."

The last sentence sent a shiver down Karl's spine.

"What're you planning to do with me?" he asked, not really wanting an answer.

"Four years ago," said Cohen, as if he hadn't heard Karl, "three children were burned to death in their home, in Ballymena..."

Karl snatched newspaper headlines from the stressed regions of his brain. *Family killed in tragic fire. Father commits suicide two months later...*

"Yes, I remember. Terrible."

"The media said it was a tragic accident. Tragic? Yes. Accident? No. The family were Jews; the arsonists, members of a neo-Nazi gang. The murdered children were my grandchildren."

"Dear God..."

"God? Like justice, there is no such thing," Cohen said. "The youngest child, Judith, was only three years old. What harm could she do? Murdered for simply being a Jew, and you dare speak of a god?"

"I...my mother was raped and murdered when I was young," Karl said, his voice barely a whisper. "I witnessed it and tried hiding in a clothing cabinet. I was attacked, left for dead. God ceased to exist for me from that day onwards."

Cohen looked as if he had been slapped.

Karl continued: "You don't know the half of it. Years later, I had the chance to avenge my mother's death, to kill the fiend. I failed, through cowardice, and he went on to kill two children. I hold myself responsible for their deaths."

"Not everyone is geared in life to take a life."

Karl shook his head. "Had I the courage to kill the beast, those children would be adults now, with children of their own. That fact torments me each and every day of my life."

In the stillness, broken only by the ticking of the clock, Karl and Cohen reflected on each other's life, and the cards dealt to them.

"Why did you leave the hand in my alleyway?"

"Panic." A wry smile appeared on Cohen's face. "The police had mounted a sobriety check, near your place, stopping drivers before testing them. I threw the hand up the alleyway. I'm afraid it was nothing more than a very bad coincidence. My original plan was to leave the hand outside the home of Harkin."

"Why leave the hands about the city? Those sausage machines look to be doing a grand job."

"Do you know the best way to flush out a rat, Karl?"

"A flamethrower?"

"A dead rat. Its corpse carries a special smell exclusively to other rats. They panic. That's the best time to capture them. The hand you found was to be a personal message to Harkin. He's been financing the hate gangs."

"Your daughter was the young woman who visited my office," Karl said. "I suspect her name isn't Judy Martin, and that the burns on her face and hands were caused when she tried to rescue her children. I suspect she confirmed my identity when you took the picture of me. She's the spitting image of him." Karl nodded in Joseph's direction. "Brother and sister, no doubt."

Joseph came rushing forward. "He knows too much, Father."

"Two days ago," Karl continued, "I went back to her place of business only to find that she had left unexpectedly. She wasn't the owner, but a part-time worker filling in for the holiday period. I presume that Uncle Benjamin is the semi-corpse whose eyes are staring directly at me now?"

"Father, don't you see? We have no other choice than to dispose of him."

Cohen shook his head wearily. "You would spill innocent blood, Joseph? Mingle it with the guilty?"

"He'll tell the police, collect the blood money. We'll go to prison for life."

Cohen looked tired and very old. "Yes, you could be right on all accounts. But you had nothing to do with any of this, Joseph. I'm sure Mr Kane will give me his word that he will in no way involve you. Isn't that right, Mr Kane?"

❦

Naomi climbed into bed beside Karl. "Is that the book that came in the post this morning?"

"It's the Jewish version of the Red Hand of Ulster," he said, holding up the hardback.

Naomi frowned. "You assured me after getting mugged at the abattoir that all that nonsense was over."

"I've admitted there was nothing to my abattoir theory, so can you stop rubbing my face in it?"

"Promise me you'll leave it to the police to find the serial killer."

Karl sighed. "I promise I'll let the cops *try* and find the killer. Okay?"

"Okay. You can read me one page before you we get down and dirty." Naomi's hand crawled down the sheets like a tarantula.

"Why does that remind me of a James Bond movie?"

Naomi giggled. "Pussy Galore?"

"It says here that some Jewish scholars believe the O'Neill's were the actual descendants of the Biblical Jeremiah. According to the story, Jeremiah fled from Palestine and travelled via Egypt and Spain to Ireland. Supporters of this theory propose that the Red Hand of O'Neill's originates from a scarlet thread — an umbilical cord — Jeremiah held in his hand at birth."

"Sounds a bit flaky." Naomi began cupping his balls.

"However," Karl said, trying gallantly to focus, "they could be mistaking it for another Biblical story. Jacob's fourth son, who was called Judah, had twin sons called Zarah and Pharez. When the twins were due to be born Zarah put his hand out of the womb and the midwife tied a red cord around his wrist to mark the first-born and his birthright — thus the 'Red Hand'. But Zarah of the Red Hand pulled his hand back and his brother Pharez was born first and so breached Zarah's birthright. Because Zarah lost his birthright he went into exile to Hibernia — Ireland."

"You must have some Jewish blood in you." Naomi smiled seductively at his circumcised penis before guiding it into her mouth.

Karl dropped the book on the floor and hammed a Sean Connery voice: "My dear Miss Moneypenny, I suspect your intentions are somewhat circumspect!"

MYTH

SHE WAILS THROUGH THE FAIR

WRITTEN BY KEN BRUEN

I chose the banshee because my father, who was the most sceptical and cynical of men, truly believed he'd seen the banshee before his mum's death and the story always stayed in my mind.

And he was a man who never took a drink his whole life!

—

Do I believe in ghosts, goblins and all that shite?

Take a wild friggin' guess.

I believe in:

Cash...cold.

Guns...primed and stolen.

Women...available and hopefully dumb.

Makes me a nice guy.

Like I give a fuck.

I'm not quite as hard-arsed as all that sounds, but it's a game face.

You play the pitch I do, you need all the front going.

I'd just finished a stretch in the Joy.

No, not an English barmaid, Mountjoy the nick in Dublin.

A credit card scam that went belly-up.

And I went down for four.

My lady, Shona, met me at the gates, with a:

Kiss

Bottle of Jay
Bundle of attitude.
She's a looker.
Swear to God and His mother.
And...
You're thinking,
The fuck is she doing with this whackjob?
She's nuts.
Straight up, certifiable.
Reason she is with the likes of me:
Guys see her, go,
"Holy shite."
Then they get to chat with her, realise she is like deranged, and head for the Connemara hills.
Fast.
She keeps me in cigarettes, booze and rent money.
I have the schemes, usually very bad ones, but she brings such an outrageous spin to them that most times we get by.
It's when I fly solo I go to jail.
Her first words to me on me being released:
"Frank is home."
Fuck on a bike.
My childhood mate.
He'd been in New York for ten years and for Christ's sake, now he comes back?
When we're shite-deep in the worst recession of our history?
He stays away for all the years of prosperity and comes home when we've lost it.
How dumb is that?
Seems he had little choice.
He had an uncle in Queens, a heavy hitter in the Unions, and Frank was doing real fine 'til he took off with the pension fund.

He has a gambling jones.

The eejit.

I always envied Frank.

He has the movie star looks, spoiled by a mean mouth, and Jesus, he could charm the ladies.

One of those guys, build it all up then blow it to hell and gone.

Shona had found a new flat for us on the promenade on Salthill.

Huge front window, looking right out on Galway Bay.

I love the ferocity of the sea, the fierce storms that make chaos seem attractive.

I didn't ask how she got such a place.

Best always not to probe too deep.

She might tell you.

And it's never good.

Never.

First off, we tore into the Jay, then we tore into each other.

It was rough, wild and just a bit scary.

She liked to bite.

Hard.

Did I complain?

Nope.

After, she lit a roach, blew hard and passed it to me. I said, "Don't do dope no more."

Got the look.

The one that says,

"You're the friggin' dope."

I let it slide, like most of her utterances.

She paid the freight, I paid in other ways.

Like keeping me mouth shut.

She flicked the dead roach across the room and I tried not to worry about fire. She said,

"Frank is meeting us in McSwiggan's this evening."

The only pub in Galway with a tree growing in it.

Don't ask.

I asked,

"How's he doing?"

She gave her enigmatic smile, a blend of grimace and malice, said,

"He has a plan."

Sweet Jesus.

I was only out of jail.

I didn't push as to the details, *soon enough*, I figured.

Shona made stew for dinner, it was good but had a kick.

I said,

"Has a kick."

She didn't even look up, muttered,

"That's the Jameson."

Uh-huh.

She'd gotten me some new gear, 501s, Doc Martens and a nicely battered black leather jacket. A T-shirt that had the logo:

Those who weep

Did I ask?

No.

We got to the pub close to seven.

Frank was already there, chatting up the lady bar keeper.

He had an Armani suit, dazzling white shirt, very flash boots.

Closer inspection showed he's had all these for quite some time, not so much frayed as over worn.

His long black hair was showing grey and his pallor accessorised. His former devil-gives-a-toss eyes had a new wariness.

You screw with the Unions in NY, especially Micks, you're going to be jumpy.

Like having the Boyos on your case.

Maybe the same gig.

He was drinking Bushmills, doubles, and I had me pint of black. Shona had some shite called a Wine Spritzer. She was so out there, she didn't need alcohol.

Frank and I did the polite dance of:

"How've you been?"

"You look mighty!"

And other usual Irish lies.

Then, five drinks in.

I was counting?

Always.

I liked Frank, but I didn't trust him.

Guy who gambles like he did, trust isn't on the agenda.

His eyes, showing the Bush, were bleary. He said,

"I'm a little short on the readies."

I tried not to sigh.

He stared at me for a length then continued,

"And time isn't on me side, some fellahs from the States are going to be arriving soon and I need to be gone."

I asked,

"You have something lined up?"

He slapped me on the shoulder, not gently.

Then he laughed, went,

"A sweet, sweet gig, post office on the outskirts of town, taking in the shit pile of cash for pensions, Social Security, other charitable crap."

I put up me hand, said,

"Whoa mate, things have changed, the fecking army guards post offices these days and no way am I going up against them."

He looked to Shona, but she gave him the blank stare.

He gave a deep dramatic sigh, said,

"You think I'd go half-cocked at this?"

Well, certainly half-pissed.

He spoke slowly, like I was deaf, said,

"That same day, your esteemed Minister of Health is due to address a huge rally in Eyre Square and with the train wreck of the Health Service, all the protection is going to be focused there."

Before I could comment, he snapped,

"You in or out?"

And with a smirk, added,

"Unless you've lost your balls since I've been away."

Nice.

Shona said,

"We're in."

End of discussion.

Later, leaving Frank outside the local kebab shop, his mouth smothered in grease and red peppers, he said,

"She's a good one, Mike, dumb as a donkey but she's got balls. Lucky one of you has."

That night, I was in a deep sleep, when Shona pulled me from it, screaming,

"Mike, come quick."

She seemed totally out of it, I mean more than usual, her hair as if she'd been trying to wrench it out, her eyes wild as she dragged me to the bay window.

I wasn't fully awake and trying to remember where Shona had put our nine-mill.

Shona was pointing at the window.

I couldn't see anything save heavy rain. I asked,

"What?"

She was shaking, asked,

"You don't see her?"

"Who?"

Her voice was cracked, and she went,

"The banshee, she was sitting at the window, combing her long grey hair and keening. Sweet Lord, the keening was like dying babies."

Right.

I said,

"Well, she's gone now, okay?"

She gave me a look of such pleading, then,

"Mike, you believe me, don't you?"

"Sure."

Then,

"You know what it means, Mike?"

Oh yeah, that Shona was even more bat-shit than before.

She said,

"Somebody is going to die."

I got her medication, added a shot of Jay and got her to bed.

Banshees...gimme a fucking break.

As I turned out the lights before I got back to bed, I avoided looking at the bay window.

Madness can be catching.

※

A week before the Robbery, Frank invited us for a night out, finalise the plans.

A time there, we'd polluted the world with Irish themed bars. Exported all the worst of our pub culture.

Payback.

We were now getting the same shite from other countries.

Los Lobos.

Jesus.

A tapas bar allied with every brand of designer beer. The staff were dressed in some kind of matador outfits, and at least looked suitably mortified.

Worse, they had karaoke evenings and yeah, Frank had selected our night to coincide with this horror.

Frank was drinking Margaritas, Shona and I settled for

Corona's. Frank, barely suppressing a sneer, said,

"You're supposed to have lemons with those."

We didn't have an answer and the staff seemed short on lemons. So Frank added,

"Bitter enough, yeah?"

Meaning me?

He outlined the plan. He and I would go in, fast, waving sawn-offs. Those, he told us, made maximum noise and had the effect of being lethal in appearance.

Shona would drive.

Few days before, Shona had taken to wearing a tiny Celtic cross to ward off the banshee.

She even had it dipped in holy water.

Frank, biting noisily down on a fajita, grease dripping from his mouth, leaned over to grab a napkin. His open neck shirt revealed a cross, the twin of Shona's.

I nearly dropped the Corona.

On stage, a parade of woesome singers continued to massacre popular songs.

If I heard one more version of *Bleeding Love*, I might shoot some bastard. Then a young girl did a version of *She Moves Through The Fair*. It's one of those songs that can almost sing itself, such is the feeling in it. But this girl, she brought a wealth of pain, hurt and dammit, tenderness that people were wiping at their eyes.

Shona was mesmerised, said,

"It's like she's wailing, like...keening."

I was going to suggest that maybe she'd like a Celtic cross?

That night, in bed, when Shona reached for me, I cried off. Her cross shining in the darkness burned me soul.

I had a real bad feeling about the post office.

I was wrong.

It went like clockwork.

We were in and out in like, jig time.

None of the stuff you hear, like the car stalling, none of that came down the pike.

We switched cars outside Oranmore and were back in the flat in Salthill within two hours.

Go figure.

Three large bags of euros, notes spilling out on the floor. It was major.

I was building large Jamesons, turned to hand a tumbler to Frank. He was standing over the bags, the sawn-off levelled at me.

"Sorry, mate. But I need to cover the lads in America and, you know, need some start up cash."

Shona was standing at the door and Frank turned, said,

"I enjoyed you, babe."

Gut shot her.

To me, said,

"Bitch betrayed you, me oul mate."

Pulled the other trigger.

Jammed.

I reached in my waistband, took out the nine-mill, said,

"Don't think the crosses are quite doing the job."

Shot him twice in the face.

Wiped that freaking smirk.

Buried them out in the bogs in Connemara, buried them deep.

I still haven't counted the money.

Shona was usually better at that.

Most nights, now that the heavy rains have really settled in, I'm lying in bed and I hear a scratching at the window, and if I listen real hard, I can hear...a wailing, a keening.

Do I go look?

Do I fuck.

Would you?

A PRICE TO PAY

WRITTEN BY **MAXIM JAKUBOWSKI**

Mea culpa. *I've only been to Dublin twice. The first time was a fleeting visit, which involved taking a cab from the airport to the railway station and then a train to County Westmeath to work with J. P. Donleavy on a book he was writing for the publishing house I then worked for. We completed our edit discussions, had smoked-salmon sandwiches and I got back to Dublin around midnight to find my hotel reservation had been lost. The next occasion, two decades later, was for New Year's Eve and I inevitably made my way to Temple Bar. Felt like the right thing to do, even though I'm a non-drinker (purely taste; no principles involved). So, I'm no expert, but the spirit of the city did somehow connect with me.*

I'm also a die-hard fan of the way that traditional Irish music has influenced so much of modern folk and rock 'n' roll in strange and wonderful ways that speak to my heart and guts. So, when the invitation to write this story came about, I knew it had to be a ballad of some sorts. A dark ballad, with death and soul heartbreak at its centre. I was working on a novel about an involuntary private eye seeking a missing young Italian girl, a story that took both characters to Paris and Rome, amongst other places, and couldn't get the theme out of my mind. So the new tale subconsciously became a variation on this story I couldn't escape, albeit with both characters somewhat changed to protect both the innocent and the guilty.

As for the Morrígan, I needed an angel of death, and three for the price of one was a temptation I could not resist. I willingly succumbed.

—

I was looking for a missing girl and the trail was growing cold.

Drunks ambled up and down the wide pavements of O'Connell Street, clutching cans of beer or empty bottles of cheap whatever as the curtain of night fell slowly over the autumnal Dublin weather. Only it wasn't autumn.

It was New Year's Eve.

I crossed the river and made my way towards Trinity College.

The University grounds were only partly open, of course, but an acquaintance of an acquaintance had hinted I might touch base there with Declan Connolly, a local snitch who might have some useful information. The *Book of Kells* exhibition was closed for the holidays, but earlier in the day I'd managed a visit to the Writers' Museum and paid my mental tribute to Irish literature. But now it was time for business again. In my business, there was no such thing as holidays.

Connolly was standing on the corner, close to the spot where the tourist buses disgorged their hordes of digital camera-waving visitors on the obligatory halt on the 'See Dublin in 20 Stops' circuit. Most were still sober, as the Guinness Brewery came later on the itinerary. Slung over his shoulder was a cavernous Strand Bookshop tote bag. I somehow guessed there were no books in it. Call it gut instinct. Under his black leather ankle-length coat, he was similarly dressed in black slacks and a black cashmere long-armed sweater.

We nodded to each other, acknowledging recognition, and walked on to the nearest pub.

Money changed hands. We drank.

Within minutes I knew the trail I had been following for the past weeks had grown cold as ice. The Italian girl he'd caught sight of the month before — a student hard up on her luck who was stripping to make ends meet in the top rooms of local disreputable clubs, and was on the slippery, druggy slide to oblivion — was not the one I sought. Connolly's girl was called Grazia, or at any rate, that's the name he had been given. More importantly, she was blonde.

"Maybe she's dyed her hair," I suggested, "and is using another name?" I was clutching at straws.

Connolly roared with laughter, and thin pearls of beer spluttered in a falling arc from his open mouth all the way across to the shoulder of my jacket. He was a fair few inches taller than me.

"The gal was stripping, man. I can assure you she was a natural blonde." He winked at me, mischief illuminating his ruddy face. "This Italian wench stood out, you know. Most working girls like to shave down there, you see. She didn't. She was different—"

I was about to interject, but he silenced me.

"Nah, I can tell when a woman colours her pubes, man. Looks damn unnatural, if you see what I mean." He gulped down another mouthful of beer. "And I had a front seat view. Real blonde. You can tell. No doubt about it. Absolutely."

He put his glass down on the bar counter and smiled, no doubt recalling the proximity of Grazia's pudenda. Waxing rhapsodic as he attempted to explain his certainty. "The colour of the skin around, the inner folds of the cunt a touch darker, the curls, the hair, it all sort of conjugates, you just sort of know when part of it is not real..."

A thin veil of hopelessness began rippling down my mind.

I was getting nowhere fast.

"Hmmm," I muttered under my breath. My glass of orange juice was empty.

Connolly jettisoned his obscene memories and gave me a sharp look. "Sorry, man."

"So?" I said.

"Maybe, just maybe..."

"Yes?"

His eyes swept the bar area, checking out the other punters. He lowered his voice.

"Maybe you could go and see the Morgan..."

"Morgan? Who's he, when he's at home?"

"It's a she," he said.

"Oh."

"If anyone knows anything that's going on, she would."

"Sounds good enough to me," I said.

"But there could be a price to pay..."

"My client is wealthy," I answered. "How do I find her?"

There was this restaurant on Temple Bar. Maybe one of the waitresses on the nightshift there in the downstairs room might know. She was Morgan's sister, it seemed. There was another sister, but she hadn't been seen for some weeks. Three sisters in all, it appeared. Morgan, Bab and Macha. Almost sounded like a trio out of a Russian play.

I paid for the drinks, crossed the road and made my way towards Temple Bar. It would be midnight in an hour or so, and the streets were fat with crowds, milling shiftlessly, ambling, parading up and down with drinks in tow as the New Year approached. It was getting colder and I turned my coat's collar up.

A doorway beckoned. Peering through semidarkness, a flight of wooden stairs. On the first floor to the right, a pub's saloon. Quiet noises of glasses clinking on counters and serious drinkers mumbling against a background of muffled traditional music. A welcoming night shrouded the deep room. And the prevalent smell of stale beer. Not my favourite fragrance.

Beyond the landing the stairs continued, cushioned on either side by yellowing posters advertising Guinness or forgotten Irish beaches that even desperate tourists might have ignored. Finally, I reached the top.

A sliver of light beneath a closed door. I moved towards it. Listened. Utter silence on the other side. I knocked. There was no response. Standing there, I felt a deep chill in the air. Knocked again.

This time there was a rustle of fabric, then steps. The door opened.

"Yes?"

It was a woman's voice, not that I could see a damn thing in the heavy penumbra beyond the threshold. There was a soft country lilt in her voice.

"I'm seeking Morgan," I said.

At first she didn't react to my question.

I waited. There was no point repeating myself.

The darkness lifted in part. I began to see her eyes. Green. Catlike. Piercing.

"Which one?" she finally answered.

"Just Morgan," I said.

"There are three of us," she answered, as if surprised I was not aware of the fact.

"I don't know," I indicated. "I was sent here. I was only given her name as the sister who could assist me. I have some questions I need answered."

"Ah..." She paused. "In that case it's my other sister you need."

Her eyes backed off towards the furthest end of the dark room and another set of eyes neared, every bit as green and piercing. It might as well have been the same woman.

"And what is it you wish to know?" Her voice was sharper, sustained by quiet anger.

By now I was becoming used to the darkness inside the dank room. I could distinguish her shape. Tall, wild-haired, a velvet robe of indeterminate colour ending at her feet.

"There's a young girl. Italian. She's been seen around here. I seek her."

The woman sighed.

"Then you need our other sister," she said.

Ah, I was now getting the whole deck of sister cards! But she did not retreat. She stood her ground. I waited for her to say more. But she failed to do so, just quizzically peering at me through the silence.

"So, is your third sister here?" I asked.

"Maybe," she replied.

"Should I wait for her?"

"That's entirely up to you," the first sister said, her green eyes now shining at me beside her sister's, like parallel sets of beacons in the Dublin night.

"In that case, I will wait," I said to them.

A set of eyes moved sideways and quiet steps softly shuffled across the room, and a pale light came on as she flipped a switch on the wall to our left. A meagre 30 watt bulb. It was larger than I imagined.

There was a sudden movement in the corner of my eye. I caught the swift movement of a small black bird racing across the room just below the ceiling. A crow. But when I looked for it again, it was nowhere to be seen. Maybe a trick of the pale light.

The two sisters were clothed in identical garb. Heavy green robes, almost like monks' habits. Tall, slender, but what stood out most was the burning fire of their red hair, myriads of untamed curls clustered together as well as exploding like a galaxy of circular stars in every possible direction, as if neither head had ever felt the caress or the pull of a comb or a hairbrush. For a brief moment, I thought of Medusa and the representations of the twisted Gorgon I had come across in books and paintings. And indeed, standing there in sepulchral silence, gazing at me, they were truly in the image of goddesses. Imperious. Come back to Earth. Or banished from the heavens.

Their gaze was unstinting. Full of anger. Like goddesses of war.

One of them spoke.

"There will be a price to pay," she said. I no longer knew which one had uttered the words.

There was a strange coldness, almost indifference, in her tone of voice.

"I know," I replied. "It's OK with me, absolutely."

They both smiled.

The sounds of the bacchanalian ocean of drunkards parading up and down Temple Bar outside began to fade in the distance, as if banished by time.

"So be it," the two sisters whispered in unison.

They moved towards me.

A different sort of music replaced the confused, modern sounds of New Year's Eve. Ancient, hypnotic, eternal, curiously faraway in time and space.

They were now so close to me that I could smell their breath.

Sweet, strong, intoxicating.

In one rapid movement, they both shed their robes and stood naked, facing me.

I drank in the regal pallor of their skin, the jutting angles of their breasts, the way their lower deltas shared the same shade of fire that adorned their heads.

It was beauty untamed. Consuming. Dangerous.

"Pay the price,'" one of them said.

I undressed.

They converged towards me in unison and smothered me in their embrace.

※

When I awoke in the bleak cold morning of New Year's Day, the memories of the past night made me retch, as if the abominable obscenities of what we had all done had literally sucked my soul out and spat it back into my body forever deformed, tainted.

As we had fiercely fucked, as they shared me between themselves, they had feasted on my flesh, my secretions, my emotions and left me empty, an abandoned shell of a man.

Goosebumps spread across my naked flesh. My penis looked even more shrivelled than ever, the surface of my skin a terrible shade of grey. I looked around for the clothes I had shed and dressed quickly, as if ashamed of my pitiful nudity, as if I had been used.

I remembered little of our lovemaking, save the tangle of limbs, the gaping of openings, the hunger of their kisses, but what I did clearly recall were the strange dreams I had travelled through between the repeated fucks. Images of bloody battlefields, of despair and pestilence, war and pain.

And surveying our intimate pornography in motion was the bird, the crow, flying high above the battleground as if giving us his blessing, his damnation, his approval.

I shook the torpor out of my limbs, tied my shoelaces and straightened my crumpled trousers.

Checked my wallet.

Everything was there; nothing had been taken from me. So why did I feel I was now less of a man?

And I remembered about the Italian girl I was seeking.

Paused for a moment's thought.

Looked around the now empty room as a thin sliver of

daytime peered hesitantly through the crack of a shuttered window in the far corner. There was a sheet of paper lying on the dirty wooden floor. The same filthy floor I had spent hours writhing on, rolling around, thrusting, being spread and flayed by the women's sexual greed.

I walked over.

It was just a crumpled sheet with rough drawings of an eel, a wolf and a cow. A curious trinity of animals. A child's bestiary? I peered at the page again. Turned it round.

On the back of the sketch, just a few words.

A name, an address.

The gift of Morgan.

I made my way to the door and the stairs and, holding unsteadily on to the rail, stepped hesitantly down to the Temple Bar pavement.

The smell of booze lingered in the air. Here and there, men with bloodshot eyes stumbled along the road, sometimes accompanied by hiccuping young women with short skirts hiked even higher, vulgar, hungover. This was the landscape after the bacchanalia. But did I look any better, I wondered.

I finally found an available cab near the river. Negotiated a rate, as the address I had been given was way out of town.

The driver dropped me off just a hundred yards from my destination.

The actual farmhouse was empty, but steps in the mud led to an outer building, a sort of barn.

The two men were still sleeping. Snoring loudly, empty bottles strewn across the ground, their attire in disarray.

In one corner, a naked woman, hands cuffed to a low beam, hung like a puppet. As if crucified.

I tiptoed silently towards her.

Dark blood still dripped down to the straw-covered floor of the barn from between her legs.

I pushed her chin up gently so that I could see her face.

Her eyes were open.

She was dead.

Her blonde hair hung limply, the ebony roots clearly showing through her parting.

It was the Italian girl.

I had no need to check her genitalia to confirm Connolly's lies. Not that I would have seen much due to the horrendous mutilations she had suffered there.

I felt sick to the core.

I closed her eyes as delicately as I could. There were dried tears on her cheeks. Tiny diamonds shining in the emerging light of the day through the open door of the barn.

I turned towards the sleeping men.

One of them, of course, was Connolly.

How could I have not guessed?

I picked up a pitchfork and with no hesitation dug it deep into his gut. He woke up, a look of pain and despair spreading across his ugly face. I pulled the pitchfork out in one rapid movement and plunged it straight into his face.

He never had the chance to say a single word.

Not that I required any explanation.

The other guy kept on dozing.

He was sleeping on his stomach, and I broke his neck with one savage stamp.

I searched for a key to the handcuffs still holding the dead girl up, but couldn't find it in the dead men's pockets.

I couldn't allow her to be found this way, strung up, defiled.

There was a can of petrol in the nearby garage. The whole place would be consumed before anyone in the area even spotted the fire. Better that way.

I walked back to Dublin with bile in my throat.

Yes, the Morgan sisters had been right. There had been a price to pay.

RED MILK

WRITTEN BY T. A. MOORE

I love mythology, all kinds of mythology, anyone who has dipped into the world I created in **The Even** *won't be surprised to read that. I have well-thumbed copies of* **The Heroes' Journey** *and* **The Masks of God** *by Campbell on my shelves and I am fascinated by the similarities and even more by the differences in myth cycles. If I'd known it was an option when I was a child, I'd have told people I wanted to be a mythologist (instead, I told them I wanted to be a jockey).*

Irish mythology has a special place in my heart. Amidst all my promiscuous myth loves, it's the one I always come back to. It resonates with me, my ideas and my narrative aesthetic.

So when the editors approached me to write a story for this anthology; I wasn't lacking in ideas, if anything I had too many of them. Partholon and his sorry fate? Fercherdne's homicidal loyalty to his lord? How could I choose? In the end, and again no one who knows me will be surprised, the story I picked is one of the less heroic of the heroic tales: the fate of King Bres.

It was the pragmatism that appealed — there is a surprising vein of it running through Irish myth. Once I had that idea in my head, the rest of the story took shape around it. My shabby, seedy world of drug dealers, mother's grief and compulsion. I hope you like it. I certainly enjoyed writing it.

The shaven-headed boy in a cheap grey suit lay in the coffin in the middle of the drawing room with his hands folded over his chest. The undertaker had slathered on the foundation, but the cheap black tatts he'd got in Hydebank Young Offenders showed through on his knuckles and throat like stigmata. Seventeen years old and already a bad wee bastard. Heavy gold signet rings hung loose on his fingers and chains were strung around his neck.

He'd been a spide in life and he was a spide in death.

Nothing an undertaker could do to fix that.

There wasn't much they could do to hide the hammered dent in his skull that killed him either. It had been spackled over and painted in, but you could still see the disfiguring outline of it. The priest had suggested a closed casket but Brigid wouldn't hear a word of it. Ruadán was her boy and she'd not close the lid on him 'til she had to.

Lugh stood over the casket and sucked on a beer. It was flat and warm as a mouthful of piss, but he wasn't going to confront the covey of old biddies in the kitchen just to get a cold one. They sat around the table in their shabby black plumage, drinking sweet tea and saying the faults of the dead like a rosary. Go in there, and they wouldn't be backward about coming forwards with the sins of the living either.

"Brigid ain't gonna let this go," Dagda said, joining him. Lugh's lieutenant smelt of cheap beer and fruitcake, a yeasty sourness sweating out of his pores. He put one hand on the coffin and crossed himself with the other. The ink on his fingers was faded from age and the backs of his knuckles were bloodied and scabbed over.

"I know." Lugh tilted another mouthful of beer down his throat and wiped his mouth on his sleeve. His suit was better quality than Ruadán's, but they were only ever worn for the same things: courts and corpses. "Fucking everyone's been telling me."

Dagda coughed and shifted his bulk uncomfortably on flat feet. He blamed prison for his fallen arches. Cheap fucking guddies they gave you in there. He said they should pay for his chiropodist.

"You gonna do something?"

Irritation twitched Lugh's upper lip tight over his teeth and he worked his jaw from one side to the other, listening to the crackle of an old break shifting. It all came down to that. To him. Every bastard at the wake had one eye on the *vol-au-vents* and the other on him to see what next.

He wasn't the hardest man in the room — bad feet or no — that was Dagda. Lugh, though, was the guy that got shit done.

"Yeah, I am." He handed his empty to Dagda who checked it for dregs. "I'm gonna talk to Brigid."

After one last glance at Ruadán's body, Lugh turned and walked away over the faded, patterned carpet. People shuffled to the side to give him room.

"Talking isn't what she wants," Dagda called after him as he started up the narrow stairs. "Last thing she wants."

It would have been easier if she'd just cry. Lugh was used to tears. Half the time they were shed for, or because, of him. It was normal. People died. All the fucking time, people died. The survivors would pay their tithe in tears and when they were done, pick up the threads of their life.

Brigid hadn't shed one tear since the doctors had told her that her son was dead. She just wailed quietly to herself. It was a weird, wild sound in the back of her throat that sounded like someone screaming from very far away. Rabbits made that sound. People shouldn't.

The door to Ruadán's bedroom was open a crack. Lugh paused outside and listened to that attenuated howl while he got up the courage to open the door. He wasn't a coward, but Brigid's grief was a hungry thing. It clawed at you when you talked to her.

Feel bad, it demanded, feel as bad as me.

He gave the bottom of the door a tap with a booted toe and it swung slowly open. The room was small and ill-kempt, with torn wallpaper and ripped carpets in stark contrast to the flatscreen TV and tower of gaming systems. Brigid sat on the end of the bed in Primark's best mourning, hugging a bundle of clothes to her chest. She rocked back and forth slowly, hunched over painfully as if her loss was located in her appendix. Her eyes were dry and filmy, her mouth red and wet.

"Brigid," he said, trying to gentle his voice. "Time to come down. Pay your respects."

She lifted her slipping, lop-skew face and fixed him with a contemptuous look. Bell's Palsy, the doctors said; it was caused by stress. It would pass. Brigid held out the balled jumper she'd been holding, letting it dangle from her hands. It was a new, black wool jumper with the price still hanging from the arms and a name-tag sewn crookedly onto the neck.

"He never even got to wear it," she said.

Lugh crossed his arms and leant against the door. He felt the ridge of the frame digging into the space between his shoulder blades. The pickled ghost of smoked tar lingered in the room; it crawled up his nose, found the addiction and kicked it awake.

"I thought he was expelled." He glanced around the room and only realised he was searching when he saw the crumpled tinfoil kicked under the TV. His mouth dried and his tongue stuck and he wondered if there was anything left.

"Suspended," Brigid corrected. She hugged the jumper tight to her chest, digging her long pink nails into the wool. "He was going back. I talked to him. He was going to get out."

Lugh breathed out through his mouth and scratched his throat. Only way Ruadán had been going back to school had been if he was hawking gear on the playground. That wasn't what Brigid wanted to hear. Least of all from him. Everyone knew Lugh hadn't liked the little shit; that he'd have kicked Ruadán out years ago if not for Brigid.

"Everyone is here."

She buried her face in the jumper and breathed in. Her brassy hair hung in draggles over her face and tangled in the curtain-ring loops of gold in her ears. Snot left a snail trail on the wool. She lifted her head and wiped her nose on her sleeve.

"Fuck them," she said, careful to get the words out clearly. "I don't owe them anything."

Lugh's mouth twitched. "You owe Ogma a tenner."

"Fuck you, too." Brigid pulled her legs up to her chest and lay down on the bed, curled up in her son's wrinkled sheets. "I will bury my son when I can bury his killer along with him. You kill Bres, then I'll come down."

"I can't," Lugh said. "I made a deal. I gave my word."

Brigid lifted her head stiffly, as if her neck was made of unjointed wood. "Your word?" She swung her legs over the side of the bed and lurched to her feet. "You gave your word? He killed my son! Bashed his head in over some cheap gear and left him to die in the gutter."

She went for him, raking at his face with clawed fingers. The edges of those French-tipped acrylics were sharp as knives and she aimed for his eyes. He grabbed her wrists and shook her, snapping her head back and forwards violently before tossing her back onto the bed. Lugh stepped forwards and cocked his fist back, his fingers curled so tight his bones creaked.

"Do that again," he said, pressing the back of his wrist to

his scratched cheek, "and I will beat you 'til both sides of your face match."

Brigid sat up carefully and wiped her face, sniffing noisily. She licked her cracked lips.

"I want someone dead," she said. Her mouth twisted and puckered tight around her pain. "Someone to bury with my son. Word to the wise, Lugh — you should have protected my boy and you didn't. Kill Bres before I decide you'll do instead."

The anger slipped through Lugh's fingers and left him nothing to feel but guilt. There should be something he could do. He rubbed his hand through his cropped red hair.

"I gave my word."

Two years ago. Him and Dagda had just gotten out of prison and they'd had a grudge to collect on. He remembered the rain. His first night of freedom and it had been pissing down on him.

※

Wet scrawls of paint tagged the battered brick walls of the alley, crawling from the ground to halfway to the roof. Condoms stuck to the wet ground where the whores had thrown them out the windows when the johns were done. Most nights Bres would be inside the club, doing deals behind the door of his office or test-driving a new girl. Tonight he knelt in a puddle with his hands on top of his bald head. Give the old bugger his due, his grey eyes stared into the barrel of the gun without a flicker.

"Didn't know you were out," he said.

Rain plastered Lugh's hair flat to his head and soaked through his thin T-shirt. He leant forward and pressed the gun to Bres' shiny forehead.

"Told 'em not to let you know," he said. "Thought it'd be a nice surprise for you."

For the first time Bres' eyes flickered and the steel went out of his spine.

"Since when do they listen to some jumped-up punk like you?"

Lugh lifted the gun and brought the handle down on top of Bres' head with a crack. The tight skin of his scalp split open, peeling back. Bres grunted and blew blood from his lips, struggling not to fall over.

"Since they found out it was you that told the police where to find me and Dagda," Lugh said. "We did three years because of you."

No point in denying it. Bres didn't even try. He squinted up at Lugh. "You're a young guy. What's three years to you?"

The trigger was smooth under Lugh's finger, warmed to body temperature. He started to squeeze. "Longer than you have left."

"Wait," Bres said sharply. He blinked and swallowed hard. It did Lugh's heart good to see him afraid. "You didn't answer my question. How much are those three years worth?"

"You think you can buy your way out of this?"

"I've fifty grand worth of tar stashed in a farm down near Ballymena. Yours. Free and clear. We forget this ever happened."

Lugh stepped back. He felt his mouth twist into something ugly.

"Too little," he said. "Too late."

Bres' eyes flinched and he struggled to keep his voice even.

"Fine. You get the shipment and the organisation. All you have to do is let me walk."

Lugh hitched one shoulder in a shrug. "I figure I'll find the farm one way or another." He'd been twenty-one when he went into prison. First time as an adult. Those three years were worth a lot. "I've been looking forward to this."

In a grace note to the moment that Lugh could not have hoped for, Bres pissed himself. It stained the crotch of his jeans and dribbled in lines and spots down his thighs. He breathed in through his nose and the tendons in his jaw bulged in shame and fear.

"Go to hell then," he hissed through tight lips.

"You first," Lugh said. "Unless..."

It was too late to offer hope and not have it be an insult. Hatred glittered in Bres' small, stony eyes. He'd just pissed himself, it was crueller to let him live when everyone would know that.

"What?" Bres asked.

Lugh crouched down, balancing on the balls of his feet, and stared intently at Bres.

"Your suppliers," he said. "Their names and their contacts. You give me that and I'll let you walk out of here alive."

Bres took two shuddering breaths and spat onto the ground. "Your word on it?"

Lugh kissed the gun. "My word of honour," he said through lips that tasted of oil. "Give me that and I won't kill you or order it done."

※

Lugh left Brigid to her keening, got Dagda and dragged him out into the back garden. It was a tiny handkerchief of crazy paving, cat shit and weeds. There were long planters full of dead herbs balanced on the two kitchen windows.

"Told you she didn't want to talk," Dagda said.

Lugh lit a cigarette and sat down on a dirty white plastic chair. It wobbled under his weight and wet his arse. He sucked hot smoke into his lungs and tried not to think about the acid bite of tar.

"She wants Bres dead," he said.

"You can't do it," Dagda said. "You gave your word."

Lugh exhaled and squinted at Dagda through a haze of bluish smoke.

"Did you think I'd forgotten? Bres has been boasting of that vow since he dried his dick and got into a new pair of jeans."

It didn't take much to amuse Dagda and he sniggered to himself at the memory of Bres stumbling out of the alley, smelling of piss and fear and sweat, to join his lieutenants. While Dagda was distracted, Lugh tried to think. His brain tried to tell him he'd think better after a taste of H, but he knew that was a fucking lie.

"Bres has gone too far," he said, trying the idea out on Dagda. "He has to die, vow or not."

Laughter vanished from Dagda's open face and he frowned, pointing a finger at Lugh. "You can't touch him, Lugh." It was the reaction Lugh had expected, although not the one he'd hoped for. "Break one promise and your word won't be worth shit from here to Chicago."

"We don't need Bres' friends in the police sniffing around either," Lugh said. "I don't plan to go back to jail over him." Three years had been enough.

Dagda leant on the wall and shifted his weight onto one foot, giving the other a rest. "So what will we do then?"

Lugh wished he had an answer to that. He made himself smile and wink one bright blue eye at Dagda.

"You'll see," he said.

※

A message made its way from Lugh's fiefdom in Twinbrook to Bres' place in Poleglass. It was muttered in pubs and passed on scraps of paper from one nervous man to the other in the street.

It was one word.

Truce.

When it reached Bres in his club — where for a reasonable price you could fuck the Thai girls upstairs any which way you wanted — he laughed, screwed the message up and tossed it aside.

That night his brand new Jag was boosted from outside his house. It came back two nights later, the interior fouled with shit and stinking of piss, the engine ripped out of it and the tyres slashed.

"Fucker!" Bres screamed. When he got angry he flushed red and the jagged scar on his scalp glowed white. He kicked the car in a fury until he collapsed on the street, exhausted and out of breath. "I'll fucking kill the little prick. Does he think he can fuck with me?"

Then the police raided his club. His whores were wrapped in blankets, led down the stairs and out into the street by sympathetic policewomen. Bres' protests that he didn't know anything about what happened upstairs rang hollow. All of a sudden his old friends on the force were too busy to answer his calls.

"My bribes put Inspector Fat-arse Harvey's kid through college," Bres said sourly. He topped up the whiskey in his tumbler and knocked it back. Opposite him his one-eyed lieutenant still nursed the first glass he'd been poured. It wasn't wise to abandon your wits around Bres, his moods were unpredictable. They sat in the empty club, torn yellow police tape fluttering from the door. "I had the boys beat the fuck out of his wife's boyfriend and run him out of the province. And yet now, all of a sudden, I'm a liability!"

His lieutenant shifted uncomfortably in his chair and turned his one eye towards the crumpled piece of paper that sat on the desk.

"Maybe we should listen to what Lugh has to say?"

Bres lifted his head from his chest and glared at him. Sweat rolled off his scalp and soaked into his collar.

"Don't be a retard. Truce, my arse." He picked the bit of paper up and squeezed it between his fingers. "This is one of that clever git's wee plans to get back at me for what happened to Ruadán. That mad bitch of his blames me for what happened to the kid."

"He *was* selling your gear—" The lieutenant stopped and hunched his shoulders, breathing shallowly. He nudged his glass away from over the table. He'd only had a few sips, but it was obviously too much.

Luckily Bres hadn't been listening.

"Don't know why Lugh gives a fuck," he muttered. "He should be thanking me for getting Brigid's bastard out of his hair. Wee shit was a liability."

He threw the bit of paper in his lieutenant's face and slouched back in his chair. His fingers drummed a tattoo on the polished wood.

"No truce. I need to show Lugh, show everyone, that I'm not afraid of him and his freaks."

A glitter from eyes sunk under heavy brows challenged the lieutenant to call him a liar, but the man hadn't drunk that much. He ducked his chin and held his tongue. Bres nodded once and poured another glass of whiskey.

"I just need a way to prove it."

Thirty cardboard boxes stamped with Clover Field Creamer were stacked where the coffin had been. Brigid had come down in the end, for the funeral, but she spent most of her time in Ruadán's bedroom. She wandered the house at night, and in the morning Lugh would find the vodka drunk and bits of bread on the floor. It was if the sin-eater had come for the funeral and not left again.

"Creamer?" Lugh pulled one of the boxes open and lifted out one of the ten cartons. He shook it to hear the powder shift inside. "That's new."

Diancecht twisted the cap of a bottle of pills and shook a single white tablet out into his hand. He'd been a doctor once and still preferred his pharmaceuticals processed and with child-proof caps. The long thin man crossed his legs and rolled the tablet between his fingers.

"His wife had a baby." He popped the tablet into his mouth and swallowed it down dry, grimacing at the taste on the back of his tongue. "Apparently he feels weird, packaging the shit in baby food now."

The flap of the carton had been glued shut. Lugh wriggled a finger under the seal and pried it loose. He held his breath as he squinted into the packet so he didn't inhale any of it.

"Still cuts it with baby laxative though?"

Diancecht propped his head up on his index finger. He raised narrow eyebrows at the question and nodded.

"Far as I know," he said. "That a problem? I always figured it'd do its bit to stop the holes from backing up. Never did figure how your eyes didn't go brown when you were using."

"Cos I'm your ma's blue-eyed boy." Lugh took another carton of creamer from the box and tossed it to Diancecht. The doctor caught it just before it bounced off his pinstripe shirt. "And I think we could get away with cutting this lot a bit more."

Diancecht pushed himself up out of the sofa.

"Junkies will be shitting themselves in the street," he said. "But if you don't have a problem with that, I sure as hell don't."

Lugh just smirked. "Oh, I got something other than a laxative in mind."

Looking puzzled, Diancecht followed him into the kitchen. The supplies lined up along Brigid's counters and piled up in her sink made Diancecht go a sallow colour.

"Lugh," he said. "I don't do this shit. I facilitate and patch up. That's it."

"Yeah?" Lugh fished a bag from the sink and dropped it onto the counter. He pulled a switchblade from his pocket and thumbed it open. The blade sliced through the black plastic likeness of a rat and let out the grainy powder. "Think of it as a promotion. Now get to work. We got a lot to do before tonight."

※

The farmer sat in his old armchair and stared at the slowly dying embers of the fire. He could hear the dogs howling from their kennel out back. They weren't used to it. His da had thought a dog's place was outside but the farmer was softer on them, and it wasn't as if he had anyone else to keep him company. He rubbed the end of his nose with his thumb and snuck a sidelong look at the three men crowded into his cramped living room.

Not usually anyhow.

They knew his name but he didn't know theirs. It was safest that way, but he'd given them names in his own mind anyhow. One-Eye and Monster and Blackie. They used to visit quite a lot but he hadn't seen them in years. Not since the new guy — the skinny red head with the flaying smile and smirk-blue eyes — took over.

This wasn't going to be a good night

"Can't you shut those fucking dogs up?" Blackie asked.

The farmer hunched his shoulders and rubbed his hands together, hard skin and thick calluses rasping.

"They don't like strangers much. It makes 'em nervous."

Blackie flicked the side of his heavy wax jacket back and put his hand on the gun slung under his arm.

"If they don't shut up," he said, "I'll give them something to be nervous about."

One-Eye stirred and looked away from the window. He'd taken his glasses off and the sight of the ruined socket on the left side was sickening.

"Give over," he told Blackie. "And don't waste your ammo on a couple of sheepdogs."

Blackie scowled but moved his hand, the jacket falling closed again. "Lugh and his boys hear that racket coming up, they'll know something is wrong."

The farmer swallowed dust and tried to pretend he'd never heard that name. Bury it down in the bottom of his mind, bury it deep enough and maybe he'd forget it.

One-Eye cocked his head to the side to listen to the banshee wail of the dogs. It was the bitch making most of the racket, the farmer could tell.

"What do you usually do for deliveries?" One-Eye asked.

"Lock 'em in," the farmer lied. He didn't want his dogs in the middle of this, whatever this was. "The other lot are used to the noise."

One-Eye stared at him for a moment, then shrugged and went back to looking out the window.

"Leave the damn dogs alone."

Blackie spat onto the carpet and went into the kitchen. Monster just sat by the fire, toasting his feet in their expensive Nike trainers, and watched the farmer with eyes so pale they looked like water. Sweat itched between the farmer's shoulder blades and in the small of his back. He'd been there when the Monster knee-capped some poor sod with a hammer. The sound of snapping tendons was the only thing he'd seen make the Monster smile.

The farmer fidgeted in his chair, tugging his sleeve back to check the time. Ten past eleven. They weren't late yet. Five more minutes until he had to worry about what he'd do if fate had cancelled tonight's run.

Five minutes passed and then seven. The farmer hadn't

had a sip to drink since he last went to the bog, but his bladder still cramped urgently on him. He was just about to ask to go to the toilet — ask, in his own house — when One-Eye backed quickly away from the window.

"They're here." He bent down and pulled an automatic from the bag they'd brought with them. "Get ready." He tossed the gun to Monster, who snatched it neatly out of the air, and got another one out of the bag himself. Both men checked the guns over quickly: ammo, firing mechanism, barrel.

"We need to leave any of them alive?" Monster asked.

One-Eye put his glasses back on, hiding the ruined socket behind a blacked-out lens, and shook his head.

"No. Bres wants to send a message about his car. Make it messy."

Monster's lips curled slightly: could have been humour, could have been contempt. Outside the dogs went spare at this second invasion, throwing themselves against the wire and barking 'til they choked on the sound. The farmer hunched down in his chair, trying to disappear between the cushions. It didn't work.

"You." One-Eye slapped him on the side of the head. "Get up. Go out. Let them in. Don't do anything stupid."

The farmer got up and went outside. It was cold. His breath steamed on the air in front of him as he stamped his way down to the gate. The van was stopped on the other side, on top of the cattle-grate. The headlights blinded him. He squinted and shielded his eyes but whoever was driving tonight didn't take the hint. The lights stayed on.

He fumbled at the padlock with cold fingers. It slipped out of his fingers twice and he dropped his keys into the mud.

"Sorry, sorry," he muttered to no-one in particular, crouching down and groping in the dark. Mud and cow crap slipped through his fingers and clogged under his nails. He finally grabbed the keys, scrambled to his feet, unlocked the chain and pulled the gate open. He hoped they'd think he was just shaking from the cold.

The van drove into the yard and turned right towards the house instead of left towards the barn. That wasn't right. They never did that. Standing there in the dark, with dirt under his nails and a stone in his bladder, the farmer stared after the van's tail lights. He clutched the gate tightly with one hand, imprinting the pattern of rust and dents on his palm. It occurred to him that they were all occupied and he could run. He shuffled over the cattle-grate, scrambled through the fence at the side of the road and cut away across the field.

From the farmhouse Corb watched him go through a pair of night vision binoculars, the farmer's body picked out in murky shades of green against the dark field. A coward's shield of arms.

"He's rabbiting."

"Let him." Mell scratched the scarred edge of his empty eye and then smashed the window with the butt of the Steyr. "We know where he lives."

He aimed at the front of the approaching van and squeezed the trigger. Recoil jammed the gun into his palm and jarred his shoulder. Bullets made the dirt in front of the van dance. He adjusted his aim and blew out the tyres. The nose of the van pitched forward; it lurched to the side and crashed into a fence-post. Smoke belched from under the crumpled hood. The driver's door opened and someone in dark clothes slid out and crouched down, using it as a shield. Another gunman scrambled out the back of the van. A single gun fired into the side of the farmhouse.

"We work for Lugh!" the driver yelled, peering out the gap

between windscreen and door.

"Not Dagda," Mell said.

Corb said, "We got lucky."

"Just don't get cocky." Mell squeezed the trigger again and stitched bullets from one side of the driver's side door to the other. It jolted and juddered under the impact, smacking back into the man hiding behind it. Mell batted the curtain aside and yelled through the gap. "We work for Bres."

A bullet winged its way past his head and killed a picture on the wall. Mell touched his stinging head and brought his fingers away bloody.

"Fuckers," he said, without heat, and wiped his fingers on the nets. "Where's Dub got to?"

Corb fired two shots at the van from his window and pointed with his gun towards the corner of the yard where they'd parked their car. The Barrack Buster had been hidden under the floor in back. Now it was balanced on Dub's broad shoulder. Mell could see his teeth gleaming.

"Down!" he snapped.

Both men dropped to the floor and wrapped their arms around their ears. The dull whomph of the RPG firing was followed by the window rattling explosion of it hitting its target. The old stone house rattled on its foundations. What little glass was left in the window showered over the two men. The photographs dropped off the wall and shattered on the ground.

Mell unwrapped his arms from around his head. His ears were ringing. He staggered to his feet and shook off splinters of glass.

"What the fuck?" He leant out the window and screamed. "You've gone and blown up the fucking gear!"

Dub swung the RPG off his shoulder and propped it up against the car. He yelled something back that Mell couldn't hear, rolled his eyes and pointed.

"...hit the road!" The words filtered through the buzz of Mell's affronted ear drums. He looked. The white van was still where it had been when he dropped. The road behind it was burning. "Van's fine. Just...flattened them."

Mell grabbed a groggy Corb by his collar, hauled him to his feet and shoved him out of the house. They staggered over the yard and slipped and skidded their way down the muddy road.

"See?" Dub said when they reached him. He thumped the side of the van with his hand. It made a hollow, echoing noise. "I told you it was fine."

Mell checked for himself. The van doors were scorched, paint peeling off in big, cracking blisters, but when he wrenched them open the boxes inside were intact.

"Should we check it?" Corb asked eagerly.

"No." Mell lifted a box out and tossed it to him. "Just start moving them into the car."

While a muttering Corb unpacked the van, Mell made his way around the smouldering crater blasted in the road. Lugh's men lay on the ground. One of them was already dead, his back charred and a piece of glass in his head. The driver was down but stirring weakly. He groaned and propped himself up on his elbows. Mell shot him in the back twice and left him sprawled in the mud.

❧

It was a bad night. The wind cut through fabric and right down to the bone. Lugh stood in the shelter of a shop door with his hood pulled up over his head. The ground under his feet was littered with the butts he'd chain-smoked to keep warm. He'd just lit a fresh one, filling his lungs with harsh smoke, when a battered old Vauxhall drove past. It turned left on the corner. He was halfway through the cigarette when Dagda came walking down the street towards him.

He'd changed out of his courts-and-coffins suit into jeans and a pair of Docs, the leather worn through to the steel on his toes. Lugh handed him the cigarette when he reached the shop door. Thick fingers pinched the filter, cupping it in his palm. He took a drag.

"Bres had the farm torched," he said. "Blew a fucking great hole in the road too." Smoke slipped from his lips like steam from a pot. "I nearly drove into it."

Lugh took the cigarette when it was offered. He took a last draw and dropped it to the ground, grinding it under his foot with the rest.

"Van got back here half an hour ago," Lugh said. "Time enough."

"For what? Two men dead. A whole shipment just handed over to Bres. We've gone along with it, the least you could do is tell me what's going on."

Lugh stepped out of his sheltered doorway and clapped a hand to his lieutenant's shoulder.

"I'll tell you if it works," he said.

Dagda heaved a sigh and shook his head, but stepped aside to let Lugh pass. He pulled a spare gun from under his jacket and handed it to Lugh. They headed over the road.

The door to the club was closed but the lock hadn't been fixed since the police raid. Lugh kicked it open and sauntered inside. Two of Bres' men scrambled up from a table, another whipped out a shotgun from under the bar. Lugh and Dagda turned on their heels and raised their weapons. Smooth as greased shit.

"What the fuck! What the fuck!" One of the gunmen stuck on the obscenity, jabbing the gun in the air for punctuation. His one-eyed friend let him rant and backed away from the table.

Lugh held up his hands. Open, empty, relaxed. His attention was on the one-eyed lieutenant. "I'm here to talk to

Bres, Mell."

The barman's finger twitched on the trigger and he swayed his weight nervously from one foot to the other.

"We gonna do it?" he asked.

"What if Bres ain't here?" Mell said.

"Trust me," Lugh said. "Lying for Bres ain't going to do you any good."

There was a silent moment of communication among the three gunmen. Mell was the first one to move. He let the gun dangle from his fingertips and leant forwards to set it carefully on the table, between the beer and the bag of nuts.

"In his office." He pointed with his chin. "If he wants to kill you, he can do it himself."

The other two followed his lead.

The barman suddenly thought better of letting them walk in on his boss. He snatched the shotgun back up, aimed it and Dagda shot him. Blood sprayed from the back of his head and a bottle of Aftershock exploded. Dagda gave the other two a flat look to see if they were inclined to loyalty too. They weren't.

Lugh pushed the door open and walked into the office.

※

The office stank, a sickening mixture of vinegar and the sour milk odour of puke. The stolen boxes were stacked up in front of the desk to form a flimsy cardboard parapet. A ripped-open carton of what claimed to be creamer lay on the desk, spilling white grains out over the polished wood. Bres sprawled dead in his chair, frothy vomit still wet around his mouth and on the front of his shirt. His eyes were wide open, bloodshot and bulging. His throat was a mess of torn flesh. The missing skin was clotted under his own fingernails.

"OD?" Dagda poked the parapet of boxes with his toe. It trembled under the assault. He shook his head in reproof. His appetites were huge and frequently indulged, but he had little sympathy for those who couldn't handle their own. "How much of our H did he snort?"

He wiped up some of the H with his finger and went to stick it his mouth. Lugh caught his wrist before the powder touched his tongue.

"Bres kept Naloxone in his desk," he said. "He knew his limits too. I couldn't count on an OD. Rat poison was more reliable."

Dagda spat onto the floor and wiped his finger on his trousers, scrubbing his hand over and cursing. One-Eye appeared at the door and looked in, his eye finding Bres' body. His tongue touched his lips and he gave the slightest nod of acknowledgment to Lugh. Dagda kicked the door shut in his face and glared at Lugh.

"You gave your word."

"I swore not to kill him," Lugh said. "And I didn't. He killed himself by gorging on bad skag."

"That you poisoned."

Lugh tugged his sleeve down over his fingers and picked up the toppled carton, setting it upright. A red cow beamed beatifically from the front.

"What the fuck's your point?" he asked Dagda. "Can't a man poison his own product anymore? I didn't make Bres steal it and stick it up his nose. TV's been telling us for years that this stuff is poison."

Dagda didn't look convinced, but he nodded acceptance and rocked from side to side on his bad feet.

"And now?" he asked.

Lugh tipped Bres out of his chair and onto the floor. He gave the dead man a kick, rolling Bres' head around so his staring, bloodshot eyes glared up at his killer. A reproach without effect. Lugh fished his mobile from his pocket, framed the image and snapped it.

He wasn't dragging the stinking corpse back to Twinbrook. Brigid would have to content herself with a photo to gloat over. A tap of his thumb sent it.

"Get rid of him," he said. "Put the word out, Dagda. I'm in charge now. Of everything."

"And if they don't believe me?"

"Give them a demonstration."

Dagda grabbed Bres' ankles and dragged the dead man out of the room, leaving Lugh alone. The chair wouldn't see use again — he wasn't going to sit in Bres' piss —so he leant back against the wall. His phone chirped and he checked the message.

"Hail to the new King."

BOG MAN

WRITTEN BY JOHN MCALLISTER

When the editors of **Requiems for the Departed** *asked me to write a story for the anthology, an image of a bogman immediately clicked into my head. And that's where it stayed for month after month until near the deadline.*

All I had to go on was the fact that bogmen were either the victims of murder, or sacrificial victims. Then memories came to me: a story I read years ago about pre-historical life around Stonehenge, where the Druid chose as that year's offering a woman, who had annoyed him; a lone hill near Coalisland, in County Tyrone rising out of the bogs; and the seeming chance that some bog roads are maintained as important county roads and others abandoned to nature.

I don't particularly believe in ghosts and things that go bump in the night, but I do have experience of something out there, of portents and signs, so I buy into the crows and the old washerwoman foretelling the death of Cúchulainn, which I have used in my story.

The rest came from two evenings spent turf cutting as a child and the feel of freedom that open spaces give me.

It also allows me to make a belated apology by dedicating the story to Sorley O'Dornan. On the way to the bog, riding on the bar of his bike, I managed to poke my foot between the spokes. We cartwheeled into the — luckily dry — ditch.

Bog oil leached from the turf into the water. From there it strained through the sheepskin jacket and entangled the matted hair floating on the surface. The early sun caught the oil and mixed in the dregs of a rainbow.

Blood lay there as well, and the ends of a knotted hemp rope. The unravelled ends floated free beside the mound of air-locked sheepskin.

Tarlóir leaned forward for a closer look and blinked in surprise. The dead man wore a linen shirt — once boiled white, now dark with tannin. It was most unusual for one of his station to wear linen. He couldn't have come by it honestly.

"A cruel death," said Concobhar. He was well-named after the hound, always at heel and trained to obey.

Tarlóir shrugged. "It was necessary."

"Necessary?"

"A bloodletting. It's the way of the world."

He said it in a matter-of-fact tone that surprised even him. When had he first thought that way? As a child, he had cried when his mother killed a baby rabbit he wanted to keep as a pet. He refused to eat that night and went to bed still howling.

He might not howl at death now, but he held back from touching this particular body. The feet were still under the surface, pinned down by rock. The head and shoulders and the bound hands floated free. After two weeks in the water, the skin was a slime waiting to come off in their hands.

Revolting. But one Morrigan less, and no loss.

The Morrígans, if he could believe the local shanachees, were descended from the coupling of King Oonie with the devil goddess Agrona. The Morrígans stayed within their own group except when thieving. Their widows were encouraged to whore in the outside world, in order to bring wealth and new blood into the community. The men slouched the countryside, hating people for hating them.

This Morrigan had lost part of a hand, gnawed at by some predator. Perhaps in feasting it had disturbed the restraining rocks. Large paw prints marked the edges of the bog hole and scoured channels where the animal had slipped and strained.

"That's what you get when you do a job in haste," said Concobhar in disgust.

"Bad luck will hound them," agreed Tarlóir. "Bad luck, and the fact we knew they lied when they said he had gone travelling. His sort are home-birds. They do their catting no more than a good hour from their settlement."

"But why kill him?"

"Why did they do it?" Tarlóir motioned for a group of men standing back a respectful distance to come forward. They advanced in broken formation, each man with his head down, eyes watching their step on the rough, turf-cut ground.

Not waiting for them, he walked upwind from the body before continuing. His gravelly voice softened as he speculated, "Spring is in the air; as good a time as any for a clearing out. He had no friends, or was vulnerable, or threatened the leadership in some way."

He could go the same way himself. Very few of his station were allowed to retire in peace. Old men with wandering minds could embarrass the Council of Elders by telling of things best forgotten.

He grimaced in distaste at the oil and dirt staining the tops of his boots. At least the rubbed-in goat fat had made them waterproof, but splashed dampness edged its way down through the socks, chilling his feet. He hated cold feet.

Bred in the mountains, he had the hill-man's disdain for the sucking bogs. Only his job of bringing the region to heel could keep him here. The men who had come with him were few in number, and not even the Council's alleged supporters among the locals could be trusted.

"What?" asked Concobhar who, like a good hound, sometimes sensed his thoughts.

"One of them, the girl. The two of them were seen together on Fair Day. He was buying her ribbons off a bagman."

"She'll not talk, not that sort," said Concobhar.

"Maybe they think she might, which could be dangerous for her. And she's starting to show. My woman noticed that."

His woman had noticed the ribbons as well, and the sweet honeycomb sold by the traders. No wonder her teeth were bad.

They stood in silence for a time. It wasn't often Tarlóir had peace to enjoy the wind in his face and the sun on his closed eyes. A smell came off the bog. Rancid, but overlaid with the sweetness of new life. He opened his eyes again as a flight of three lapwings blurred past his feet, skimming the heathers. The birds banked between the gorse bushes and flicked out of sight.

Three, a good number. The priests of the new god, Jesus, preached the mystic power of seven, but even their leader Padraig had to fall back on the shamrock. Better than that, the lapwing was a sign that good luck would follow.

Seeing the lapwings made Tarlóir willing to take a chance. Normally he favoured the slow, methodical approach, preached it to his men. Perhaps this time he should be like the roe, and leap.

"We'll walk," he decided.

"What?"

He shrugged. "How else did they get the body here?" He looked around him. "You don't see any tracks, do you?"

From where he stood, scrawny trees blocked the horizon. In the mountains, those trees would have been like grass in the far fields. Here, instead of fields, were clumps of heather and sudden drops where turf had been cut away. Soon it would be time to go home again for the feast of Beltane, to feel the spring grass brush his feet and the ache of the hills in his legs.

When he first dared go back, he had built a house in the hills; not much of one, but it did for him and the wife. They liked to turn the sod and help root out the harvest. Share religious ceremonies ingrained in the soil with his brothers and sisters. Only among family was he liked and accepted for himself and not greeted with fear because of his job. A job that had him walk the lowlands with Samhain. In the mountains the old gods sang in his blood.

※

They set off northwards, with the spring sun more behind them than to the side. The persistent wind gathered speed over the open ground, found a gap at his neckline and chilled his back. It made him long for the honest cold of winter when he could wear his cloak and hood. Three crows flapped their way overhead, going in the same direction. The sight of them made him shiver.

People had passed this way — they saw footprints in the mud and crushed heather — but whether it was to cut the turf or carry a body, they couldn't say. At one point they stopped at a patch of cleared ground. Someone had used a flachter to cut through the heather and roots into the raw turf below, and had thrown the scraw into the adjoining bog channel.

Tarlóir made an impatient noise with his lips. "Always the easy way out. They block the channel with that mess, then someday there'll be a surge and a poor innocent will find himself drowned."

With any luck it would be one of the Morrígans, but they had the goddess Carlin on their side, and thrived where others failed.

Tarlóir and Concobhar stood on a turf mound in order to see the cleared ground better. Its humus was ridged by circling feet and, was it their imagination, or did they see the handle of a flachter edging the surface of the still water?

"It couldn't be that easy," said Concobhar.

Tarlóir had a ghost pain in his shoulder, as if a bird sat there, talons hooked into his skin. He needed peace to have the gods speak to him.

He said, "Fetch the men. I'll wait here to mark the spot."

While he waited, he walked the ground around the clearing. Vague footprints were there, telling their own story, if only he could make sense of them. He spotted something else in the channel, almost buried by a last handful of scraw.

He walked the ground again, putting his feet where others had trod, looked at what they'd looked at. Noted the caked patches on the raw turf that had to be blood, and the violent tears in the heather where a man had clawed for life.

Part lapwing and part crow, the good and the bad came out of the ground and spoke to him. When he thought he had things correct in his head, he took his ease on a low turf bank.

For once it was pleasant to merely sit and not have to answer questions or make decisions. Upholding the law of the Feni was a lifetime penalty for his own youthful revolt. He unbuckled his sword belt and put it and the weight of its office to the side.

If only people realised that good order meant obedience to the law. Not the big ones — crime like that day's murder were exceptional enough — but respecting a neighbour's right to a night's rest, and exchanging a pleasant word instead of a curse.

In recent years the Morrígans had become greedy, their villainy organised: livestock poisoned or stolen away, and equipment sabotaged. It was time they were brought within the law.

His men came at last, just as he was getting chill. He wasn't sure if he had become soft from lowland living or from the constant damp off the bogs that brought a winter ache to his bones. Four men carried the body in one of their short cloaks. Others walked on the far side of the channel, looking for signs of a struggle there.

"Good thinking," he told Concobhar.

It had occurred to him to give that order, but he liked people under him who thought for themselves. Just so long as their thinking was about practical things. Initiatives remained his domain.

He sat on while the men recovered the flachter from the channel and brought it to him. It was cold to touch. The cutting edge remained free from rust and the wooden shaft was thoroughly wet but not waterlogged, so it hadn't been in the water for long. He hefted it and found it had a good balance. Old and well maintained, it may have been the murder weapon. Probably was, but there was no way he could say for sure.

He pointed to the heap of scraw. With a stretch and scoop of the flachter, one of his men flicked a woman's shoe onto the bank. It lay there, its leather darkened by blood. Almost certainly there was a matching one somewhere in the water, but he nodded, satisfied. He had enough evidence for what he wanted.

When the men had done their work he stood and re-buckled his sword belt.

"The body?" he asked.

"One slash to the throat," said Concobhar, pointing.

The throat could have been a second mouth; giving an extra-wide smile to a man who had never worn one in life. The arms and hands had been bound; soon after death, no doubt, for ease of carrying. The ropes had almost disappeared into the bloated body, which seeped a rancid fluid.

The cloak holding the body was spoiled. The smell would linger in it for weeks to come. Maybe it should be replaced, but that was money out of his own pocket.

He looked to the near hill, edged with bog where the Morrígans lived. "I'll go on my own," he told Concobhar.

"Are you mad? That lot—"

"We're here to bring peace, not start a war."

He could see that his men disagreed. They had already gone into battle stance: heads up, mouths tight. Even the flachter was being held ready. One way and another the Morrígans had caused them all grief, and his men resented what had happened to the local men among their number: some bribed, some frightened off, one vanished. The last time they'd gone up that hill, blood had been drawn, and he didn't want that to happen again. He had few enough left under his command as it was.

He ordered his men to meet him on the remains of the old road that gave the Morrígans access to the outside world. The Council of Elders had allowed, even encouraged, people to cut it away. With a proper road into their settlement, the Morrígans might have been less resentful of their neighbours. There again, hate and 'otherness' were in their blood and couldn't be changed.

The people on the hill were watching him. He knew that and it made him uneasy, though the only movement he could see was an old woman hurrying indoors with her washing, and the three crows circling. The crows separated, arched their wings and landed on different houses.

The houses were ramshackle, the roofs leaning into each other, the mud walls crumpling into the earth. The latticed wooden frames beneath showed more clearly with each year's rain. Built in a haphazard circle just below the crest, the gaps between houses were narrow and defensive. These suited stabbing work and not the honest blow of a sword. The path up ran steep and straight. The boundary, thorn hedges the height of a man.

"What about the body?" asked Concobhar.

There had to be punishment, not only for the killer, but the whole tribe. This was their best turf bed; he would blight it in perpetuity.

"Throw it in the channel and cover it with scraw, properly this time." He smiled at Concobhar's look of surprise. "Have a priest recite the prayers of Samhain over the body, make him this year's offering to the gods."

※

When they were sure Tarlóir was on his own, the people came out of their houses. Each of them stood different: hostile, nervous, angry. Some women wore shawls on their heads, others kept their hair in tails to ward off vermin. The clothes of both women and men hung shabby and pull-together.

Once he crossed the remains of the rutted track, the heather under Tarlóir's feet gave way to sweet grass. Primroses peered out of the hedgerows. There was no smell of dirt, he'd give them that, but maybe something of the fields and the cattle house.

Hate came at him. He stopped and waited for the Morrígans to make the first move. Two crows rose up and flew away. The third remained. He tried not to look at it.

The man who stepped forward was weedy and thin, with a bony head too big for his body. He wore a fresh jerkin and a white shirt over mud-spattered trousers, and kept brushing vaguely at the mud. Tarlóir noted it because it wasn't a nervous gesture; more one of dislike, as if he wanted something better of life.

"You want?" asked the thin man.

"To speak."

The thin man looked angry. At the same time his eyes flicked to Tarlóir's men who stood grouped on the road, blocking any escape.

"You lot always say that. Any of our men you take 'to speak to' never come back."

Tarlóir nodded. So this was the current head of the Morrígans, and not necessarily like the rest. His eyes had the blue of distant mountains after rain and his hair was surprisingly fair. Perhaps he was the product of a traveller from the isles to the far north?

His mind was wandering, Tarlóir realised: from tiredness or having done this job too long. A bit of both probably. Meanwhile, this new headman might be annoyed, but one of his people was dead, blood drawn, and could not be overlooked.

While he planned his moves Tarlóir looked at the women. They were all ages, from old crones muttering against him, to young girls pressed against their mother's skirts. The one he wanted wasn't there. He already had enough evidence to demand that she be given up to the ritual of revenge.

Tarlóir said, "You didn't ask who it is we want."

"You'll tell me in good time," Morrígan answered sharply.

All the same, he had made a mistake in not asking. Tarlóir was tempted to step forward and use his height advantage to bring pressure. He could have made two of this Morrígan. Usually the head of the Morrígans was the biggest, broadest, thickest-skulled man in the pack. This one was different. In ways he reminded Tarlóir of his younger self. He wore the same smirk as his eyes fixed on Tarlóir's torc, his badge of office. It was made of copper and tin, with a faded coating of silver. Tarlóir would never attain one of pure silver, let alone gold. They went to the sons of princes.

Embarrassment at being found wanting in bloodlines, if

not ability, made him blunt. "We want the one you call Brigit."

"No."

There was something in the tone of Morrígan's voice, something personal.

Tarlóir asked. "What's it to you?"

Morrígan smirked. "She's my mother's cousin's sister's aunt."

Tarlóir nodded. There was enough inbreeding in the Morrígans to make that true. And he was sweet on the Brigit one, may have taken her for a season as his wife.

"She doesn't know anything," Morrígan added.

"About what?" asked Tarlóir, and tired suddenly at being tactful. "The signs are in the humus and the body half-buried in the bog. She came to her lover while he was at work and lay with him as a wife would. When she told him she was pregnant he didn't want to know, maybe laughed at her. The flachter was all too handy for a woman needing to strike out."

The story was in the signs. Her footsteps had covered those of her lover, which in turn had been covered by people helping her to hide the body. Those people should be taken as well.

Tarlóir shrugged. Maybe another day, maybe not at all. He was already sick at what he had to do. With luck, someday he could school a man like Morrígan to take on his job, and retire to the mountains.

He made it easy for Morrígan, the way they had done with him about his friends.

He said. "I give you my word, she will not suffer."

Morrígan asked. "You'll deal with her as you'd like us to treat one of your daughters?"

Tarlóir looked at him sharply. How did they know that? He kept his private life to himself and the family lived well outside of the area. A woman chosen locally kept his house and saw to his needs.

"Megan, Deirdre and Ursula," said Morrígan.

"Is that a threat?" He felt a rage burn in him. If he ever got his hands on this Morrígan he'd roast in hell. Those bloody witches whoring themselves to the outside world, they'd been asking questions.

He said, "You left the girl's shoes where they could be found, with the blood still on them."

Was that done so as not to confront the law, or a peace offering, or to spite the girl for giving her body to someone else? Tarlóir didn't know which. A bit of everything, he suspected, but it boded well for the future.

Morrígan turned and raised his hand. The one they called Brigit came out of the house with the crow still perched on the roof. She was white faced from pregnancy and fear, and probably no older than his youngest daughter. The clothes she wore were cheap, the best she had for travelling: a thin cloak over a jacket, and a dress that had seen too many washes. The dress was short; half-way between that of a child and a woman. As she was. The remains of tears tracked her face.

Tarlóir secured her by placing a gentle hand on her shoulder.

She asked, "Are you going to...?" She choked into silence.

"Yes," he said. Anything else would have given her false hope.

Nobody said goodbye to her. It was the way of the Morrígans. The clan stood and scowled their hate. That night or tomorrow some innocent would feel their anger in clenched fists and flailing clubs. Not Tarlóir, he knew better than to walk alone, and never in the dark.

He looked across to Morrígan. "What you said about my family had better not be a threat."

Now the first burst of panic had faded, he approved the

way Morrígan gathered information and used it where it would cut the deepest.

"See she's treated well," said Morrígan and turned away, perhaps a little too quickly. Feeling guilt perhaps at leaving signs leading Tarlóir to the girl. Morrígan went into one of the houses. The rest followed him up the hill and soon only Tarlóir and the girl remained.

"Walk ahead of me," Tarlóir ordered her, and when she did, he drew his sword.

THE SEA IS NOT FULL
WRITTEN BY UNA MCCORMACK

The setting for The Sea is Not Full *is based on Drumanagh, a headland fifteen miles north of Dublin, where Roman artefacts have been found in the past. The question of the Romanisation of the Celtic world is, of course, a thorny one; however, the headland is in private hands, and legal proceedings on the part of the owners have prevented any further archaeology at the site or investigation of the artefacts already found. While all this mystery must be frustrating for archaeologists and historians, it is fertile territory for a fantasist interested in historical imagination and national mythmaking. David Thomson's memorable book* The People of the Sea *(Canongate, 1996) — an account of his journeys around the Hebrides and the west coast of Ireland and the stories that he heard there — was also a source of inspiration.*

People who do not fit into their skins, the slippery line between civilisation and barbarism, and the bringing of law from across the sea (look closely and you may glimpse St Patrick coming): all of these are questions which I hope this story examines.

—

> And so I saw the wicked buried, who had come and gone from the place of the holy, and they were forgotten in the city where they had so done.
>
> *Ecclesiastes 8: 10*

When the boat was securely tied, Avitus strode out onto the land, small stones crunching beneath his boots. Behind him, Gaius, thicker-set and less agile, slipped on the wet rock, all but losing his footing. He cursed, loudly and bluntly, and the sound startled a seal mother resting on the sands nearby. Quick as sunshine between showers, she slid into the sea. A little way out she stopped and turned — sleek head bobbing above the water, soft eyes bright and wary of the intruders — and she called to her pup to follow.

As the men unloaded the boats of goods and arms, Avitus took in the land around them. Grey-green grass, rain-soaked and wind-bitten, sloped upwards ahead; at the top of the hill, a low wooden hall squatted. Smoke rose greasily from its roof. "End of the fucking world," Gaius declared, with morbid satisfaction.

Avitus was inclined to agree. A small piece of land, jutting out precariously back into the sea; the unpromising hovel of a dubious chieftain: such was the sum total of the Empire's presence in Hibernia. This was no *Deva Victrix*, with its well-ordered streets and barracks, where his wife and daughters waited for him by the hearth, watched over by their household gods. Nor was it the wall of coast that stretched out to *Mona*, with its chain of stone watch-towers and solid fortlets. After these had come the great open maw of the sea and, at the far side, this bare land. The end of civilisation. The end of the world. Avitus set his gear and his men straight, and led them up the hill: a thin red line of order passing all too briefly through the wilderness.

The lord of this low hall and its weather-beaten lands was named Diarmait. His hold on both came courtesy of the Empire: in his youth, hot-blooded and too eager for chieftainship, he had been driven from this island, taking refuge in *Deva* as a guest of the Governor. When his people's raids on the north-west coast of the province again became too bold, the Empire had seen fit to put him back, and had kept him here ever since. A common enough policy along all the frontiers: putting the barbarians at odds with each other, holding them back without the trouble of conquest. Rome paid him occasional visits — such as this — to bring arms, to remind these people of the reach of their neighbours.

Diarmait stood waiting upon the threshold of his hall. He wore the clothes that the legions had adopted throughout these sodden islands: the woollen leggings of the barbarians, the tunic and red cloak of the legions. His hair was cut short. Lifting his arm, he welcomed his guests in their own language, but the words sounded odd coming from his mouth, as if he was singing them or a child was saying them. Gaius laughed quietly under his breath. Before Avitus could reply, Diarmait looked past him, at the men muttering and cursing as they set down their burdens. He frowned at Avitus. "Where is your centurion?"

Gaius laughed again. Evenly, Avitus said, "I am in command."

A cloud of anger sped across Diarmait's face. What had he been expecting? The Governor himself, brought up the hill on a litter? When Diarmait spoke again, his tone had shifted subtly. He addressed Avitus now as he might a servant. "Follow me," he said, turning his back to them and leading them into his hall.

Inside, the space was hot and dark, the fire at its heart smoking upwards towards the rafters. Avitus looked round in distaste at the cots and benches and heaped furs. Who would choose this squalor over Rome? At least there was no sign of the Christus, that cultish figure that had swept through the Empire like a storm or a plague, stealing the clothes of the bull-god to whom Avitus remained stubbornly loyal. Not this far; not yet. They would have their own gods here, strange foreign gods of the trees and the waters. There would be barbarous rites, sacrifices...

From out of the shadows a figure emerged; a woman, pale-skinned and dark-haired, wearing a green dress. A single gold bracelet snaked up one white arm. When she reached Diarmait, he took her hand and spoke to her in their language. Avitus picked out a few familiar words: *Deva*; *Legio XX*; his name, and then: "*Optio statorum*".

The woman's dark brows lifted. "*Optio?*" She studied Avitus coolly, like an equal. "My wife," Diarmait said. "Muirín." Avitus saluted her. Muirín smiled. Even in the poor light, her small white teeth shone.

As the day wore on, Avitus simmered with slow but steady fury. Diarmait, it seemed, held himself in high regard, seeing his friendship towards Rome as all that kept their coasts safe. So much for the forts and unceasing watch of the legions. But what, in the end, would this warlord amount to? A petty king; a single line in the records, a footnote. He would come and go — but the Empire that had kept him was unending. He could style himself Roman, imagine himself Roman, but they no longer bothered to send a centurion to deal with him. No, they had sent a mere *optio*.

It did not help his temper that Avitus could find no fault with Diarmait's defences. The hall stood on a small peninsula, surrounded on three sides by the sea, with cliffs on the northern and western sides bringing further protection. At the point where the promontory joined the mainland, Diarmait had ordered three long ditches dug. Behind them, a high wooden fence had been raised, with guard-posts at either end and over the gate. Here his men stood watch, able to survey both land and sea. At the southernmost of these,

Avitus stopped for a while, looking down the track that came from the village further along the coast. Gaius stood nearby, arms folded, whistling off-key.

He stopped as one of Diarmait's men came past. The new armour they had brought from *Deva* had been given out; combined with the barbarians' preference for long hair and the rough cloth they used here, it had an odd, unsettling effect. "Looks strange," Gaius said. "Like wild animals wearing men's skins."

Avitus smiled, despite himself. Gaius grinned back, all teeth, and returned to his whistling, competing amiably with a nearby blackbird. Avitus watched a cart roll slowly up the track towards the gate. Then the wind changed. Softly, inevitably, the rain started up again. Gaius stretched and yawned. "Gods, but this place is a shit-hole. Let's go back inside."

Avitus grunted in agreement. Together, they went down the wooden steps and trudged back up the slope. As they walked past the settlement that served the hall, someone called out. A young man came running towards them. He had on some bits and pieces of their armour, but no helmet; the rain was turning his brown hair sleek upon his head. When he reached the two soldiers, he started gabbling at them. Gaius, who had picked up a word or two from his previous trips, tried to follow, but he was soon shaking his head. As the young man saw he was not understood, he began to get more and more upset. And then another voice called out, a single word.

"Rónán!"

The young man's name, Avitus guessed. It had the force of a command. Rónán stopped speaking and bowed his head. Diarmait strode over to join them. He said a few short, sharp words to the young man, and sent him on his way.

"What was that about?" Avitus asked, watching him go.

"Nothing," Diarmait said. "A family matter. He should not have come to you with it."

Should he not, indeed? Avitus was sorely tempted to press for more, but the rain was coming down more heavily, and Gaius was muttering, so he let it pass. But later that evening, when they were eating together, Gaius nudged him. "What was that boy's name again?"

"Rónán."

"Rónán. Thought so." Gaius tore a piece of bread in half and nodded towards the lord and lady of the hall. "It's just come up again."

The lady was speaking in low whispers, all sibilants. She frowned at them; Gaius gave her a cheery salute. "What do you think?" he asked, when she looked away.

Avitus pondered this. "He does wear our armour," he said slowly. "Perhaps it could be seen as a matter of discipline."

Gaius popped some bread in his mouth and started chewing. "Ah, well, if it's a matter of *discipline...*"

※

Early the next morning, Avitus and Gaius slipped out of the hall and walked down to the settlement. It stood quiet as a mausoleum in the dawn mist: a dozen or so dark huts, their round roofs made from thatch; their walls, it seemed, from mud. A sorry sight to men used to city life. Light rain was falling, and the huts seemed hunched together, their backs turned to the sea. Perhaps fifty people lived here in all: the men who guarded the hall; their families, kindred, and slaves. A small host to serve the hall, and the people required to serve them. A girl walked past, a baby on one hip, a clay jug swinging in her free hand. "Rónán?" Gaius called out to her. She tilted her head, directing them across the village.

They found the young man sitting outside, sharpening his knife. When he saw the two legionaries, he got to his feet. All three men eyed each other, warily, and then Rónán's story came rushing out. He jabbed with his finger at a nearby hut; his voice rose in anger and — was that grief? Soon enough he reached the climax of his tale. He stopped and looked at them expectantly. His breathing was ragged, and there was a glitter of water in his eyes.

"Well?" Avitus said.

Gaius shrugged. "Didn't get a word."

Rónán tried again, but Gaius got nowhere. At last, the young man muttered angrily and went off. "Is that it?" Avitus said.

"No, I'll think he'll be back...Yes, here he comes. And what's this he's dug up?"

Rónán was dragging a boy behind him, a slave by the looks of him. With a brusque command, Rónán pushed him in front of the two men. What a stinking specimen. Dirty and hardly clad for this weather, his long hair fell in strands around a pinched and frightened face. Gaius gave him a wolfish grin; the boy looked away, quickly. Then: "Masters," he said, "he is asking you for justice."

Avitus and Gaius stared at each other in amazement. This was their language, but not strained through a foreign tongue, nor scarred with the harsh gutturals of the slum. This filthy scrap spoke cleanly, purely — almost, you might even say, like a patrician. Rónán spoke again, urgently. "His mother," the boy translated. "He says nothing has been done for her."

"What's wrong with her?" Avitus demanded. "Come on, boy, spit it out!"

"Master, he says she has been murdered. He says his father did it."

※

Avitus was an honest man; honest enough to admit later that

he thought no harm would be done in curbing Diarmait a little. Who was the man, after all? A barbarian; his house a stinking wooden hutch on a hill in the middle of nowhere, his people — it seemed — lawless. What harm could be done by him learning some respect for the people who kept him here — whatever their rank. But as well as this, his sense of order was offended. How could a woman be killed and no man punished? It disgusted him. Grabbing the boy by the upper arm, he strode up the hill. "Come," he called to Rónán. "You shall have your justice."

Marching past the men who guarded the door, Avitus went up to the far table where the lord and lady were sitting. Seeing Rónán, Diarmait frowned. "What is this?"

"His mother has been killed," Avitus said. "Murdered, indeed! And yet, so he tells me, there has been no justice. How could this happen?"

Muirín leaned over to speak softly to her lord. Avitus shook the boy's arm. "What did she say to him?"

"Master, I could not hear—"

Diarmait rose from his chair. "I told you yesterday, this is for the families. I know this young man, his family. I have known them all since before Rónán was born. *If* there has been a murder, his mother's kin must seek redress—"

Avitus pointed at Rónán. "Is he not her kin?"

"Her father or her brothers," Diarmait said with unconcealed impatience. "This is our custom—"

"Custom?" Avitus spat. "What about punishment? The law requires punishment." Seeing Diarmait hesitate, he pressed on. "It is the law which makes us Roman, the law which civilises us."

Muirín spoke. Avitus shook the boy again. "What did she say?"

"She said that the foreigners will find nothing. She said..." He looked puzzled. "I do not understand that—"

"What do you think she said? Come on!"

"I think she said...she said that she has gone back. Gone home. I cannot be sure."

"And what does she mean by that?"

The boy trembled in his grip. "I do not know!"

Avitus brushed him aside and took a step towards Diarmait. "Who upholds the law in your hall?" He nodded over at Muirín. "Did the women take on the task while you were snapping at the Governor's heels?"

Diarmait went red. Muirín rose from her seat and put her hand upon his arm. A heated exchange followed between lord and lady. "He's angry," the boy whispered to Avitus. "Angry with her. He says he's as good as any Roman...As good as you," he added, after a hesitation. "She has told him he's a fool. And he has told her she's a witch." He clapped a hand over his mouth, stifling a nervous laugh. "Oh, she doesn't like that!"

So it seemed. Muirín hissed a curse and stalked off into the shadows. Diarmait wiped his hand across his mouth. Then he ordered, "Bring the boy's father to me."

Two of his men bowed and left. To Avitus, Diarmait said, "You are very sure of yourself. For a man in your position."

"I am sure of the law," Avitus said steadily. "If the young man wears our armour, he merits all of its protection."

Diarmait took his seat. Gaius said, "How I love these goodwill missions."

An uneasy silence descended like a cloud upon the hall, heavy as the smoke from the fire. Avitus considered the boy standing beside him. Where had he come from, with a voice as sweet as that? Glevum, perhaps, or maybe *Deva* itself; shipped over here now the waters were safer. All to the good; trade between these islands being better than war. The lad became tense and wary under his scrutiny. Avitus cuffed him idly on the shoulder. "What's your name, boy?"

"Cotric, master." He lowered his head, hiding his face behind his unkempt hair. From behind this cover, whispered words came out in a great rush. "I beg you, master, please, help me! I am a citizen, like you. The son of a rich man. We lived near the coast. The boats came from out of the sea and took me away. I have been here three years, almost four—"

The doors of the hall swung open. Diarmait's men were returning, bringing another with him. Seeing his chance passing, Cotric tugged at Avitus' sleeve. "Help me! Master, please! My father is very rich!"

Avitus weighed the odds of his claim. True, the boy spoke well, but there were people who paid handsomely for such polish. And no rich man's son would call a common soldier 'master', surely, not even one in such desperate straits? Still, he would be useful while this business dragged on...

"Stay next to me," Avitus ordered. "Tell me what these people are saying to each other. You can start there." He gestured towards where Rónán's father knelt before his lord. Cotric nodded, and began to translate in quick, quiet undertones.

Diarmait explained to the man kneeling before him that a charge of murder had been brought against him, and that he must answer to it. The man took a long time to understand who he was supposed to have killed. When at last he grasped the accusation, he blanched. To Diarmait, he cried, "Lord, she was my wife! I loved her!"

"Then where is she?" Avitus demanded, but even after Cotric had passed on his words, the man remained silent. "Did you kill her? If not, where is she now? If so, where is the body?"

Diarmait said, with reluctance, "Answer him as you would answer me."

Still speaking to his lord, the man said, "She is gone—"

"Gone?" Avitus said. "Where?"

Clasping his hands together, the man held them in front of him. Then, slowly, he began to unfold them again. His right hand uncurled, his arm stretched out, then his forefinger...

Despite himself, Avitus followed the movement — only to realise the man was pointing at nothing. Diarmait laughed; some of his men followed suit. They stopped when Rónán stepped forwards. "I heard you!" he cried to his father. "You quarrelled! She was weeping, she cried out! Then, later, there was blood on the ground, her dress was torn—"

"We quarrelled, yes," his father replied, unwillingly, half to son, half to his lord. "But I never harmed her. I loved her!"

"And the blood?" Avitus demanded. "The dress?"

The man pulled up the sleeve of his tunic. His forearm was bound up. "A slip of the knife. I used the cloth to bind it. I never harmed her! She was my treasure. She was like no other woman." Turning, grief-stricken now, back to his son, he said, "I would not do such a thing! She was my treasure, Rónán, as you were our treasure. As you are still — our treasure."

At his words, the young man hesitated. He seemed to Avitus to be caught in some conflict, unsure which way was best. From the corner of his eye, Avitus saw that Muirín had come back. She moved forwards, but Diarmait held her arm. All of them watched in silence as the young man struggled with each part of himself.

Perhaps if his father had not spoken again, it might have gone differently. But the man could not hold back. Grief, perhaps, drove him to speak: at the loss of his wife; at the blame of his son. But there was anger too, at those who had put all these wounds on display. Pointing at Avitus, the father asked his son, "Why do you give them what they want? Why do you do their work for them?"

Whatever bound his son to him broke. Putting his back to his father and his lord, Rónán came to kneel before Avitus. "For my mother," he said, "that I loved beyond all treasure, I ask you for justice. I ask Rome for justice."

But they still lacked any proof. Avitus sent Gaius off with three of the men to search the huts, the ditches, the whole length of the fence. Cotric went along to ask their questions for them. At the end of the day, Gaius reported back: there was no sign of the woman, or of any fresh grave. The settlement had closed ranks. "If they know what happened to her," Cotric said, "they are not telling. But she is gone, for sure."

Avitus considered their news. The lack of a grave hardly surprised him. Why bury her, when the wide sea opened all round to scour away any guilt? But where did this leave him? He had no body, no witness to anything beyond a quarrel, no proof that any murder had in fact taken place.

Gone, the lady of the house had said. *Gone home, gone back*...What had she meant by that? There had been a quarrel, was that all? Had he found himself in the midst of nothing more than the usual choppy waters that lay between a man and his wife? He would look a fool, if that was the case.

"Master," Cotric said, anxiously.

"Stop calling me that! Have some pride!"

Cotric flinched, lifting his arm to shield himself. Softly, Gaius said, "The boy did well today."

Gently, firmly, Avitus took hold of the boy's arm, and lowered it. "Go on. Speak your piece. What else?"

"People were angry," Cotric said faintly. He swallowed, and carried on in a stronger voice. "They asked by whose leave your men entered their homes. They asked: Is Diarmait lord here or Rome?"

"Now, as I recall," Gaius said, to nobody in particular, "we're meant to be here to shore up this alliance." He glanced at Avitus. "Not wreck it."

He was right too. They could do no more. They *must* do no more, if they did not want to have to report back to *Deva* that Diarmait — and the seaways — were no longer so friendly. Whatever quarrel lay between this young man and his father, it would have to be settled within the family. As Diarmait had said it should...

Avitus cursed, and turned to kick over the nearest chair. It relieved his temper, but it finished Cotric. Slumping down to the ground, he sat hunched over, his arms around his knees, staring at his bare feet. "People will not forget what I did today. Nor will they forgive it. I shall kill myself rather than remain here. I shall throw myself into the sea."

He looked up at Avitus, his face bleak as the grey sky before the storm. He was a wretch, and Avitus had no need for another slave — indeed, his pay would not stretch so far. If he took this creature home, he would never hear the end of it... "Bring Rónán to me, Cotric," he instructed. "Then go and wash. Gaius will find you something to wear. We set sail for *Deva* the day after tomorrow." And the sooner the wide sea lay between him and this desolate place, Avitus thought, as Cotric kissed his hands then scrambled to his feet to obey, the happier he would be.

It was a bitter interview with Rónán. The young man came eagerly, but his face clouded over as Avitus spoke and Cotric translated. "I have no proof that your mother was murdered," Avitus told him. "I ask you — is it possible that she left of her own accord? Perhaps she has returned to her own people?"

Even before Cotric finished, Rónán had begun to shake his head. "He says that he has a young brother and a young sister. That she would not have left them. She would not have left any of them. He killed her, he says, and yet you do nothing!"

Avitus held up his hands. "I've done all that the law permits."

"The law? I came to you for justice!"

Diarmait lifted his hand, palm out. It needed no translation. *Stop.* The young man fell silent. To Avitus, Diarmait said, "This ends now. If she was murdered, the body will be in the water. If the sea gives her back, then this young man will receive his justice." Diarmait's eyes flashed. "Through me. His lord."

Avitus hesitated, remembering the insults and contempt. "Don't be a fool," Gaius breathed into his ear. And perhaps this was the best outcome. Diarmait had not lost face — but they would remember Rome here, and perhaps the memory would make them more careful. They would not forget their master's master. They might now even remember the law. "You are a friend to Rome," Avitus said stiffly. "Your promise is enough." Graciously, Diarmait bowed his head; when Cotric repeated the words in her tongue, Muirín nodded, once, as if she too was satisfied.

※

Before dawn, Avitus woke to the sound of a settlement in uproar. He grasped his sword and jumped up. Cotric, at his feet, curled up in terror and called upon Christ to protect them. The noise came closer, up the hill and towards the hall. There was a hammering on the doors, and shouts came from within and without. Avitus pulled Cotric to his feet, and brought the boy along with him to see what was happening.

Diarmait was already down at the doors. Gaius was there too, short sword ready. He put himself in front of Avitus. Then the doors swung open, and two of Diarmait's men came in, dragging a third behind.

It was no attacker, come to burn the place, to kill the men and take the women and cattle. It was Rónán, and, even in the gloom of the rush lights, Avitus could see that the young man's hands were stained darkly with blood. Cotric began to whisper to Avitus what Diarmait's men were saying. "After he saw you, he went back down the hill...got drunk, it seems...then he and his father quarrelled..." Cotric broke off with a cry.

"What? What happened?"

"He took a stick...Oh!"

"And what?" He seized the boy by the arm and shook him. "Tell me!"

"Oh, master! He has clubbed his father to death."

Avitus flinched. Gaius cursed in the darkness. "What are they saying now?" Avitus asked thickly, as Diarmait came to stand over the young man. "What do they mean to do to him?"

Cotric strained to hear the judgement Diarmait was passing. "He'll be banished, I should think," he said. "Yes, he's to be branded, and then they'll send him on his way."

Avitus, pierced with relief, released his grip on the boy. Gaius breathed out sharply. "Is that all?"

Cotric misunderstood. "Master, he's better off dead. An outcast, without lord or kin? Branded his father's killer? There'll be no welcome for him, wherever he goes."

Their lord's order given, Diarmait's men made to carry it out, pulling Rónán to his feet. Then a woman called out. Turning, Avitus saw Muirín coming out of the dark heart of the hall. She was barefoot, like a servant. Quickly she came forwards, and she knelt down before Rónán. She lifted his head so that he was looking directly at her, and she spoke to him in their own language.

"She says she knew his mother," Cotric whispered. "She says she grieves with him that she is gone and grieves that he was driven to this. She asks if he trusts her."

Rónán nodded. Then Muirín rose to her feet, and spoke

again, setting everyone around her gasping, Cotric with them. Diarmait took a step forwards, but before he could intervene, Rónán took his lady's hand and answered her. Muirín stooped to kiss him on the forehead, and then all those gathered looked at Avitus, as if it was now his turn to speak. "Cotric?" he rasped, heart sinking.

"She told him he was halfway Roman. That he wanted Roman justice. That he should receive it."

Rónán, Avitus saw, was looking at him fearlessly. "And what did he say back to her?"

"Master," Cotric whispered, "he said he will do what she requires of him."

Avitus closed his eyes. Outmanoeuvred — and by a woman. It meant an execution, and a public one at that. Bitterly, expecting nothing from it, Avitus threw Muirín's challenge back at her. "What do you think I should do, lady? What do you think would be just in circumstances such as these?"

Cotric trembled, but he repeated his words. Muirín answered, and then walked past him back into her hall. Avitus looked down at Cotric, pressed up against him for protection. "She says...Master, the lady says that you should do your worst."

※

In the chill morning, then, Roman justice was carried out for the whole world to see. The young man was strung up on the gatepost, flogged, and when that was done, the body was weighted with stones and cast over the cliff into the sea — where his mother had no doubt gone before him. The people watched it all — and whispered to each other as the Romans marched in line back up to the hall.

Muirín stood waiting in the doorway, a green shawl wrapped around her shoulders. Sourly, Avitus called to her, "Satisfied, lady?"

Cotric began to translate, but Muirín spoke over him, answering Avitus in his own tongue. She had the same singsong voice as her lord; it sounded like a spell. "There has been no victory here," she said. "But all our vanities have now, I think, been served."

※

Leaving Gaius standing solid as a rock in the stern, Avitus made his way with care towards the prow. Cotric was sitting there, his back to the land that had held him. The wind spread his dark hair back across his face and his thin body shivered beneath the cold spray. Avitus, drawing near, heard the boy's teeth chattering and, beneath this, chanted words, like a song or a spell. He stood and listened, making out at last a hard fast prayer, a promise. Taking off his cloak, Avitus put it around the boy's shoulders. He kept one hand there. Partly he wanted to remind the boy that he was indeed safe; partly he wanted to stop the flow of words, which disturbed him. "Quiet now," he commanded gently. "Be still."

Beneath his grip, the boy struggled to master himself, biting his bottom lip, enough to draw blood. He wiped at his mouth. "Sometimes," he said, "they told stories about the people who came from the sea. Seals, I think they meant. Sometimes they would shed their skins and come and walk amongst the folk of the land. That was lucky, they said. And if you found the skin of one while it was walking upright amongst men, and you hid the skin away, then they would forget where they had come from, and that would keep the good luck with you. So long as they didn't go near the sea. Then they would remember where they came from, and go back again."

Tenderly, Cotric touched his lip, and then he set his hand down, deliberately, upon his lap. It jerked once, and then lay still. "She was good to me," he said. He did not mean the lady of the hall, Avitus thought — hardly her, snake-cold — but that other woman, the one Avitus had not even seen, but whose absence had all but foundered an alliance. "The only one with a kind word. I think she knew how it felt to be amongst strangers. She often sang about the sea, but I never saw her near it. Perhaps that's what happened. Perhaps they stole her from the sea, and then she went down there one day, and remembered where she came from, and she went back, leaving her man and her boy behind to love her and miss her and fall upon each other. Like savages."

Cotric stopped. He shuddered, violently, as if to shake off a burden or a second skin. "It is a lie, of course," he said, coldly, with the kind of long-harboured anger that can remake a world. "A heathen story from a heathen land." Turning his head, he spat into the sea. There must still have been blood in his mouth, for it came out red and stained the water.

Avitus did not believe such a story either. It was clear enough what had happened, clear as the sky after rain. A man had killed his wife — through rage or love or both — and their son had exacted revenge on behalf of a beloved mother. Not magic, not a great tale or song: these were sordid crimes, barbarous, and the guilty had been punished for them, as the law declared they must, as the gods demanded. For the gods were purposeful, the invisible hands that guided men's fates, and their laws were meant to constrain men's passions and punish their disorder. Submission, obedience: that was what was asked of a man, and he went his own way at his peril. He had had no choice. He had done what his laws and his gods had required.

Turning, Avitus saw the last of the land slide into the water. Below the surface, two dark shapes were swimming, lithe and free; they followed the ship for a while and then went on their way. The boy started praying again, in hot fast whispers, calling on the new god, a god of slaves and women that was now the lord of emperors. The little boat bobbing was taken by the open sea. The world began to slip, like bare feet on wet rock, and past and future merged, the boundary no longer tenable.

THE DRUID'S DANCE

WRITTEN BY TONY BAILIE

The legend of Tuan Mac Carrell is found in an 11th century manuscript called **Lebor na hUidre** (The Book of the Dun Cow). Tuan tells a Christian monk that he was born 2,000 years earlier and witnessed many of the waves of invaders who came to ancient Ireland — the Nemedians, Firbolg and the **Tuatha Dé Danann**. As an old man he crawled off into a cave and fell asleep and when he awoke he had been reborn as a vigorous young stag. The process repeated itself each time he became old and he was reborn variously as a wild boar, an eagle and eventually as a salmon. However, during his existence as a salmon he was caught and eaten whole by the wife of a chieftain called Carrell and passed into her womb to be reborn again as Tuan Mac (son of) Carrell. The myth clearly suggests that there was a belief in reincarnation among our Irish ancestors.

So, if Tuan was reincarnated over a 2,000 year period up until the early Christian era in Ireland (circa 600-800AD) who is to say that the process didn't continue? That leaves the possibility that someone could still be running around today claiming to be the reincarnation of the ancient chieftain (although they fail to mention the bit about also being a fish). It is a scenario that was just crying out to be turned into a gory police procedural story with (at least in my head) a soundtrack by Horslips.

Detective Inspector Shane MacGowan ignored the TV crews and the dozen or so newspaper reporters and photographers who had gathered at Dunbicru. At the police cordon he flashed his ID to a young red-cheeked cop before stepping through a hole in a hedge and into a field beyond that inclined upwards. MacGowan mounted the small hill and glanced around, taking in the collapsed dolmen at the centre of a stone circle, the sniffer dogs and officers examining the area on their hands and knees, and the white tent outside the circle.

MacGowan nodded brusquely to the two guards standing outside the tent and ducked under a flap into the narrow space. Just a few inches from him a woman's naked body lay sprawled. Bile rose in his throat and he desperately needed to go to the toilet. MacGowan tried to regulate his breathing as he looked at her face, expecting to see an expression of terror fixed from the moment she realised she was about to die. But she looked quite calm...she could have been fast asleep if it wasn't for the gaping wound between her breasts and the dried river of blood that had crept along the contours of her torso and onto the grass.

He heard a shuffling behind him and turned to see Detective Sergeant Joan Moran who had been the first to arrive at the scene. She was dark and petite, barely making the minimum-height requirement for policewomen.

"Do we know who she is?" MacGowan asked.

"Margaret Cronin. She was a university student in Belfast." Moran moved into the tiny space beneath the canvas.

"Who found her?"

"A farmer who was out early trying to shoot a fox that had been bothering his chickens. He was in the next field when he heard a scream. When he got here he saw a man who has since been identified as Professor Mervyn Crawford, who teaches at the dead woman's university, standing naked with a sword in his hand. There was also another naked woman, who we believe is called Francesca Kelly, but we haven't been able to get much sense out of her. She's in shock."

"What about Crawford, has he said anything?"

Moran shrugged. "Yes and no. He seems quite oblivious to the fact that he is the main suspect and insists that he was merely enacting an ancient druid ritual. He says he's as shocked as everyone else by the discovery of the body of a woman who just happens to be one of his students."

MacGowan forced himself to look back at the dead woman Moran said, "What do you make of her hand, sir?"

"What about it?"

She looked at him quizzically. "Her left hand?"

"Jesus!" The woman's thumb had been almost completely cut off where it joined the hand. The middle finger had been cut off two thirds of the way up and then slashed close to where it joined with the hand so that it was half hanging off. The tip of the small finger had been completely severed.

MacGowan sat at his desk back at the police barracks and flicked through the interview notes taken by Moran. They had questioned Crawford in the interview room earlier that morning.

Crawford claimed he and Francesca had been involved in a ceremony to mark the spring solstice and the rebirth of the year. They'd been about to symbolically consummate the coming together of the masculine and feminine deities into a new season when Francesca screamed. Crawford claimed he had not known what was wrong until the farmer arrived and shone his torch on the body lying nearby.

MacGowan looked up as he heard Moran's distinctive rap at his office door and didn't have time to answer before she came in clutching a sheaf of papers.

"If we are to believe Crawford, the body must have already been there when he and Francesca arrived," MacGowan said.

Moran nodded and gestured to the papers she was holding. "Forensics say the time of death was probably two hours before the body was discovered, which would rule out Crawford. He says Francesca was with him at the time."

"But she hasn't spoken yet, has she? Maybe the trauma is a result of witnessing her friend being slaughtered."

"Well, there is the time factor," Moran said. "The farmer says he was at the scene within thirty seconds of hearing the scream. And the forensics report says there is no evidence that the sword held by Crawford was used to kill Margaret Cronin. Also, the weapon was too blunt to have carried out the mutilation of her hand."

"Was nothing else found at the scene?"

Moran shook her head.

"What do we know about Crawford?"

"He is sixty-three, divorced with no children and teaches Celtic Studies at the university," Moran said. "He's been there for thirty years and is fairly well respected, although there seems to be a bit of a cloud regarding his relationship with some of his students."

"Really? In what way?"

"Nothing concrete, but whispers and rumours of inappropriate suggestions to some students. Usually the poorer performing ones."

"What do we have on the dead girl and Francesca?"

"They were both taking Celtic Studies courses and shared a flat. Francesca's and Margaret Cronin's flatmates say they were both struggling with the course and that Francesca had been considering dropping out."

"Has anyone examined Francesca yet?"

"We've called in one of our consultant psychologists."

MacGowan straightened in his chair and brushed forward his receding hair. "Oh, right. Good. Which one would that be?"

"Dr Margery Barefoot," Moran said sharply.

MacGowan was startled by the slightly bitter tone in her voice.

※

As Francesca sat in the police barracks she could still feel nodules of cold sharp stone piercing her back. Still hear the old geek chanting above her.

The Professor had unfastened the laces of his cloak to reveal a gnarled body, with protruding varicose veins winding around his legs like vines around the trunks of two stunted trees. She remembered him licking his lips as he held the sword aloft and chanted.

Dawn had broken to reveal the stone circle shrouded in mist.

Francesca could still feel Crawford's legs moving between hers.

She had closed her eyes and let her head fall back so that the crown of her head was almost level with the ground, and when she opened them again she had howled in terror.

※

WPC Helen Collins touched Francesca on her arm to ask if she was all right, but Francesca snarled and yanked back, drawing her limbs tight into her body, coiled and ready to lash out at the first sign of danger. Collins withdrew and made a note of the time.

After a few minutes Francesca's limbs started to loosen

and the anxious creases on her face settled into what appeared to be a dreamy smile. She sighed a long, drawn-out syllable.

There was knock on the door and a woman in her late forties entered. She was tall and her long greying hair was tied back. She wore a baggy, multi-coloured jumper and torn jeans, and as soon as she entered the room she kicked off the sandals she was wearing to become like her name. Dr Barefoot approached Francesca.

"Has she said anything?"

"Nothing really." Collins glanced at her notes. "Just one word. It sounded like 'tune'."

※

Professor Mervyn Crawford appeared bemused at the situation in which he found himself. His straightforward, unhesitant answers surprised MacGowan and made his solicitor squirm. The professor admitted he had taught both Margaret and Francesca. Margaret had not been getting great marks in her essays and had come to him for advice. She'd heard he was looking for students to help him with his research. No, he didn't see anything amiss with asking female students to partake in ancient rites. Yes, he had to admit he was only speculating about what form these rites would have taken. Yes, they involved him having sexual intercourse with the girls, but it was all done in the name of academic research. Yes, he and Margaret had been at Dunbicru the previous morning and performed a rite. Afterwards, he had driven her home to her flat in Belfast. When she told him that she shared it with the "rather interesting looking" student who always sat beside her in class, he had indeed suggested to Margaret that it might help Francesca's results if she agreed to participate in a similar rite.

MacGowan was becoming frustrated with Crawford's

nonchalance and suspected he was trying to portray himself as an unworldly character whose naivety made him incapable of murder.

"Tell me, Professor Crawford, do such rituals ever involve cutting off the thumbs and fingers of sacrifice victims and driving a sword into their chests?"

Crawford's lawyer shot the detective a warning glance and started to tell his client not to answer, but the Professor was already vigorously shaking his head.

"Oh no, never. The druids never indulged in human or even animal sacrifices. That was all propaganda devised by the Romans and Christians to paint them as brutal pagans."

On his way out of the interview room, MacGowan bumped straight into Dr Barefoot and nearly sent her sprawling. "I'm so sorry," he blustered as he caught her by the waist and helped her stand up straight.

She was as tall as him and they briefly stood face to face with his arms wrapped around her. He could smell what he thought was the whiff of patchouli oil off her clothing and feel her breath on his cheeks. She held his gaze and MacGowan felt instinctively that the right thing to do at that very minute would be to move his lips towards hers. He might even have done so if DS Moran hadn't come running up the corridor towards them.

"I'm sorry, Dr Barefoot," MacGowan said, stepping back.

"That's OK, Shane." Her dove-grey eyes crinkled and he wanted to grab her again despite the presence of Moran.

"How is Francesca?" he asked. "Has she been able to tell you anything yet?"

Dr Barefoot shook her head. "She's suffering from severe trauma. Having read the case notes, who could blame her? Seeing her friend mutilated and murdered like that, and probably believing the same thing was about to happen to her..."

"Well, we're not sure if it's as cut and dried as that," MacGowan said, trying to ignore the DS vying for his attention.

"You don't think this Professor Crawford is the culprit?"

"Well, yes he is a suspect, but the evidence isn't quite there to definitively say he did it. We are going to release him, for now anyway."

"Oh dear," sighed Dr Barefoot. "Well, obviously you know best. It might also be an idea to release Francesca into my care for a day or so," she said. "Although your officers have tried to make her as comfortable as possible, she is still sitting in a police cell. I can look after her much better at my practice."

"Absolutely." MacGowan finally acknowledged Moran. "Joan here will see to the paperwork."

"Thank you very much, Shane," Dr Barefoot said. "Maybe we can meet tomorrow for lunch? I might be able to give you a bit more information about Francesca and what she actually saw."

MacGowan watched the psychologist walk down the corridor, her sandals spanking her bare feet, leaving a waft of patchouli oil still hanging in the air. Moran was tugging at his sleeve like a child and he could have sworn he heard her mutter, "Hippy slut."

"Sorry, what was that?" he asked.

"There is someone who wants to speak to you about the case," Moran said, indicating an interview room. "He says he may have information that could help."

"Right," said MacGowan absentmindedly. "A witness?"

"A journalist. He says he's been investigating Crawford for the last two months and had been about to expose him for gaining sexual favours in return for marking up poorly performing students."

"A journalist?" MacGowan sighed with distaste. "Oh well, I suppose I'd better see him."

Barry Crowe opened his backpack, took out a large ominous looking hardback book and set it on the desk in front of MacGowan.

"This was written by Crawford," he said. "It took me three weeks to read it and I had to read every line two or three times before I could work out what the hell he was going on about. It covers Crawford's area of research — druid rituals and beliefs. He is a dull and dreary writer, but passionate about his subject and has put a lot of himself into these texts."

MacGowan gazed at him suspiciously, waiting for the punch line. "And?"

"I know this man. I went to a couple of his classes, followed him in his daily routine. I know where he shops, eats, goes for a pint and who his friends are. I have interviewed people he works with, his students and even the woman who cleans his house."

MacGowan sighed. "What's in it for you?"

"My paper was about to expose him. The story was with our lawyers, but there's no way they'll let me publish it now if this guy looks like being charged with murder. It could be a year before a trial, then all this stuff is bound to come out anyway, but if I help you to convict him I'll get my scoop."

"Maybe he's innocent," MacGowan said.

Crowe shrugged. "Then I'll get a scoop about how I saved a sex pest from being wrongly convicted of murder."

MacGowan wanted to tell the journalist where to go, but a quick flick through Crawford's book confirmed what Crowe had said about it being heavy going.

"OK," he said non-committally. "In what way were you going to expose Crawford? We already know about his indiscretions, but that doesn't prove he's a murderer."

"It did surprise me a bit when I found out he was being questioned about the killing," Crowe said. "In his book he insists the druids were basically nature worshippers. Proto-hippies who enjoyed dancing about naked, eating psychedelic mushrooms and screwing each other while listening to the ancient Celtic equivalent of Jimi Hendrix playing harp under a rowan tree."

"Nothing about ritual sacrifices?"

Crowe's eyes lit up with excitement. MacGowan cursed himself for his carelessness. The police press office had said a murdered woman's body had been found, but omitted any mention of swords or the mutilated hand. He looked again at the ominously large book before pulling a folder towards himself and lifting out a close-up picture of Margaret Cronin's hand. Crowe winced as MacGowan set the photo in front of him. The journalist gazed at it for a full minute before a look of enlightenment spread across his face.

"Ogham," Crowe said.

"Owe him what?"

"No, Ogham. It's a type of alphabet believed to have been used by the druids. I recognise the pattern. There is a chapter about it in Crawford's book."

Crowe opened the thick volume to a page where Crawford had reproduced diagrams of Ogham script — a series of horizontal lines with shorter vertical one running along them — and given their equivalent in the Roman alphabet.

MacGowan pointed to a drawing of a hand with four letters marked along the length of each finger and the thumb. "What's that?"

"The Druids communicated secret messages to one another by inscribing Ogham into strips of wood or stone, but the letters also had an equivalent on each finger of the left hand so that the letter A — which in Ogham is depicted as a short straight line cutting through a longer one — can also be indicated by pointing to where the thumb connects with the palm of the hand."

MacGowan set the photo beside the diagram.

"Well?" he demanded. "The middle finger has been cut off from just below the nail, what would that indicate?"

Crowe consulted the book before looking back at the photo. "T."

"And then below that it is has been slashed again where it joins the hand."

"That indicates a U," Crowe said.

"The thumb has been almost severed where it joins the hand."

"A"

"And the tip of the small finger."

"N."

"T.U.A.N. Tuan?" MacGowan said, puzzled.

"Tuan mac Carrell!"

"Who the fuck's he?"

"There is an obscure eleventh century Irish manuscript called *The Book of the Dun Cow* which tells how a sixth century abbot called Finnien became friendly with a pagan chieftain called Tuan mac Carrell, who lived in Donegal. When Finnien asked Tuan his background the old chieftain told him he had been born more than 2,000 years earlier. Tuan told how his people had been wiped out by a great pestilence, but he survived and wandered from place to place seeking shelter from wolves for twenty-two years until he became old and frail. One night he fell asleep in a cave, and when he woke in the morning he found he had been reborn as a stag. Tuan was wild and vigorous again and became king of all the deer in Ireland. The cycle repeats itself and Tuan is reincarnated variously as a boar, then a sea eagle and then in the shape of a salmon. However his cunning failed him and he was caught and taken to the wife of Carrell the High Chief of Ireland, who ate him whole. He passed into her womb and was reborn as her son, Tuan son of Carrell. He recalled all of his previous lives and passed on his memories to monks and scribes in the form of poems and stories which they then transcribed."

MacGowan, who was becoming increasingly irritated by this stream of Celtic bollocks, sighed with relief as Moran entered the room with a file under her arm.

"These are all the statements we have gathered so far," she said, handing it to MacGowan.

"OK, Joan. Has everyone gone?"

"They all left well over an hour ago."

"Did you manage to get anything from the girl?"

"No," Moran said. "According to WPC Collins, who was with her most of the time, she just kept repeating the same word over and over again. Tune. At least she thinks that was what she was saying."

"*Tune,*" MacGowan said, letting the word linger in his mouth. "Could be...Jesus, maybe all that Celtic crap might have something to do with it."

"I'm not sure what you're getting at, sir," Moran said.

"It wasn't tune, Joan. It was *Tuan.* Right, Mr Crowe?"

"Maybe we should go and see Professor Crawford," the journalist said. "He wrote about Tuan and might know why his traumatised student is so fixated on that particular name."

"Exactly what I was thinking," MacGowan said. "Joan, let's go. Mr Crowe, can you please make a full statement to Constable Collins telling her exactly what you told me?"

"But would I not be better—?"

"Thank you, Mr Crowe. Helen will be with you in a few minutes."

"Fucker," Crowe muttered as MacGowan and DS Moran hurried off down the corridor.

🌀

Francesca could feel a vibration through her body and was unsure of where she was. Her eyes were closed and she didn't really want to open them. The last time she had done that she had been confronted with the mutilated hand just a few metres from her face and the pool of blood that had seeped onto the grass beside Margaret's naked thigh. She remembered screaming and looking up to see Professor Crawford — or Tuan as he'd insisted she call him — looming above her with the sword still in his hands. After that things had gone distinctly fuzzy with only an occasional impression of sitting in a room with someone and trying to speak. But that had hardly seemed real and was like a half-remembered dream. The feeling of movement and the sounds that she could hear seemed much more tangible.

...stole my identity purely for the sake of impressing others. My memories...

Francesca didn't really want to pay attention to the voice. She didn't want to deal with dead bodies and people complaining.

The vibration seemed to have a background hum and Francesca suspected — in fact she knew she was in a car — but she was trying not to let herself acknowledge such concrete facts.

He brought all this on himself and his floozies. His actions will haunt him for a thousand lifetimes and each time I meet him I will do exactly the same...How dare he claim to be Tuan!

When Francesca heard the name Tuan she realised for a brief second that she should be very afraid, but her mind could not cope with the thought and dragged her back down into the warm fuzziness.

🌀

A series of incisions had been cut into Professor Crawford's dick. A deep scar ran along one side with three smaller strokes radiating from the top, followed by three more lines dissecting the scar. Then a line by itself, followed by five smaller ones that once again sprouted upwards.

A fishing line had been looped over a chandelier and pulled tight to ensure that the hook attached to the Professor's foreskin kept his knob upright and the incisions clearly visible. A scalpel lay on the floor beside the body.

What looked like guitar strings had been tied around Crawford's ankles and wrists to anchor him to a couple of heavy sofas. By the way they had gouged deep into his flesh and from the look on his face, MacGowan suspected the professor had been alive while the engraving took place.

Then the murderer had made the killing blow. The sword still protruded from the professor's chest.

"Well, there's no better alibi for not being a murderer than getting murdered yourself," Moran said. "What do these marks mean?"

"It's Ogham script, an ancient alphabet supposed to be used by the druids," MacGowan said. "They also spelt out messages to each other by pointing at parts of their fingers and thumbs. The incisions on Margaret Cronin's hand indicate exactly the same letters as have been spelt out here." He motioned towards the professor's scarred cock.

"Tuan," Moran said.

"Exactly. Where the hell is that back-up car?"

MacGowan started poking around the living room, prodding items with a pen and squinting at random objects which lay on a mantelpiece — anything to keep his eyes averted from the stiff on the floor. He stopped and sniffed.

"Can you smell something?" he asked.

Moran looked around and sniffed the air. "Just shit, boke and blood."

"No, well yes, but there's something else." MacGowan

sniffed again. "Like a joss stick…"

He let his eyes drift around the room, looking for a candle or an incense burner, but saw nothing that accounted for the scent. It was getting dark outside and he used a tissue to press a light switch on, catching sight of a gleam of metal between two bookshelves as he did so. Attached to a wall were a series of six brackets. The wallpaper beside them had faded around what appeared to be the shape of two crossed swords.

"Joan, look at this. What about the weapon which was used to kill Margaret Cronin — did we ever find it?"

"No. But the one that we found Professor Crawford with this morning was very like the one that has been used to kill him. I'd need to check though."

"Patchouli oil," MacGowan said.

"Sorry, sir?"

"Patchouli oil. That's what I can smell."

"It's hardly surprising after that Barefoot woman rubbed herself all over you," retorted Moran.

"Moran! Despite your entirely inappropriate suggestion, I only touched Dr Barefoot for a couple of seconds." MacGowan sniffed at the arms of his jacket. "There is a slight trace on me, but only a hint. This smell is much stronger."

"As if someone smelling of patchouli oil had actually been here in this room?"

"Erm, yes."

"Recently?"

MacGowan sniffed again.

"Yes," he sighed.

"Sir," Moran said nervously. "We released Francesca into Dr Barefoot's care."

"Yeah, I know," MacGowan said. "Oh fuck, oh fuck, oh fuck…Fuck, fuck, fuck, fuck…"

"Yeah," Moran said, running out of the house after him.

"Fucking slut."

※

Dr Barefoot's clinic was in a plush town house in one of the wealthiest areas of the city. At the front door was a small plaque with the Celtic-style words, *Cneasaí anam*, which MacGowan translated from Irish as "Healer of souls". DS Moran brought a jemmy from the car and they forced open the door. The porch opened onto a consulting room where a fan of patchouli incense sticks was still burning and an ambient drone was coming from a CD player.

"She must have been here not that long ago," Moran said.

"Check the rest of the house, Joan. Be careful."

MacGowan paced around the consulting room, letting his eyes wander over Barefoot's desk, filing cabinets and a black couch. Just behind the couch MacGowan saw six brackets with an ornate sword still in place. The other space was empty. He started rifling through the desk drawers and lifted out a box of medical scalpels. The cover said it held six, but there were only three left in it.

"What's a psychologist doing with scalpels?" Moran said coming back in to the room.

"Any sign of Francesca?"

"No, the place is empty."

"Where the hell did she take her?"

"What about Dunbicru?"

"Aah...stupid, stupid, stupid!" MacGowan shouted, running from the house. "Hurry up, Joan. You drive and I'll radio for support."

※

The police car, its lights slicing through the icy night, tore down a country lane.

Before they reached Dunbicru MacGowan ordered Moran to turn off the siren.

"Turn off your headlights as well, we don't want to spook her. The back-up should be here in a few minutes. Joan, you go in at the entrance further down the road and I'll go this way."

MacGowan hurried over the damp dewy ground towards the gap in the hedge where he had passed through that morning. It was pitch black and he could see nothing as he fumbled blindly forward. Then he stumbled and landed heavily on his knee. He had to bite into his sleeve to stop himself from crying out. He lay winded for a few seconds, trying to steady his breathing.

MacGowan could hear the sound of chanting so he forced himself to his feet again and hobbled up the incline towards the dolmen. The clouds thinned and through the gauzy haze a full moon struggled to make itself visible. The extra light illuminated the circle of stones and as he came over the lip of the incline he suddenly came on the scene that he had dreaded but almost expected to see. Dr Barefoot stood naked with a sword upright above her head. On the stone altar beside her lay Francesca, conscious now, but frozen in terror.

MacGowan unholstered his gun.

Barefoot chanted: "In the name of god Crom and the goddess Danu I make this offering as an appeasement for the defilement of my sacred name Tuan." Barefoot turned the sword so the point rested on Francesca's bared breasts.

"Ah, fuck no. Stop," shouted MacGowan. He pointed the gun towards her and placed a trembling finger on the trigger.

Dr Barefoot raised the hilt of the sword higher in preparation for plunging it downwards. Even now her dove-grey eyes seemed to crease in a flirtatious wink. Her wrists tensed around the hilt of the sword.

MacGowan tried to squeeze the trigger but couldn't bring himself to do it.

Just as the sword started to plunge, Dr Barefoot's head

snapped backwards. A millisecond later he heard a bang. The psychologist's body twitched. She stumbled and the sword fell onto the grass.

MacGowan ran to where Dr Barefoot lay and saw her eyes glaze over. He stared helplessly as the body jerked and then became completely still.

He turned away to see the petite figure of DS Moran, her gun still raised.

THE CHILDREN OF GEAR
WRITTEN BY NEVILLE THOMPSON

I liked the Children of Lir *as a child. I never was really into the folklore, but I liked that one.*

For me to totally relate to most things I have to bring them back to what I know.

So in this day and age I reckon that three children getting lost for years to normality could only mean one thing, drugs.

Once I thought of that concept the story kind of wrote itself.

—

The old story goes that when on smack people feel they are Gods. On our estate the main dealer is a bloke called Lir. We all say, "When you want decent gear head to Lir." Lir had our respect. He didn't serve up shite. His was a quality product. Not that he'd always been that way. Once upon a time, Lir lived quite happily with his wife and four kids, Fionula, Hugh, and the twins Fiachra and Conn. They were the apple of his eye.

Lir was a normal hard-working truck driver; not opposed to a little bit of knock-off but decent all the same. That was until the night his wife was knocked down by a drunk-driving copper coming home from work. In the space of time it took for the car to take her life, Lir's life changed totally. The cover-up by the police for one of their own instilled a hate for authority. The need to fend for his children instilled a need for money. And his wife's sister, Aoife, was about to prey on those needs.

※

Aoife was a cute girl. She looked like her dead sister and milked Lir's need for a mother for his children. She had a lot of ideas and was there when he needed advice, even when he didn't realise he needed it. Within two months they were married. Whirlwind, some said. But those who looked closer could see it was more premeditated then that. Truth was, Aoife saw Lir as her meal ticket. They raked in the money and their lifestyle was far better than anyone else on the estate. They bought the whole block of houses on their road, gates were put up and swans sat either side of the front door. Aoife went from a Micra to a Merc, from short hair to extensions, from Penney's to Brown Thomas. But try as she might, Lir would never leave the estate. The reason? The kids. They liked their school, liked their friends being around, and what the kids wanted the kids got.

Aoife knew things had to change. She knew Lir idolised the kids, but then again, he had idolised her sister and had got over her. Maybe it was time to help him get over them, too.

※

It wasn't hard. Lir was busy with his business and the kids were her concern. All he wanted her to do was feed his kids and keep the place clean. Easier said than done: four kids, and all their friends, meant continual cooking. Breakfast had just ended and they were looking for lunch, then it was, "What's for dinner?" And then, while watching telly, they wanted more food, finishing off with supper before bed. She hated it, hated being tied to the cooker. For fuck's sake, they had bucket loads of money, but she was finding it increasingly hard to get to spend it. She had asked Lir about getting a cleaner and a cook, but that had got a steely silence. It was time for action.

※

The plan was simple. Lir might deal in drugs but he hated them, despised anyone on them. All she had to do was get the children addicted.

It started with a trip to the pictures. They were all teenagers now and wanting to stretch their wings. A film over their ages ("our little secret"), a beer ("just the one"), a cigarette ("only in the garden") and a bit of weed.

A bond grew between them. There were the knowing nods, the winks, the cheeky smiles every time Lir came in. Every time he failed to see what they were doing they went a little further. They soon progressed beyond weed.

※

They woke up one day and asked Aoife to take them to town. She refused.

Within an hour all four felt as though they had the flu. Within another couple of hours they were cramped up, sweating like pigs and crying for help.

Aoife drove them into town and dropped them off at a place she knew they could score. The children moved like shadows through the streets, hurriedly paying for whatever they could get. They couldn't go home, what would their father say? Besides, they were having fun.

Soon their savings were gone and they still needed to score. They begged on the streets, but could not make enough money to feed their habit. One night, as they huddled in the doorways trying to get heat from one another, the twins asked if they could not head home.

"What about Daddy?" replied Hugh.

The twins wanted it so much.

"He won't mind, may be a bit annoyed to begin with but he loves us."

"You think?" Hugh asked excitedly.

"Of course, we are his pride and joy!"

"His pride and joy," replied Fionula, looking at their reflection in the glass door. "Just look at his pride and joy now."

All four saw their images and were ashamed. They knew they could never go home, no matter what.

🙞

Lir raged. He could not understand why his children had just decided to up and go without a by-your-leave. Aoife tried to play for time, to give him a chance to get over them like he had his wife. But Lir raged night and day. He didn't care about the empire he had built and soon it started to fade. If he wasn't out searching the city streets for his children he was at home drunk and narky.

🙞

One day, while out shopping, Aoife's credit card was refused. The shop said she had insufficient funds. Time to give Lir a few home truths. She walked in to find him drunk. She threw water over him, slapped his face and walked him to the car, drove him to the part of town where his children now roamed. Rubbish blew up the streets, and in doorways waif-like figures sat huddled from the night breeze. A young girl, skinny and unkempt, stood on the pavement. She leaned into a car and on demand flashed her body. The men laughed and drove away. She cursed them as she scrabbled for the coins they had thrown her way.

"What are we doing here?" Lir asked.

Aoife drove to where the girl was. "You wanted to see your children, didn't you?"

Lir sat as the girl approached the car.

Aoife wound down the window. The girl leaned in, her gaze vacant. "You looking for biz?"

For a moment he could not see who she was, but there was something in her eyes, something that reminded him of his first wife. "Fionula?"

"N—No, you must be mistaken."

Before he could answer she was gone, scurrying back into the night. He followed her down a lane calling, crying, wanting. And, as he did, Aoife drove away knowing he would never be hers again.

※

Lir found all four of his children hiding in cardboard boxes, weak and malnourished. The twins rolled into little balls expecting a beating from the latest man to come into their alleyway. He held them close, and as they explained what had happened he cried and told them all that they were coming home and that everything would be OK.

But it wasn't.

Having seen the damage his drugs had done to his children, Lir realised the damage they had done to other people's children, too. He stopped dealing and lost face. His empire quickly became a hunting ground for all the up-and-coming dealers who saw his decision to stop as a weakness.

The children had changed.

Their journey into drugs had robbed them of the innocence of youth and their journey back from it was pitted with disaster and failure. Lir sent them for the best treatment his money could buy, but there was no quick-fix. It required them to work hard and it took years. The counsellors recommended they didn't see Lir until they felt ready. They remained locked in their own world.

❧

Lir waited patiently. He did not think of them as the ghosts he had come across in the lane, but as the beautiful bundles of joy he and his wife had held when they were born. At night he would hear them crying for him as he slept. He would find himself waking in a sweat and running to their rooms.

One day, while walking to the shops, he died, knifed by a man he had never seen before in his life. As Lir lay bleeding the man leaned down and whispered that his sons had died from Lir's drugs.

With his last breath, Lir grabbed the man's sleeve and asked for forgiveness.

❧

No one recognised the four ghostly people who stood at the front of the church. No one knew it was Fionula, Hugh and the twins, Fiachra and Conn. They had been lost forever. Four lost souls. The children of gear.

FIANNA

DIARMAID AND GRAINNE
WRITTEN BY ADRIAN MCKINTY

When I was eight years old I read the novel The High Deeds of Finn MacCool *by Rosemary Sutcliffe. The most compelling part of the story for me was the tale of Diarmaid and Grainne. I've never forgotten it and I liked the idea of putting a contemporary spin on this classic.*

—

A dream about a girl. A draught from the open window. Silence.

The quiet woke him.

His adrenalin spiked and he reached under the pillow. There wasn't anything there. He breathed hard. Opened his eyes.

The walls were pink, the curtains taffeta, the carpets white. His wife was asleep next to him.

This was the other house.

"Jesus," he said.

Quiet unnerved him, unbalanced him. Quiet made him think of poisoned dogs and picked locks.

He slipped from between the sheets, walked to the window and pulled across the hanging blinds.

Fog.

Fog that had damped the halyards on all the boats in the marina. That's why it sounded so odd. You got used to the dissonant, incessant chime of rope line on aluminium mast, you heard it all the time, you filtered it into the background and you noticed it when it wasn't there. Or at least, *he* did.

He slid open the doors and walked onto the balcony. Couldn't see the boats today. Couldn't see twenty feet. And of course it wasn't *completely* silent. Traffic on the dual carriageway and, in Belfast, fog horns. That, like so many things, irritated him. Fog horns were ridiculous in this day and age, completely unnecessary, what with radar and sonar and GPS. If you remotely knew your arse from your elbow, fog shouldn't be a problem. They were for the incompetent and the foolhardy.

He looked at his watch.

Six fifty-eight.

He went back inside, picked up the alarm and tried to turn it off, but it wasn't on. Her doing. Last night, after the wine, after the argument.

He sat on the edge of the bed.

Six fifty-eight.

Six fifty-nine.

Seven.

That's how your life went — in increments of nothingness.

He went to the kitchen, flipped the switch on the kettle. He made coffee, booted the laptop and carried both to the deck.

He shivered. The sun still wasn't up and the mist was cold and heavy. You could just make out the lights from the one vessel in Carrick harbour, a Latvian hulk arrested for non payment of dues and the crew stranded, living on the charity of the town's people. Probably vodkaed up, the lucky beggars.

He sipped coffee, scanned his email. It was a Sunday so he wasn't expecting anything. He checked all of his accounts. No big developments. He put the laptop on the chair and went to the balcony rail. The apartment overlooked the marina and the harbour and the lough, and they made you pay through the nose for such a view. He yawned and peered into the gloom. He was anxious to see the water. It was a luck thing for him. He'd been born and raised and always lived close to the sea. As long as he could get a glimpse of the grey tongue of water in Belfast Lough, or the green North Channel or the blue-black Atlantic, he felt he would be okay. Lyr, the god of the sea, would protect him from his own weakness. Nonsense, of course, but it was a habit he'd fallen into and was hard to break.

"Eejit," he told himself.

That was his ninth or tenth minute of consciousness and now he began to think only of *her*. She consumed most of his waking hours. On the job, off it, driving, reading, watching TV. He smiled and went back into the flat.

He showered, dressed, fumble-dropped his mobile phone on the dressing table.

It didn't wake Jenny. She slept well and long now with her new job. Now that she'd made partner she always came home exhausted.

"Hard day?" he'd ask, and she'd grunt and pour herself a vodka tonic. There'd be three or four more, a frozen dinner; she'd say nothing or pick a minor fight and then watch telly and go to bed.

Still this tiredness wouldn't last. It was just the newness. Once she got into a routine it would all be the same again. Back to normal. Back to the way things were supposed to be. She was efficient and clever, and would soon learn to delegate and better manage her time.

Then they'd start going back to the golf club, the bridge nights, dinner parties...

He looked at the side of her face.

A handsome woman, some man would be lucky to have her. And of course she could be tired for other reasons. Perhaps she had met someone. A new co-worker, one of the young solicitors. He nodded at the thought. It was not impossible. He wondered if she was any good at dissimulation.

He tried to care but he just couldn't manage it.

"Bye," he whispered. He wrote her a note and left it on the TV: *I'll be back Tuesday. Don't worry. Wee surprise: I've tickets for Van Morrison on Thursday. Don't thank me, they're Bertie's. He couldn't go. Love you. D.*

He looked about for his duffle coat. He searched the cupboard, then the storage closet and then in unlikely places around the flat. Finally he discovered it there in the first cupboard lying on the floor. It had fallen off the hook and she'd put her boots in on top of it. There was mud down the sleeve and all over the back. He returned to the kitchen, crumpled the first note, wrote another, leaving out the bit about Van Morrison and "love you". He'd sell those bloody tickets. He put the old note in the bin, turned off the light and went towards the door. He stopped, came back, fished the old note out of the bin, set fire to it with his lighter and put the ashes out the window.

"Always the paranoid," he told himself sourly.

For a second the car wouldn't start. But it was a reliable old brute and after some coaxing it roared into life. 1980 Volvo Estate. Two hundred thousand miles. He turned on the fog lights. "Swedes make good cars," he said, for something to say. Some words to resist the quiet and the chill. He drove down to the harbour's edge, but the tide was out and still he couldn't see the water. A real pea-souper. He'd have to be careful on the motorway. Maybe the bloody motorway would be closed.

He turned on the traffic report but there was nothing

special. Only a few words of warning from the peelers. 'Drivers are urged to proceed with caution...'

Of course, when he hit the M5 everyone was still roaring along at sixty, seventy.

He was doing fifty in the slow lane and people were giving him dirty looks as they went past. Oh, but even so, he could feel the tension easing off with every mile. For most individuals in his line of work, the anxiety increased as they got closer and closer, but for him it was the reverse. The safe life in the apartment with the wife and the sea-view and the widescreen TV and multimedia system — that was the double place, that was the fake reality, that was the lie.

And where he was going now. That was truth. That was where he felt at home. Where he could be the person he should be. Where the pretence was only skin deep. Where the lie was white.

He noticed a receipt on the dashboard from a car park near Stormont. He grabbed it and tossed it out the window. You were supposed to do a check of your car, your pockets, your bags. It was a precaution so that you didn't accidentally bring in anything of the other world. He'd done it last night and he thought the car was clear. But you could never be too careful. Some idiots he'd heard about kept their warrant card in their wallet. Others had left their cell phone lying around with all those incriminating numbers. They'd been caught. One had only just gotten out with his life and he knew another, back in the old days, who'd been tortured over a weekend and dumped in a bog on the other side of the border. The farmer that had found him thought, at first, that it was a dead animal, so patiently had he been transformed from a human being into a punching bag, a quivering object, and finally, a corpse.

Over the years about a dozen undercover RUC and PSNI men had ended up this way. A very low percentage. And those had been either stupid or unlucky. He wasn't stupid and luck generally avoided him, bestowing neither fortune nor disfavour.

No, he would be fine. He was so relaxed only someone really looking would suspect anything.

His op zone was a small town just a klick over the border.

Old days, real bandit country. Now drugs, smuggling and quite a few dead-enders. The locals had been suspicious when he'd first showed up, but he was supremely well-trained, affable, confident, and this had gradually disarmed them. He hadn't asked any questions, he hadn't done or said anything silly. He was playing a long game. He was never nosey and he was free with information about himself. He didn't inquire into anyone's back story and he certainly never inquired about illegal activities or the paramilitaries. God, no.

His role was clear, simple. He was a businessman, he spent a lot of time travelling, sold tractors and bought used farm machinery. He did well for himself but not in an ostentatious way. He was originally from Belfast, and had bought a wee place locally because his da used to take him fishing on the Tavnamore River nearby.

He was popular. He always stood a round in the pub. He was only ever in town a couple of days a week because of the travelling, but he was well-liked when he was around. After about a year most people there knew him and most ignored him. He was a fixture. Some of the older lads down the bar even thought they remembered seeing him with his da, fishing on the river. One even recalled showing him how to tie trout flies. People were funny like that.

But he didn't push it. He was experienced and could play them. In the nineties he'd worked a gig in Larne for two years before someone told him about a crystal meth shipment coming in and wondered if he could help distribute it. He had helped out and that had led to other wee jobs and finally he'd gathered enough information on a local hood to put him inside for twenty years. They'd pulled him after and put him on regular peeler work for a year or two, but his talents were wasted there and now, once again, he was back undercover.

Some coppers cracked. You'd hear about them playing Russian roulette with their sidearms or the old hosepipe in the car window, others went prematurely grey or ended up addicted to drink, cigs, uppers or valium. Not him. He loved it. At least this assignment. This place. This...

This girl. And there she was again. The thought of her killed the last remnants of his bad mood and his face broke into a broad grin for the first time in days.

They'd met almost immediately. She worked the bar in the Railway Arms but was taking a certificate in information technology at the tech in Dundalk. She wasn't stupid by any means, she'd just messed up in school, falling for some lad who she ran off with and married. He was a bad lad and he was doing hard time now for shooting a man in London. They got divorced and for a while the town had turned against her. How could she abandon her man while he was in the clink over the water? But she had a winning personality and soon they'd all come back again. And the fact that she was drop dead gorgeous hadn't hurt either.

He'd met her and it had taken six months of constant campaigning to get her into bed. Not that that had been his goal. No, nothing so base. He'd loved her from the first. Her green eyes, red hair, her skin like marble. There was something of the faery folk about her. Bewitching, but not sinister. For her you'd want to listen to the siren, you'd want to slip to *Tir Na nÓg*.

He thought of her every moment he was on the border and a good deal of the time when he was home. It maddened him and he sometimes had to force her out of his awareness to get things done. They'd been together for nearly a year now and he was reasonably sure that she loved him. She said she did, but what did that mean? When he said it he meant it. They weren't just words. There was something tangible about the phrase. It was the truest, least false thing in his false, made-up life.

Their affair was supposedly a secret but in a small town nothing is a secret. Word went out.

Grainne's shacking up with yon boy from Belfast.

Is she now? He has some nerve. Lifting our lasses from under our noses.

Ach, he's a fine character so he is, sure I used to know him when he was this high.

No one had warned him to stay away. No bricks had come through his window. And no one had bothered her either. Why would they? He was well-liked. So was she. People were happy for them and when gossips talked about her husband the prisoner, or the age gap, they were hushed and chastened.

Her complexion was ruddy, tanned and there was something earthy, chthonic about her. Her hair was unruly and wild, and she preferred T-shirt and jeans to outfits from Next or designers in Dub. She was the opposite of the blonde, anaemic thing lying back in the flat in Carrickfergus.

He'd fallen hard, but it was a necessary fall. Without her, he knew that sooner or later he'd be one of those cops with his gun pointed at his temple. Without her, there would be no worthwhile life at all.

He followed the A1 until he hit the Mournes and stopped for a bottle of water in Newry. He got back in the car and looked at himself in the rear-view.

"Well, mate, is today the day, is tonight the night?" he asked himself for the hundredth time. Would he tell her? Did he have the courage? Did he believe sufficiently in her?

The expression in the mirror changed.

His face fell.

No, he wouldn't tell her. Perhaps he would never tell her. But, oh God, he wanted to. He wanted to end the other life, the ghost life, the days in exile away from her.

Carrickfergus might as well be on the other side of the planet.

A1 to M1.

The fog had followed him from the north and it was raining now. As usual, as he got nearer, the scene played itself out for him: "Grainne, listen, sit down, I've got something to tell you. Something important."

Her brow would furrow, perhaps she'd be frightened.

"Listen honey, I'm just going to come right out with it. I'm a peeler, a cop. I've been sent down here as a sort of a spy. I report movements, suspicions. I'm prepping the territory for deep cover. Not just me, a few others. We're plugging into the Real IRA's networks. We're playing them. But listen, Grainne, I've fallen in love with you and I know you love me. I want you to come away with me. To England or Scotland or anywhere. I want you to leave with me. I'm quitting the force. We'll get a ferry tonight. A plane. Doesn't matter. I've money saved, we'll be fine. Grainne. Please, what do you say?"

What would she say? In the dreamscape she'd kiss him and cry and he'd help her pack and they'd drive to the ferry and from then on life would begin.

But he wasn't a fool. There was the fantasy in his head and the truth on the ground. What would happen? He had narrowed it down to four main possibilities. He rated them in the order of the most likely to the least, trying to be as logical and unemotional as possible. First, the Hollywood Ending — perhaps a shade more probable than the others. She would say that she loved him too and that she was willing to go away with him.

The second possibility was that she would say that she loved him and for a few hours he would believe her, but then, on the sly, she would make some pretext and slip out (to pack, perhaps, or give her notice down the pub) and she would come back with her friends and they would point guns at him and take him away and over the next few days they'd make him tell them everything.

In the third scenario she would simply go nuts when he told her about his deception. She'd feel betrayed and furious. She'd make noise and throw things and there'd be a fuss and she'd kick him out. She wouldn't grass him, but she wouldn't want him either. Nothing would end decisively. This might be the worst of the possibilities.

The fourth and last prospect would be a reaction that was no reaction. A coolness. She cared for him but it wasn't enough. For her, this was just a piece of fun. She didn't love him. She wasn't serious. How could she be, a man ten years older than her? And now he wanted her to run off with him to England? It was ridiculous...She'd ask him to leave her, leave town. She'd be embarrassed in a way. He'd have to admit to his superiors that the operation was compromised. They'd discipline him, suspend him, but none of that would matter because, more significantly, he could never be with her again.

There were other denouements but it would most likely be one of those. He was hoping for the first but there was a pretty good chance it would be number two. He knew her intimately, she liked him a lot, but her tribal loyalties were deep. Her ex-husband was, after all, a romantic rebel, even if that did boil down to shooting a fellow drug dealer in the back in some dank amp lab in Hackney.

Not too long over the border he got off the M1 and headed west. Ten minutes later he was at the outskirts of town.

His cottage was just off the old Dublin Road and after waving to a couple of people he knew he pulled into his garage.

He went inside the house, opened the windows, picked letters from the hall and sauntered upstairs. He showered and shaved.

In the bedroom he took the revolver from its hiding place behind the bookcase and put it under the pillow. Had to be somewhere easy to get and easy to hide when Grainne stayed over.

It was eleven-thirty, the pub would be just open. He changed into a checked shirt and jeans and grabbed his wallet and his coat.

She was pleased to see him. "I thought you might not be coming down today. You know the fog," she said, and smiled like the goddamn sun after a thousand year winter.

He sat opposite her at the bar. There were a couple of locals in already.

"What are the oul' contemptibles having?" he asked loudly.

"Mine's a Guinness," McCarthy said.

"Ach, you couldn't stand me a wee whiskey," Georgie Flinn added.

"Set them up there, Grainne love, and mine's a Black Bush if you don't mind," he said.

She grinned.

He watched her get the drinks. She had lost her scrunchie and several times she had to push long wavy strands of hair back from her face. He could watch her doing that all day. Watch her doing anything.

"I've news for you," she said.

"What news?" he asked anxiously.

"It's a secret. Tell ya after I knock off at lunch."

"Well, what's it about?"

"It's a secret, weren't you listening?" she insisted.

"Okay, but what's the nature of the secret, the general subject area?"

"It involves travel," she said, and went over to give Flinn his whiskey.

He let the matter drop. Probably she wanted him to take a holiday with her. She had mentioned such a plan before. Of course, it would be next to impossible. The peelers would never allow it and how could he explain such a thing to his wife.

No, it wouldn't do, he'd have to talk her out of it.

Father McCawley came in and they had a few words about the football. Father McCawley hated to see Arsenal play so defensively. He agreed and bought the old man a gin and tonic and they talked for a while.

Once, in an insane moment, he'd thought about going to Confession and unburdening himself, telling Peter McCawley that he was: married, a Protestant, an undercover cop and that he'd been lying to everybody for the last sixteen months. Clarity had convinced him of the foolishness of this idea. The Priest wouldn't break the sanctity of the Confessional but he'd blurt it out in other ways, drop unintentional hints. His body language would change his attitude. He was a nice old bird but not the subtlest of God's agents on planet Earth.

No, there was only one person he could tell and he wondered if he would ever have the bottle for it.

When the pub closed after lunch he walked her home. She was chatty and excited. He'd let her down gently about the holiday. Tell her they could go for a weekend somewhere.

She showered. He cleaned the grate and got a fire going with newspapers and a wedge of turf.

He went into the kitchen and put the kettle on.

"I made some tea," he said when she came down in jeans and a long-sleeved Undertones T-shirt that he'd bought her.

"Oh thanks," she said, and took her mug.

He waited for as long as he possibly could and then asked: "Okay, so what's the big news, hon?"

"Jesus, I wondered when you'd get to it. I've been offered a job in Wales! At a software firm. They were recruiting at tech a couple of months ago, never heard anything, and then they emailed out of the blue. They do interfaces, American company, European HQ's in Swansea, but they had places in either London or South Wales. Of course, I picked Swansea. I couldn't live in London, not with Martin being in the Scrubs and everything, you know?" It all bubbled out of her like a happy little stream.

He was thrown. She wanted to go and she *would* go, that was for sure. Could he go with her? Quit the force? He couldn't keep his assignment here and spend time in Swansea too. Move? What would he do over there? Nothing. He was fit for nothing. But what was the alternative?

"I'll go with you," he said.

"What?"

"I'll go with you, I love you, I, I, can't be without you."

"Oh my God, oh my God, I didn't want to even hope, I love you too," she said, delighted.

Tears. They hugged, kissed. She cried.

"What will you do?" she asked.

"I don't know, I'll think of something," he said.

"You could still do your business, you'd make contacts. I'm sure the Welsh need tractors," she said with a little laugh.

He smiled. Well, here it was. This was the opportunity he'd been waiting for. He would either tell her now or he would never tell her. She loved him. They were going together to Swansea. They were starting a new life. Her hair was red. Her eyes emerald.

"I don't sell tractors," he said.

"What?"

He took her hand.

"Listen," he said, and told her everything.

She did listen. She was quiet. She didn't interrupt. She took it all in and at the end she didn't say anything for a long time. Finally she looked at him and, leaning over, kissed him.

"It doesn't matter, I love you, the real you. I know the real you, that's all," she said, and he could have wept with relief.

She got up to make another pot of tea.

"Shit, we're out of milk," she said.

"Are we?" he asked. There had been a half a pint there a minute ago.

"Aye, we are, look. I'll just run to O'Neill's before he closes. Skimmed, right?"

He nodded and out she went.

He got up, went slowly into the kitchen and looked into the sink.

Milk still there around the drain. His knees buckled.

He grabbed the counter top and steadied himself.

"That's that then," he said sadly.

He wondered if he would ever see her again.

Almost certainly not.

He walked back into the living room. Sat down.

He knew he should run, but as the moments ticked by, the window for escape closed.

He took out his wallet and threw it on the fire. At least they wouldn't have the satisfaction of spending his money.

A mere ten minutes passed.

The sound of a car.

The front door opened and it was as he had expected. Two men in ski masks. One was holding a revolver, the other a semi-automatic. He put his hands up. The men said nothing and motioned him outside. A Land Rover was waiting. Someone thumped him. He fell into the black earth. He felt the boots fly in. He curled into the foetal position to protect himself. Someone kicked him in the head. He lost consciousness...

He woke intermittently throughout the night, the pain

almost immediately knocking him out again.

Finally it stopped for a long time and he knew that he was sleeping. It was a beautiful sleep and he was glad of it.

A hand shook his head from side to side.

"Okay, gorgeous. Wakey wakey. Time for the old chop," a voice said.

He woke. He'd been stripped. Everything hurt. He was blindfolded.

"You do it, Barry," the voice said.

"Do I have to?" Barry asked. He was young, frightened.

"*Finnbar!* Let's not get into this now, you know you have to," the voice said.

They cuffed his hands behind his back and marched him along a concrete floor. He could hear animals. He could barely walk. Barry's hand shoved him gently from behind. He tried to say something but his teeth were broken and his tongue swollen.

He was on grass now. He could sense through the blindfold that it was daylight. Barry marched him for two minutes. He was desperate to speak but his jaw seemed broken too. He could only moan and he didn't want to moan.

Barry prodded him a little more and then stopped him.

"On or off?" Barry asked, his voice trembling.

"Oaaafff," he managed.

Barry leaned forward and removed the blindfold. "Don't turn round," Barry said.

Barry didn't want to see him, to look him in the face. That was understandable.

He opened his eyes. They were near the border. He recognised the hills, the boggy fields, the barbed wire fences. It was a desolate spot. Far from any frontier posts or villages or farms. Far from the nearest *Garda* station or customs men.

They were utterly alone. There would be no cavalry, no last minute dramatic appearance by the cops or (he mocked himself) her. No sudden countermand of orders, no rescue, no histrionics. It would be quick and calm. It would all be over.

The boy put the gun to his neck. He felt the coldness of the metal. The gun jerked as Barry chambered a round with his left hand. It was a semi-automatic. Perhaps they wouldn't have cleaned it well. Perhaps it would jam. Sometimes they did.

He smiled at himself. No, not for the kid's first time. The poor wee lad probably spent half his waking hours making sure it was oiled and piped.

The barrel was wet with dew. It was shaking. The boy wasn't keen, but he had to be blooded sometime. Had to resolve himself. Psyche himself up.

"Okay," the boy said.

This was it.

He could see down into the next valley: trees, a hint of blue water in a lough.

The fog was finally clearing up.

"Good," he said.

THE FORTUNATE ISLES
WRITTEN BY DAVE HUTCHINSON

I think the first time I heard of Tir Na nOg was on the sleeve notes of The Book of Invasions by Horslips. That would have been back in the late 70s, and Tir Na nOg wasn't actually mentioned by name, if I remember correctly, but the story of the Tuatha Dé Danann outlined in the notes stuck in my mind. And it really is a cracking album, too.

The next time I heard of Tir Na nOg was sometime in the mid-80s, in the booklet that accompanied a computer game called, reasonably enough, Tir Na Nog. If you were a Spectrum or Amstrad gamer in the mid-80s, the chances are you know what I'm talking about.

The idea of this land of the ever-young, this far-off place beyond the edges of the map, has stuck with me for years.

—

A television is playing in the corner of the room, a big LCD flatscreen model, maybe thirty years old, its picture speckled with malfunctioning pixels. The sound is turned down, but the screen is showing a reality show, this one involving fifteen celebrities — including, improbably, the last surviving and very aged member of U2 — locked in a decommissioned Russian nuclear submarine on the floor of the Arctic Ocean off Novaya Zemlya. The show's been airing for a couple of weeks now, and the participants are starting to look bored and listless.

The two men ignore the television and continue walking around the room.

They're walking in opposite directions, facing outward, along the wall, unhurriedly, looking at everything, taking photographs with their phones. The wall is covered with lining paper and painted what was probably once a sunny lemon yellow rendered a shabby nicotine colour by the years. The light switch has been plumbed in by running a cable down from the ceiling and stapling it to the wall. Neither of the men touches the light switch.

When they cross over by the door, they go round again, covering each other's ground, taking more photographs, bending down to examine marks on the skirting, looking up at where the wall meets the high ceiling, checking under the furniture.

"I think I'm coming down with a cold," says Pawel.

"You should be so lucky," says Daniel, who is beginning to be annoyed by the smell in the room.

"There's a lot of it about," says Pawel, a tall, sandy-haired young man who looks as though he could manage a walk-on part in one of those new World War Two epics — Third Nazi From The Left (the one who gets his throat slit by a British commando during the daring raid on the German radar station in Occupied France).

Daniel takes some more photographs of the mess on the wall behind the armchair. "Ready?"

"Just a moment." Pawel leans forward until his nose is almost touching the wallpaper. Leans back. "Okay."

The two men turn and face the room.

It's not a big room and there's not a lot in it. Shabby armchair and sofa upholstered in green velour, to which a grey long-haired cat has added its own touches. Low coffee table in some cheap wood, with a scratched glass top. Television attached to a number of add-on boxes by a cat's cradle of mismatched cabling. Pawel and Daniel go around the room again, clockwise and counter-clockwise, looking under the furniture again, looking at the bottle of whiskey and two glasses and the scatter of magazine printouts on the coffee table. They ignore the dead man in the armchair. They go around again, taking photographs.

Daniel's phone hums. He looks at the screen and touches the answer icon. "It's yourself, Gard Lockhart," he says with all the Biblical opprobrium he can load into his voice.

As responding officer, it was Gard Lockhart's job to secure the scene until Daniel and Pawel arrived, but in a fit of compassion, Gard Lockhart felt it necessary to accompany the hysterical widow to the local hospital, and now Daniel and Pawel have to assume the scene is contaminated even if it's not, which means they'll have to regard any evidence they find as suspect, because any future defence counsel will certainly tell the jury about it.

"No, Gard," says Daniel after listening to Lockhart's explanation for longer than strictly necessary considering how angry he is. "Go back to Ballymena Street. Go into my office and sit down. Don't stop off in the canteen for a coffee and a chat. Go into my office, close the door behind you, and sit down and wait for me. And don't touch anything." He listens again. "No, Gard," he replies, "it will *not* appear on your overtime sheet. Not even if you have to wait for me until the end of time. And if, at the end of time, I do finally turn up, and I discover that you've fucked off again, I will find you and I will do things to you that will *entirely* change your outlook on life. Now repeat what I just said." He listens. Then he hangs up without saying goodbye.

"Bit wordy," Pawel comments.

"Wordy is the least of Gard Lockhart's problems," says

Daniel.

"You could go straight home from here and leave him in your office overnight," Pawel suggests.

Daniel thinks about it. It does appeal, for a moment. He shakes his head. "So," he says.

"Mm," says Pawel, and they both walk over to stand in front of the dead man.

He's sitting in the armchair, white male, in his eighties. He's wearing a brown pair of corduroy trousers, a white shirt and a tatty grey cardigan. His legs are sprawled out in front of him and his arms are resting on the chair's armrests. His head is tilted back until he's looking at the ceiling with an expression of calm puzzlement, slightly cross-eyed, as if he's trying to focus on the neat little hole in the centre of his forehead. On the wall behind him are a large proportion of the contents of his head. There are blood-spatters all over the armchair and the carpet. Daniel steps forward and palpates the fingers. Rigor hasn't set in yet, the eyes are still moist, there's a stench of blood and cordite and voided bowel in the room but no smell of decomposition. All of which unscientific testing appears to mesh with the facts as he knows them. The widow called the police at half past three this morning, about an hour ago, saying that she had gone up to bed and then heard a gunshot and when she came back downstairs she found her husband like this. The widow is, of course, the prime suspect at the moment — the only suspect at the moment — and it's annoying that she's now at the hospital under sedation and unable to answer questions. Daniel adds another black mark against Gard Lockhart's eternal soul.

"I don't recognise him," Daniel says, stepping back and lifting his phone to take more photographs. It's not exactly a fatuous statement; this is a small city, but it's certainly big enough for one person not to know everybody. A disproportionate number of murder victims tend to come from the criminal classes, though, which is handy because they come attached to priors and files and known associates and probable motives, and Daniel knows most of them personally.

"According to the wife, this is Mr Glenroy Walken," says Pawel. "And that's about all Lockhart managed to get out of her before he took her to the hospital."

"Glenroy." Daniel moves to one side of the body and takes more photographs. "Well, good morning, Mr Walken. I'm Detective Inspector Snow and this is Detective Sergeant Cybulski and we'll be your investigating officers for today." He takes more photographs. "What do you think?"

Pawel stands in the middle of the room and looks at Mr Glenroy Walken, his head tipped to one side. "No sign of a struggle. No sign of forced entry. Drink and glasses on the table." He looks at the sofa, snaps a couple more photos of it. "We should bag this."

"So he's entertaining a friend," Daniel says. "And at some point around half past three this morning the friend pulls out a handgun and shoots him in the head and then lets themselves out before the widow comes downstairs."

"Works for me," says Pawel.

"Or he's been drinking with his wife all night and about half past three in the morning she just gets sick of listening to him and pulls out a handgun and shoots him in the head."

"Works for me too," says Pawel.

Daniel sighs. He rubs his face, says, "All right—" and there's a commotion outside the room. The door opens and a tall white-haired man wearing a rumpled suit walks in, followed by a flustered-looking Gard Kennedy.

"Snow?" says the white-haired man, walking confidently towards Daniel and Pawel. "What have we here, then?"

Detective Superintendent Tweed, well beyond retirement age and famously insomniac, drives around the city through his endless nights looking for something to occupy his mind. Over the years, Daniel has developed a kind of Zen calm regarding his superior's habit of striding unbidden into the heart of crime scenes. It's an attitude Gard Kennedy, who Daniel stationed outside the door in the stead of the disgraced Gard Lockwood, has not had time to cultivate, and he's mugging and rolling his eyes behind Tweed's back like a Kabuki performer. Daniel waves him back outside.

"Sir," he says sternly to Tweed. "You really shouldn't be — sir, please." Tweed has gone over to Mr Walken, seized his hand, and is repeating Daniel's unscientific test for rigor. Daniel grabs the Superintendent by the shoulders and steers him back into the middle of the room, where Pawel has switched off his phone and put it in his pocket and is standing looking up into the corner of the ceiling so that one day, if a canny defence barrister ever questions the security of the scene he can say, quite truthfully, "No, sir, I never saw Superintendent Tweed enter the room."

"Sir," Daniel says to Tweed. "We've spoken about this before." He lowers his voice until he's barely whispering. "Uncle Billy, *please.*"

Tweed is a legend, a myth, a story told in hushed voices in canteens and locker rooms in police stations all the way up and down the West Coast of Ireland, an Olympian policeman, the yardstick against which generations of detectives have measured themselves and found themselves wanting. On his good days he's still as good as he ever was, but the good days are getting further and further apart, and he's taking on the aspect of a ruined monument. Daniel doesn't know what pursues him out of sleep, but he has an idea that after more than forty years as a policeman the inside of Tweed's head must be a terrible place.

"Sir," he says more gently. "I must ask you to—" and the door opens again. This time Wee Rab O'Connell, all done up in his sterile white romper suit, is standing in the doorway. Daniel blinks. "Doctor O'Connell," he says. "Join the party."

O'Connell, Chief Forensic Officer, gives the room the once-over and Daniel sees his shoulders slump, although his face maintains its usual deadpan. He sighs fractionally.

"Sergeant," Daniel says to Pawel, "would you show Superintendent Tweed back to his car, please? And then go and see how we're doing with the door-to-door."

Pawel comes out of his testimony-protecting trance ("No, sir, I didn't notice the presence of Superintendent Tweed on the scene until after Doctor O'Connell was in attendance") and gently walks the unresisting Tweed out of the room.

O'Connell remains blocking the doorway. "A moment, Sergeant," he says, taking out a phone and aiming at the white plastic overshoes Pawel's wearing. The phone scans the overshoes' barcodes and logs them into the evidence database. O'Connell looks at Tweed's brogues for a moment, then scans them too. He sucks his teeth and moves out of the way to let Pawel and the Superintendent pass.

"Don't say a word," Daniel warns when they're gone.

O'Connell thinks about it, then says, "What have we got?"

"White male, seventies or eighties. Single gunshot wound to the head. No signs of a struggle." Daniel tries to be deliberately vague, to let O'Connell come to his own conclusions from the evidence. "We'll want everything in here bagged and blitzed, but concentrate on the sofa and the bottle and the two glasses. Check the bathroom in case the shooter used the loo. And dust the lock on the inside of the front door and the button on the doorbell."

O'Connell bends over until his nose is inches from Mr Walken's. He sniffs the wound in the forehead and then straightens up and looks at the mess on the wall. He looks at the sofa and nods. He looks at Daniel, starts to say something, thinks better of it, and goes back into the hallway to unpack his gear. Daniel hears the sounds of scenes-of-crime officers arriving, O'Connell bollocking them for taking so long to get to the scene. He looks at the serene corpse of Mr Glenroy Walken and takes a deep breath and lets himself fall into the familiar rhythms of a murder investigation professionally conducted. It feels like coming home.

There's an old joke: Little Jewish chap's walking through one of the insanely sectarian parts of Belfast — doesn't matter which one — and he comes upon this group of paramilitary hard men — Republican, Loyalist, it doesn't matter.

"So," says one of the hard men, "are you a Catholic or a Protestant?"

"I'm Jewish," says the Jewish lad.

The hard man thinks about it for a while, then he says, "Yes, but are you a *Catholic Jew* or a *Protestant Jew*?"

Okay, so not very funny. The funniest thing about it is that someone actually once asked Daniel the very same question, in all seriousness. Are you a Catholic Jew or a Protestant Jew?

Some years later, it occurred to Daniel that if he'd had his wits about him he would have told the truth, which is that he's not really any kind of Jew. Judaism descends through the maternal line, and his mother, the sainted Siobhan, for whom his father threw aside a promising career with the Metropolitan Police in order to relocate to this little city in the West of Ireland, was a Humanist who had left instructions in her will that she was to be buried in the back garden of their house in a biodegradable wicker coffin.

Big Sam Snow wasn't having any of that. He loved his wife to the fringes of insanity, but there was no way he was putting her in the ground in a laundry basket.

This immediately posed the problem of *where* exactly the interment would take place. Siobhan had been raised a

Catholic, but she had spent the latter years of her life politely but gleefully alienating any priest who came within earshot. The local priest, a man who knew how to nurture a grudge, dolefully informed Sam that it would be impossible for Siobhan to be buried in a Catholic cemetery. Sam tried a number of parishes — some of them tens of miles away — but everywhere he went Siobhan Snow's lonely battle against Catholicism had been waged there ahead of him.

Eventually, Sam found a Protestant vicar some miles from the city who was prepared to perform the ceremony and allow his wife to be buried in his cemetery, but after the service the vicar posed to Sam a question which he had been too busy to think about: how was the boy to be brought up now?

To be truthful, neither Big Sam nor Siobhan had given it much thought. Daniel had been baptised a Catholic, but that was where his involvement with organised religion had stalled. His parents had thought that perhaps they'd cross that bridge when he was old enough for school, but now Sam, the polite refusals of the priests still ringing in his ears, decided it was time to take the bull by the horns.

So, one day shortly before his fifth birthday, Daniel accompanied his father on the train to Dublin, there to visit a *mohel* of Sam's acquaintance.

Returning three days later, bemused, in quite a lot of pain and a fraction of a gramme lighter, Daniel listened to his father telling him that he wasn't really Irish. He was actually descended from a race of people whose history went back to some awful distant vanishing point and involved a great deal of fighting and slavery and wandering in deserts.

When he got old enough for it to matter, Daniel found it in his heart to hate his father for the decision he'd made. His religion initially confused and then enraged his schoolmates and the bullying dogged him all through his schooldays. His father's cack-handed attempts to keep a kosher kitchen only lasted a couple of years, and by the time he went to university in Manchester they were both ordering Chinese takeaways heavy on the pork dishes with barely a twinge of guilt. They were, Big Sam told him, Jews. But they weren't *orthodox*. You had, Big Sam said, to be *adaptable*. Daniel remembers a conversation with his Rabbi around the time he left for university where the issue of *adaptability* had almost resulted in physical violence.

But he went to Manchester, where he had his eyes opened in too many ways to count. And then, his father's son, he went into the Metropolitan Police. And then, after a few years, he went home, this English-Irish-Jewish-Catholic-Humanist copper, to find his father and his Sergeant, the nearly occult Billy Tweed, more or less running Ballymena Street nick as a private fiefdom.

In truth, it wasn't an onerous job. The Traveller Wars, the biggest thing that had ever happened to the area, were long finished. In the early years of the century two traveller families, the Mitchells and the Copes, had squared off over control of the local drugs trade, which any rational person would have realised was barely worth fighting about. For a very brief period the city resembled one of those lawless towns in the Old West, and questions were asked in the Dáil about whether the local Garda were up to the task of keeping order. And then the Mitchells surprised everybody by providing their very own solution to the problem.

At some point the Mitchells came upon a paramilitary arms cache — doesn't matter from which side — long-forgotten in the white heat of Decommissioning. The passage of time had, in fact, rendered a lot of the weaponry beyond use, but enough of it remained operational — including a number of shoulder-launched anti-aircraft missiles once meant to be introduced to Brit helicopters — for the Mitchells to mount what they obviously conceived of as a mighty hammer-blow against their opponents.

The problem for the Mitchells was that the paramilitaries had not forgotten about the arms cache at all, and now they were in government in the North, its deployment became something of an embarrassment. An embarrassment which they resolved with elegant simplicity by erasing the Mitchell family.

In the aftermath, nobody could ever prove anything, which was as intended. And the police didn't fall over themselves to investigate the deaths and disappearances associated with what became, in local legend, The Massacre. It was hardly a shining moment in law enforcement, but as far as they were concerned, Big Sam once told Daniel, the problem was resolving itself and they weren't going to interfere. When it was over the Mitchells were broken and the Copes, taking the hint, moved on to pastures new.

Since then the city has been like pretty much any city in impoverished, financially bruised Western Europe. It has a small but muscular drugs scene, several protection rackets, some rather half-hearted prostitution, and its share of gangs and cowboys, all seeking 'respect' and periodically becoming enraged when nobody gives them it.

And today it has one more murder.

Daniel gets back to Ballymena Street around seven o'clock in the morning, after almost four hours watching O'Connell's men logging the scene and bagging up various bits of furniture for later trace evidence examination, and when he walks into his office he finds Gard Lockhart sitting fast asleep in his visitor chair. He feels a faint and entirely transitory pang of guilt for having forgotten about the young Gard, but he can't raise the energy to bawl him out.

"Oh, fuck off home, Lockhart," he mutters, settling himself in his chair behind his desk. "Don't do it again." And as

Lockhart, still half-asleep, stumbles out of the office, Daniel docks his phone so he can upload its pictures of the Walken crime scene to the nick's expert system, which will stitch them together, along with Pawel's photos and the pictures O'Connell's team took, into a zoomable three-hundred-and-sixty degree walkthrough for future reference. "Get me a coffee before you go," he tells Lockhart's gratefully retreating back. "Black. Put all the sugar you can find in it."

And he turns to his keyboard and starts writing his report of the night's events. After about fifteen minutes, he stops, and the members of the morning relief in the outer office, shrugging off their coats and quarrelling over who gets the canteen croissants and who gets the Danishes, hear him shout, "Fuck! What day is it?"

*

Big Sam Snow lives a mostly blameless life these days. Early on there were episodes of wandering, sobbing, begging and attempts to negotiate with the nurses and perhaps even God Himself, and on one notable occasion the hurling of a chair through a window and Sam's attempt to follow it into the Great Outdoors. But those days are long gone. Now Big Sam exists in two states — asleep and awake. And the awake state is divided into two positions — in bed and in his chair.

Today is a Chair Day. "He had a good night," says Helen, the nurse who looks after Sam and the thirty or so long-term cases on the ward. A good night for Helen is one where only a third of her charges were doubly incontinent. She's in her early forties, attractive but entirely worn out, and in an alternative universe she and Daniel would have established a Relationship. He'd have started by maybe giving her flowers now and again, and it would have progressed to little presents and then a trip to the cinema to see a thriller, which he would have scoffingly but charmingly deconstructed afterward over dinner. Eventually there would have been Affection, two similarly afflicted souls living outside normal diurnal existence. Later would have come an Understanding, and after that maybe Love.

But this is not an alternative universe. Helen is a nurse overworked beyond the point of exhaustion, and when Daniel visits the hospital he's usually running on caffeine overdrive. Every time they see each other it's like the meeting of two distantly related species and the idea of a relationship, if it ever crosses their minds, is entirely ridiculous. All they have in common is Big Sam, and, all respect to Big Sam, it's not enough.

The hospital has seen better days. Back at the turn of the century, in the time of the Celtic Tiger, it was very nearly state-of-the-art. But the Celtic Tiger stumbled, got to its feet, then stumbled again and went down for good as economies across the world blew away on the wind. Since then, investment in public services has been thin indeed. Big Sam's pension and health insurance barely covers his upkeep; it's nowhere near enough to pay for private care.

So here he is, the Big Man, sitting in a threadbare armchair beside his threadbare bed at the far end of the threadbare long-term ward. As usual, Daniel tries not to look at the other patients as he makes his way with Helen to Sam's bedside. Hard though it might be to credit, there are people here worse-off than his father.

The worst thing is that he doesn't look ill. He looks...thoughtful. Distracted, sometimes. He sits in his chair by the window and looks out over the city. The ward is high enough in the building that you can see the hard sheen of the Atlantic beyond the clustering rooftops, and sometimes you might think Sam is looking out at the horizon and imagining the endless miles between here and America. But the odds are against it.

He's neat and clean in his pyjamas and dressing gown, freshly shaved and hair combed. Helen says to him, "Look who's here, Sam, Daniel's come to see you," but he doesn't pause in his examination of the horizon.

Daniel thanks Helen and pulls up a visitor's chair beside his father. "Well," he begins. "*That* was an interesting evening."

The sad thing is that the only thing Daniel and his father really have in common is The Job. If any of the other patients were able to pay attention, they would hear Daniel on his visits giving Sam chapter and verse on his latest cases, in nitpicking detail because Sam used to be a nitpicking sort of policeman. So Daniel tells Sam about the call-out this morning, about Mr Glenroy Walken and his unusual living arrangements.

It turns out that Mr Glenroy Walken was not really Mr Glenroy Walken. There's no record of a national ID card in that name, no passport, no National Insurance number. His fingerprints are still making their weary way through the National Fingerprint Database, and it'll be days — weeks, probably — before there are any results from his DNA. A quick Google brought the news that 'Glenroy Walken' was a character in *The West Wing*, a turn-of-the-century American television drama.

Whether this is relevant or not, nobody knows, and it's impractical to ask the widow because about an hour after Gard Lockhart brought her to the hospital she suffered a massive heart attack and is now in a coma in the intensive therapy unit four floors below Sam's chair. 'Widow', indeed, is a misleading term because, while Mrs Ellen Wright is certainly a widow, she is not Mr Walken's widow. The late Mr Wright died of cancer fourteen years ago, and since then Mrs Wright has lived alone. According to statements by neighbours, Mr Walken is a new addition to Mrs Wright's life. He's been living at her house for between two and six weeks and he didn't go out much. So far, a search of the house has not turned up any documents belonging to or pertaining to him.

Daniel tells his father this much, tries out a few half-formed theories on him, but Sam just sits looking into the West like a character from some old story, and when it comes time for Daniel to leave there's no sign that his father ever knew he was there.

On his way out of the hospital, Daniel stops off in ITU and checks on Mrs Wright. There's a Gard stationed beside her bed in case she comes out of the coma and makes a statement, but so far the old woman's condition is unchanged. Daniel stands by her bed for a few moments looking at her, a bone-thin old lady with long white hair and the blue smudges of old tattoos up both arms. What was it with her generation and tattoos? These days it's rare to find young people indulging in any form of body modification more extreme than earrings, but Daniel has seen the bodies of old folk adorned with sometimes astonishing decorations. He remembers a local councillor who died of a heart attack aged seventy-five, a staid and upright citizen and a figure of great probity. There was a brief question about the cause of death, and the body was given the once-over at Antrim Road mortuary and, once undressed, turned out to be an alien landscape of piercings and jaw-dropping old decorative scarification. That was the day Daniel learned the phrase 'Prince Albert'.

Standing there, a thought occurs to Daniel. He takes out his phone and takes a couple of snaps of Mrs Wright's tattoos. It's a long shot, but anything they can learn about her would be useful.

Outside in the late afternoon sunshine, he stops and takes stock. He can't think of anything else they could be doing in the Walken investigation. He's visited his father. He's managed some shopping. What else? Oh, yes. Sleep. Ought to make time for some sleep.

※

A week on, and no one is any the wiser about the Walken killing. Mrs Wright remains in a coma and things are not looking so hopeful for her. Mr Walken remains a mystery wrapped in an enigma, although like Mrs Wright he has many tattoos and a number of the designs are similar to the old lady's. Cause of death was indeed the single gunshot to the head; a bullet dug out of the wall behind the armchair turned out to be a .38, but too damaged to provide reliable comparison evidence, even if they do find the murder weapon. Local CCTV has proved inconclusive, mainly because budget cuts have eaten into the camera network's maintenance and only a third of it is currently in operation, none of it in the area of Mrs Wright's house. Daniel takes on new cases, visits Sam in hospital, returns to his flat above Ballymena Street nick, cooks himself solitary meals, works works works.

And then one morning Wee Rab O'Connell knocks on the door of Daniel's office and comes in with a briefcase in his hand and a smile on his face.

"Have a win on the Lottery?" Daniel asks over the top of his monitor.

"Not far off," O'Connell admits, sitting down on the other side of the desk. "We got an identification on Glenroy Walken."

Daniel sits back in his chair. "Do tell."

"The DNA results came back about an hour ago. It turns out Mr Walken's on the database under the name of Mitchell. Alan Mitchell."

Daniel thinks about it. "You know, that rings a bell."

"It should. Mad Dog Mitchell. The Traveller Wars?"

Daniel sighs. If only he had a euro for every hard man who styled himself 'Mad Dog'. But that isn't what's ringing the bell. "You think that's started again? After, what, sixty years?"

O'Connell shrugs. "I don't know. All I know is that Alan Mitchell went missing during The Massacre. At which time he was sixty-two years of age."

Daniel raises an eyebrow. Then the bell rings again and he starts pulling up the Walken file from the expert system.

"We also got DNA off one of the glasses you found in the living room," O'Connell continues, "and that also was in the database. We have a positive identification of one Gordon Cope."

Daniel opens another window on his monitor. Cope, Gordon. One previous arrest for joyriding fifty years ago, which is when his DNA went into the database. He's in his early seventies now, lives in one of the grim little estates over on the northern edge of the city. Daniel shouts, "Pawel!"

Pawel comes to the door of the office. "Boss?"

"Get a car from the pool. We're going for a drive."

Pawel nods and goes back through the office.

Daniel looks at the Walken file again. Yes, there's that little ringing bell. Mrs Ellen Wright, *née* Ellen Mitchell. "They're related," he says.

O'Connell can't see the screen, but he knows exactly what Daniel's talking about. "We took DNA from her at the hospital, for elimination purposes. We need more careful tests, but off the record I'd say she's his daughter."

Daniel sits back again and tries to rearrange all of this in his head to make a meaningful narrative. O'Connell's phone rings. He takes it out of his pocket and says, "Yes?" Then a puzzled expression crosses his face. "I didn't authorise that." He listens again. "Who did they say they were?" He listens again. Looks at Daniel and says, "Did you order the Walken body moved?"

"Me?" Daniel asks in surprise.

"No," O'Connell says to the phone, "he didn't either. How long ago was this?" He listens, nods, and hangs up without saying goodbye. "Someone's stolen the body," he says to Daniel.

⚜

When O'Connell and Daniel get to the mortuary it's strangely difficult to get a straight story out of anybody, even allowing for the fact that no one wants to be blamed for the mess. It seems that no one can exactly remember what happened, but it looks as though, while O'Connell was on his way to Ballymena Street, a police officer arrived with documents signed by Daniel authorising the removal of Alan 'Mad Dog' Mitchell's body. The body was loaded into a police van and the Gard drove away.

Except nobody can agree what the Gard looked like, and at least one member of O'Connell's staff has a *feeling* it wasn't a police van at all. Another, who was there through the whole thing, can't remember anything about it. The supposed documentation signed by Daniel turns out to be a blank sheet of paper torn from a notebook. O'Connell looks at it and starts shouting at people. Daniel takes out his phone and puts out a crash bulletin for vans — *all* vans — travelling around the city.

Two hours later, fifteen miles south of the city, a patrol unit pulls over an unmarked blue van. Inside is a driver and a biodegradable plastic utility coffin containing the earthly remains of Alan 'Mad Dog' Mitchell, latterly Mr Glenroy Walken.

⚜

A veteran of police interviews, Daniel used to think he'd more or less seen it all. He's seen suspects in tears, he's had suspects attack him. He's had them deny everything, he's had them confess the moment he sat down across the table from them. Once, he had a suspect get down on their knees and pray to him. Not to God or Jesus or Allah, but to *him*, which was an experience that stayed with him for some time afterward.

But the moment he steps into the interview room at Ballymena Street nick this evening he knows that everything has gone wrong.

Sitting at the table is the van's driver, a man who has only given the name 'Rhuari'. Rhuari is almost a cartoon of a Black Irishman. Black curly hair, handsome smiling face, twinkling blue eyes, devil-may-care air. He's wearing jeans, a black sweatshirt, a denim jacket and battered workboots and he's sitting there as if he not only owns the interview room but the police station and the entire city. His self-confidence is so intense that it's almost a physical thing. Beside him, Mr Spode, the duty solicitor, is sitting quietly writing on a notepad.

Daniel takes a breath and walks over to the table and sits down, Pawel beside him. Pawel fiddles with the recorder while Daniel takes a moment to consult his notes.

Rhuari, however, chooses to occupy the silence. "We're getting short of time, Inspector." His voice is low and musical and as twinkly as his eyes.

Daniel looks up. "Oh?"

Rhuari grins. "Well, *you* are," he says. "I've got all the time in the world."

Daniel clasps his hands on the table before him and looks levelly at Rhuari. "Perhaps we should hurry, then."

Rhuari sits back and beams at Daniel. "I have a story for you, Inspector."

"Good."

"It's a story about a place. A place a long, long way away. And then again, it's not a place. It's more of a *metaphor* for a place."

Daniel sighs. "I think I'd prefer it if you told me why you stole a corpse from a Government mortuary."

"Well," Rhuari says with a shrug, "we'll get to that. May I go on?"

Daniel spreads his hands in assent.

"This place isn't on any maps and no one will ever find it by accident, and that's where my employers live."

"Your...employers," says Daniel, bemused.

"It's an old place, you see," Rhuari continues. "Almost as old as...well, *everything*. My employers have been living there for a very, very long time and they're quite content to keep themselves to themselves. But on occasion they find it appropriate to interact with the outside world."

Daniel stares at him. "This is bollocks, son," he says finally. "Why did you steal the body?" Actually, the question is just as much *how* he stole the body. According to O'Connell, nobody at the mortuary now remembers the body ever being there in the first place. And when Daniel spoke to him a couple of minutes ago, even O'Connell sounded as if he was struggling to recall the details.

"When my employers need to interact with the outside world," Rhuari continues as if Daniel hadn't spoken, "they prefer to do it at arms' length. They prefer, in fact, for people like me to do the work for them." He grins again. "It's a dirty job, Inspector, but someone's got to do it."

"You steal bodies for them?"

"Now, I have to admit, Inspector, this was a first for me. But I've done stranger things."

"Like what?"

"Oh, stuff I can't tell you about."

"Are you trying to tell me you're with Intelligence?" says Daniel. "You're a secret agent or something?"

Rhuari thinks about it. "Well, yes," he allows. "And then again, no."

Daniel stands up. "I think we'll continue this conversation when you've decided to stop telling fairy stories."

Rhuari grimaces. "Ah, sit yourself down and stop interrupting, Inspector," he says amiably, and Daniel finds himself sitting down again without the slightest memory of having done it. He stares at the young man on the other side of the table.

"Now then," Rhuari muses, "where were we? Oh, right. Yes. Fairy stories. Well, there are times when it's useful for my employers to send me and my friends to do a job here. But to be honest with you, it'd be counterproductive to have us stay here all the time. We're sort of high-maintenance. No, for the everyday stuff, the meat-and-potatoes stuff, the occasional odd-job, they like to recruit native talent. And that's where Mr Mitchell comes in."

It has become very still in the interview room. Spode is writing on his notepad...no, now Daniel looks more closely, Spode is *doodling* on his notepad, like an absent-minded professor sitting in on a particularly dull lecture. Daniel glances at Pawel, who is staring at the wall above Rhuari's head with a faraway thoughtful expression on his face. Neither Pawel nor Spode seems interested in the conversation. Or even aware that a conversation is going on. Daniel feels a prickle of apprehension in his stomach.

"Mr Mitchell was a bad man," Rhuari continues. "But my employers, well, their general rule of thumb is that morality's just something that happens to other people. Over the years, Mr Mitchell did some useful work for them. So when he had his little *contretemps* a few years ago and asked my employers for asylum, they agreed to grant it him." He leans forward a little and lowers his voice conspiratorially. "Actually, between you and me and the gatepost, he paid them for it. My employers aren't stupid. And they're easily as venal as the next man." He sits back again. "What you have to keep in mind is that time in the place where my employers live isn't quite the same as it is here. You could live there forever and always be young. Yes, Inspector, you've heard of that place, haven't you? People still tell stories about it and sing songs, and that really is rather sweet, you know?"

Rhuari's musical voice, the rhythm of his story, the strange sense that some of the details of the case — the dead man's address, for example — are starting to get hazy, are all combining into a strange, soothing state of mind. It does not occur to Daniel to disbelieve anything Rhuari is telling him.

He makes an effort and says, "His daughter."

"Well, yes." For a moment, Rhuari looks disapproving. "Mr Mitchell thought of himself as a feudal warlord, really. And he thought his association with my employers made him superhuman. Which it did in the end, I suppose. All he thought about was his own survival. He never even asked for asylum for the rest of his family. Not that my employers would have granted it. But he never even asked."

"He came back," says Daniel.

Rhuari nods. "And we may never know why. Someone else, I would have said he had second thoughts or he wanted to see his daughter, but as I said, Mr Mitchell wasn't wired that way. Possibly there was something here that he wanted." He shrugs. "He was warned what would happen if he came back. My employers told him that as soon as he was here the years would catch up with him very quickly."

"They don't seem to be catching up with you," Daniel says dreamily.

Rhuari nods. "Yes, well, I'm a lot younger than Mr Mitchell," he says. "And of course, I'm not human, strictly speaking."

Daniel makes another effort. "No one is ever going to believe this," he says.

Rhuari shrugs again. "By this time tomorrow there won't be anything for them to believe." He glances at Spode, looks at Pawel, both of them lost in their own reveries. Away with the fairies, Big Sam used to say when Daniel was daydreaming as a boy. Rhuari looks at Daniel and smiles. "People don't want to remember, in general. It's an effort — so much stuff to try and keep track of, some of it not very nice. Much easier to forget."

"Particularly if someone helps."

Rhuari sighs. "Sometimes there are situations which need...tidying up. Things which might be problematical for my employers but don't warrant their direct intervention. Direct intervention is rare — and really you ought to be grateful for that. Most of the time, it falls to people like me to tuck in the loose ends."

"There are documents," says Daniel. "Computer files."

Rhuari holds up his hands and wiggles his fingers. "We always move with the times."

Daniel looks at Pawel and Spode and wonders what's going on in their heads at the moment. He says, "Why are you telling me all this?"

Rhuari grins. "Because I have something you need."

"You've got nothing I need."

"Ah, now." Rhuari leans forward. "Think about that a little, Inspector."

❦

"So who killed him?" Daniel asks.

"Who?" says Rhuari.

Daniel jerks his thumb towards the back of the van.

"Oh." Rhuari smiles. "Well, from what I can gather, Mr

Mitchell was admirably circumspect for the first couple of weeks after he came back. My employers told him where to find his daughter, and he moved in with her and kept his head down. But Mr Mitchell was not the sort of man to hide himself away. He wanted to have a look at his old kingdom, and while he was out and about someone recognised him."

"Gordon Cope."

Rhuari takes his hands off the steering wheel and claps, and while he does so the van slows down, brakes, waits to let an oncoming bus pass, and then makes a right turn, all on its own. It's not actually a van at all, Rhuari told him when they left Ballymena Street. It's more of a *metaphor* for a van. Daniel has decided, in order to maintain his sanity, that he's going to keep thinking of it as a van.

"So the old man let Cope into the house? Why would he do that?"

Rhuari takes hold of the steering wheel again. "I think you're going to have to resign yourself to never solving this case, Inspector," he says. "One of the people involved is dead, and the other one can't remember anything about it. This time tomorrow it'll be as if it never happened."

"What about the daughter? Have you visited her?"

Rhuari looks sad. "I'm afraid Mrs Wright isn't going to regain consciousness." He glances at Daniel. "No, that *doesn't* have anything to do with me, Inspector. That's just life."

They're having this conversation around Big Sam Snow, who's sitting between them in the front seat of the van staring out through the windscreen with the same look of distant concentration with which he used to look out of the window of his ward.

Daniel looks at his father and says, "We're Jewish."

"Ah," Rhuari says with a wink, "but are you *Catholic* Jews or *Protestant* Jews?" He chuckles and shakes his head. "Why do you think it matters?"

"Aren't we the wrong religion or something?"

Rhuari gives an astonished little bark of laughter. "At least you believe in *something*, Inspector. Your average little fecker these days can't even be bothered." He looks out through the windscreen. The buildings are thinning out now; they're passing through one of the city's modest little suburbs. Tidy houses with tidy gardens. "You're an outsider, Inspector, and we work best with outsiders. You're a policeman, you're Jewish, your Dad's a Brit, you're not married. All you do is work and sleep, and if you'll excuse me saying so, I don't think you sleep a lot. I wasn't sent here to recruit people, I was sent to tidy up the mess Mr Mitchell left behind. But I made a command decision; we don't often interact with people in your position and you might come in handy. Don't let yourself think we're doing this out of the goodness of our hearts. You *will* wind up paying for this, one day." He glances over at Daniel. "Ach, don't look like that, Inspector. We do you a favour, you do us a favour. How can that hurt?"

Daniel looks at his father. "And he'll be better?" he asks.

"Good as new," Rhuari promises, looking out of the driver's side window, where the view has given way to fields, the road curving west towards the coast. "Better than better."

"He's going to be angry when he finds out what we've done."

Rhuari laughs. "He'll learn to live with it, Inspector. I promise you."

A loud snore sounds from the back of the van, where Superintendent Billy Tweedy is stretched out, fast asleep, alongside the coffin containing the earthly remains of Mad Dog Mitchell. Rhuari sucks his teeth.

"You know," he says, not quite so amused any longer, "it was well within my operational boundaries to recruit you and bring your father back. But *this*..." he jerks his head backward. "I had to bring in backup to cover *this* guy's tracks."

"He and my Dad were inseparable," says Daniel. "Snow and Tweedy, supercops. After Mum died, he...he was a big man and he helped us get through it, and in a year or so he's going to be..." He gestures at Big Sam. "My Uncle Billy. You want my help, you help him too." He adds, "How can it hurt?"

Rhuari looks over at him and grins, as if Daniel has suddenly learned how to play a complicated game and has managed to take some points off him at the first try. They have passed through the city in a storm of forgetting, Daniel facilitating the second theft of Alan Mitchell's body, spiriting Big Sam out of the hospital, leaving in their wake people who can't remember any of it ever happening. Rhuari and people like him have already made all the evidence of the Mitchell murder disappear. The same people have erased the recent memories of Superintendent Tweedy, tampered with records, done some other things. Billy Tweedy truly has passed into legend.

The van pulls to a halt at the side of the road. "That's us, then," says Rhuari.

Daniel looks at him, at his father. He opens the passenger door and climbs down, stands there looking into the van. "Dad?" he says, but Big Sam just sits looking through the windscreen. Daniel says to Rhuari, "You take care of him."

"As if he was one of my own," says Rhuari, and Daniel can't suppress a shiver. "We'll be in touch."

"Look after yourself, Dad," he says, and he slams the door shut and steps away as the van pulls out into the road and drives off into the West. As it gets further down the road it starts to look sort of vague, and the sound of its engine could be the sound of horses' hooves, or the sound of the ocean lapping against the side of a wooden ship. Daniel wipes a tear away and the van's gone.

He sniffs and puts his hands in his pockets and looks

around him, registering for the first time where he is.

"You could at least have dropped me off on a bus route, you gobshite," he mutters, and starts to trudge his way home.

FIRST TO SCORE
WRITTEN BY GARBHAN DOWNEY

I wrote this piece in late 2004 for a book of short stories I was finishing, called Off Broadway *(Guildhall Press, 2005). The collection, set in the North's post-ceasefire underworld, owes considerable stylistic debt to New York's finest son Damon Runyon. And in deference to the master, most of the yarns were blackly comic escapades, loosely based on unprintable stories I'd come across as a working journalist.*

First to Score *was a little different. As a ten-year-old Horslips fan, I'd become enthralled by the legend of Diarmaid and Grainne after hearing their take on the story in the song* Warm Sweet Breath of Love *(Book of Invasions, 1976). So, almost thirty years on, in a bid to leave a subtle Celtic stamp on my new book, I thought it'd be fun to transfer the couple's doomed elopement to present-day Derry, to see if they'd fare any better.*

–

The five-a-side indoor football game at Brooke Park Leisure Centre has been running every Wednesday night for more than ten years now. And although Stammering Stan the Radio Man has been practising hard, he is still no better at all.

So this evening after a particular stinker of a game, Stan is sitting in the changing room, thinking maybe he should give it all up and concentrate on his drinking, when Danny Boy

Gillespie comes over to commiserate.

"Never mind," grins Danny Boy, who is no great shakes either. "It could be worse. 'Stead of just having no left foot, you could have no legs at all."

This raises the hair, as expected.

"You're some man to talk about legs," snaps Stan. "If you could keep your eyes off Orange Jillys on a Tuesday night, you'd run a lot faster in here on a Wednesday."

"Ouch," chuckles Danny. "Am I right in saying, Stan, that you're originally from Donegal?"

"That's right."

"So you can play for the Republic. And your father's from England, so you can play for them too. What about your mother?"

"She's from Scotland," says Stan, "so I suppose I'm eligible for them as well."

"Yeah," replies Danny, "and, of course, you can always play for the North."

"How's that? I've no relations here."

"Aye," laughs Danny, "but you're crap."

※

Danny Boy tells this yarn about Stan so often that I know it by heart. Stan, of course, swears it is really the other way about. But you and I both know that the story is as old as the hills.

Despite the after-match to-ing and fro-ing, the Wednesday game is the highpoint of the guys' week. It's more or less the same personnel who have played there since the early nineties — apart from a few unavoidable departures due to retirements, cruciate ligaments and extradition laws.

The ten regulars are as thick as thieves, which is hardly surprising as that is precisely what most of them are. Dumpy Doherty and Get-em-up Gormley operate the market on the Foyle Embankment. Tommy Bowtie, the lawyer, is of course the greatest stick-up man never to use a gun. Gerry the Hurler runs his brother Harry the Hurler's video and DVD department, while the youngest Hurley, Jimmy Fidget, looks after their cigarette depot. The numbers are made up by the city council's head of engineering, Mickey 'Bangers' Johnston, who was previously an unpaid demolition expert for the revolution, and the hospital pathologist Sean 'Doctor Death' McGoldrick — a handy man in the bandaging department when Gerry the Hurler lets loose with his slide tackles.

Harry himself retired from playing about three years back, in his mid-forties, when he discovered he could no longer cut it using just fear alone.

But like all those who never quite hit the top ranks, he has a hankering to go into management. Only problem is, who would have him?

Harry still likes to hook up with his old teammates for a pint after their Wednesday game. And despite their best efforts this night, he finds them anyway, upstairs in the Celtic Bar on Stanley's Walk.

"To be a good boss, you need to know what makes players tick," Harry tells them as they squeeze over to accommodate his size 46 jacket and pants. "Football is just like politics. They are games for professionals, played by greedy little amateurs. And while players and politicians pretend to be in it for the good of the team, it is all about grabbing the glory and the headlines for number one. There isn't one of them, when they get a brown envelope, won't tell you that they'll be looking for a bigger one next time. If either of the two lots tells me it is raining outside, I will wait until I can swim from here to the top of Shipquay Street and jet-ski across the Bog, before I say I believe them. There's not one of them who will do their job for the love of it — there has to be an angle. Which is why it takes a guy like me — who understands these things and can deal with them — to run a team. All of which brings me to my point..."

Everyone freezes, aware that something big, stupid or crazy — and probably all three — is coming.

"I think," says Harry, "we should set up our own football club and enter it in the Irish Cup."

Everybody cracks up, everybody that is except Harry and Tommy Bowtie, who is a lawyer and thus completely devoid of humour.

But when the merriment subsides, in deference to Harry's well-known reluctance to be laughed at, he looks round the table slowly from face to face and says, "There is a lot of money in this, a hell of a lot. Hear me out. Earlier today, myself, Tommy Bowtie there, and Mike the Knife are over with Switchblade Vic McCormick in his pub in the Waterside sorting out a bit of business. A few young Planters in Nelson Drive are taking pot-shots at our taxis every time they go past — and our lads are starting to return the compliment as soon as they see the Planters' plates coming across the bridge. Anyhow, we're sorting out a protocol, that we'll each kick our own lot's arses. But afterwards, we get chatting about football — 'cause, as you know, Vic's daughter Gigi is now in charge of Londonderry Legion's first team. And Gigi, it seems, is currently in a bit of a pickle..."

※

Switchblade Vic's only child, Gigi, is as pretty as a poem. Her mother Maria, who's originally Catalan, was once a famous catwalk model in London, and Gigi is her double — only better built. Her name isn't Gigi at all — but Grainne Gael, in honour of the famous 14th Century Irish buccaneer. As you'll expect, Vic hates the name, but Maria insists the full version goes on the birth certificate. "The father thinks he's a damn

Irish pirate," she says, "so the daughter can be one as well."

Gigi, however, is a good and gifted child and turns out to be a clean-living sports nut. In particular, she shows a great aptitude for shooting, fencing and cross-country running — just like her father. Unlike Daddy, however, she never actually uses any of these in her day job. She's also happy to avoid the other track sports, which pleases Vic no end. Up to this point, she's showing no real interest in boys, and he doesn't want her trying out for the wrestling team.

A couple of years back, after she gets her physio degree, Gigi takes some football coaching badges and is put in charge of the Londonderry Legion Under 14s. She works her way up the ranks and proves such a dab hand at it, that earlier this season at the age of twenty-four, she becomes the first ever lady manager of the full team.

In fact, Gigi is the first ever lady manager of any Irish men's team — even if the Legion are languishing in the nether regions of Division Three.

Not surprisingly, the appointment of a new lady boss — and particularly such a tasty one as Gigi — makes a number of the senior players forget their manners. But the new chief tackles the mischief-makers quickly, by demonstrating that not only does she have her mother's looks, she also has her black Spanish temper.

The message is relayed in no uncertain terms after the first training session, when the Legion captain, Red Roger Rogan, a remarkably ugly man-mountain with the manners to match, remarks that maybe Gigi should join the team in the shower.

Without blinking an eye, Gigi kicks him so hard and so quick that not even his jockstrap can save him. And poor Red wakes up with a large crowd around him and a seven-stitch cut on the back of his head.

"Another crack like that," warns Gigi as she pulls Red to his feet, "and you'll be lining out with the ladies' squad. As a fully paid-up member."

From that day on, Red and the others just dote on Gigi. They fight among themselves to carry her physio kit, time the laps and cut the half-time oranges. They even swipe flowers from the neighbouring gardens for her little office. But she refuses to take them on at all. She has the players where she wants them — scared and eager, and most importantly, starting to get results. Within two months of her arrival, the Legion are top of their division and knocking all-comers for four or five goals a game.

But last week, after the Legion hit Ballykelly for nine — including a Red Rogan hat-trick — Gigi lets her guard down a little and tells her captain well played.

"Okay, so," he asks her, "what will it take to make you go out with me?"

"A loaded gun and no visible means of escape," deadpans Gigi.

"What if I score the first goal against Glentoran in the Irish Cup next week? The Glens are second in the Premier, and the smart money is on them hitting us for double-figures."

"No way," says Gigi, "you're far too lucky. That third goal today just bounced in right off your knee."

"What if I get a hat-trick against the Glens?" persists Red.

"Nah, their bus could crash on the way down here and kill half of them. Besides, Red, no offence or anything, but ginger-headed muscle-men just don't do it for me."

"Okay, so," concedes Red, "one last go. What if I'm the first to score in this year's Irish Cup final?"

"Do that," laughs Gigi, "and I'll marry you." Well, the words are barely out of her mouth when she's trying to bite her tongue off.

Red just stands there shocked. The odds of the Legion even reaching the final are exactly two hundred to one, but all Red can see is himself standing at the altar with Gigi in a white satin dress.

"It's just a figure of speech," she protests.

"No backing out, now," retorts Red, "you have to let a guy live in hope."

"Okay, okay," snaps Gigi, calming down a little, "but you so much as look at me sideways from now to the end of the season, and remember what I'm telling about the ladies' squad..."

Harry the Hurler laughs as he fills us in on Gigi's dilemma, and Vic's complete lack of sympathy for his unmarried daughter.

"But that still doesn't explain how we can make serious money forming a football club," says Mickey Bangers.

"I'll take this one," says Tommy Bowtie, on Harry's nod. "Switchblade Vic is actually quite a fan of Red Rogan and would be quite happy to see Gigi hook up with him. As we all know, being big and brainless is no crime in Vic's book. So we're chatting on for a while, when Harry asks Vic what odds he'll give on Red being first to score in the final. Vic thinks for a minute, then says about a thousand to one. So Harry then says, 'What odds will you give me getting the first goal in the final?' To which Vic, who's enjoying the fun, says, 'I'll give you ten thousands'. But Vic gets the shock of his life when Harry steps forward, shakes his hand and announces, 'Right, I'll have a grand on the nose, and Tommy Bowtie and Mike the Knife here are my witnesses'."

Harry eventually lets Vic whittle the size of his bet down to £50, which will still give him a cool half mill if he does the business. Though as part of the deal, Vic specifically bans Harry from buying his way into any team in the top three divisions.

Harry might as well throw his £50 away in the street. But

ten other men sitting upstairs in the Celtic Bar see possibilities. And that very night Derry Fianna FC is formed.

※

The planning goes on well into the wee hours with Tommy Bowtie appointed chairman, so he can sort out all the paperwork with the Irish Football Association. Harry the Hurler is, of course, manager. HurH.

None of the indoor squad are signed to any club — nor indeed is Harry — so there'll be no difficulty registering them.

"We've only one real problem, now," says Stammering Stan.

"And what's that?" asks Tommy Bowtie.

"We're a bunch of fat drunks who couldn't beat a team of little girls."

"That's where good management comes into it," explains Harry, nodding. "My young nephew Dee Dee will be joining the ranks tomorrow on a free transfer from Derry City. They won't let him play Gaelic on Sundays anymore, so he's itching to move. He's coming in as head coach."

This is impressive news. Diarmuid 'Dee Dee' Dunne owns what is widely believed to be the best right leg on this island, only slightly bettering his left. He is the first centre-forward ever to average a goal a game in the League of Ireland premiership, and is also a GAA all-star — all at the age of just twenty-five.

If that isn't enough, he is as handsome as a prince — though some might say a little too swarthy and dark-haired. In fact, he's so hairy that opposing fans sometimes throw bananas at him during games to wind him up. But he never bats an eye. And from what Harry tells us, his quiet, gentlemanly nature could charm the chickens down from the trees. But, he's generally way too shy ever to switch it on.

Dee Dee's day job is as a manager at a meat plant out in the country and, says Harry, he is very pally with a squad of Chechen refugees who fix the machines there. Apparently, half of them were full time pro footballers before falling out with Old Mother Russia and they're eager for some action.

"So, does this mean we're all dropped?" asks Danny Boy.

"Yes," says Harry. "All except Stammering Stan."

"No way," protests Gerry the Hurler.

"You're joking," pleads Danny.

"That's right," grins Harry. "I am joking. Stan's dropped as well. Let's face it, you're a bunch of fat drunks who couldn't beat a team of little girls. But on the bright side, you'll all get turns on the subs bench. Look, this is going to require a lot of organising. So, help me pull this off, and each and every one of you gets two percent. That's ten grand a man to you, Stanley."

*

There is considerable crying and roaring from the IFA about Derry Fianna's decision to enter the Irish Cup — particularly when they find out Harry himself is registering as a player. But as he has no previous convictions that are relevant, and is not the subject of any specific banning order from any league ground, there is very little they can do. They do raise the issue of a possible clash against the RUC Old Boys, but Tommy Bowtie argues that, in that unlikely event, the two balls will go back in the bag, and no-one will see nothing.

The IFA are also still reluctant to allow games on Derry's west bank, since the unfortunate incident of the Ballymena team bus, an incident which four independent witnesses can tell you has absolutely nothing to do with Harry the Hurler. But Mickey Bangers pulls some strings at the council and manages to get the Swilly Stadium, in the safe and leafy confines of the Buncrana Road, registered as Derry Fianna's home ground. And the IFA — who already allow Oxford Stars to play from here — have no choice but to accept this.

Stammering Stan, who now edits the *Derry Standard*, sponsors a set of rigs and organises a big write-up about the new team for the back page. This will ensure a big crowd for the first game, which will be against the Division Two side, Stranocum.

Gerry the Hurler and Jimmy Fidget, meantime, are helping Dee Dee with the coaching — a sensible arrangement given that both men exude a natural authority and have extensive experience of running training camps.

And also in the dugout is Dr Death McGoldrick, who is very excited to have live specimens to play with. He is busy designing diet sheets and psych tests for the Chechens, who are overjoyed to be doing anything other than fixing stinking machines and drinking cleaning spirits.

Danny Boy Gillespie is put in charge of hospitality, while Get-em-up Gormley and Dumpy Doherty will take care of the gate receipts.

❧

Derry Fianna's first match is a total disappointment. Although the team are making great progress, Dee Dee is worried that they still aren't at full pace. So he warns them not to try anything too clever. As it turns out, it's his backroom staff he should be talking to.

More than a thousand fans are gathered at the Swilly Stadium for the game, when a call comes to the Sports Complex to say that that the Stranocum squad are pulling out. It seems a cardboard box containing lots of protruding wires was left under their team minibus the previous night. There is nothing else remotely inside the box, other than a gift card signed "A present from Derry Fianna FC". But, as Tommy Bowtie argues at the hearing three days later, there is no proof whatsoever that his clients are involved — and both witnesses who put Jimmy Fidget at the scene are now withdrawing their evidence.

Stranocum are ultimately disqualified for failing to field a team. And Derry Fianna, on the chairman's casting vote, are through to the next round, though in line with tradition, they are forever banned from playing matches at their home ground.

By the time the second round comes around, the Chechens are raring to go. The six weeks off the juice, eating pasta and fresh fruit is starting to show. And Dee Dee's tireless training sessions, along with Doc Death's instructions to remember that every opponent is a filthy Russian Para, have them all ready to jump through fire.

This time, the Fianna are drawn away to First Division Drumcree United in a tie the *Irish News* says will have more blood than The Alamo — and most of it will be Harry's. Harry himself reckons that they could possibly parachute the team into Portadown for kickoff, but he's damned if he can figure a way back out again that doesn't end up with him starring as Davy Crockett.

Even the IFA recognise the potential of this one and step up to demand that the game is played behind closed doors at Windsor Park at eight o'clock on a Sunday morning. Windsor Park, of course, being a Neutral Venue.

A few Concerned South Belfast Residents stay up late to throw lighted bottles at the arriving Fianna bus, but it matters little. The Derry men are too focused and rout Drumcree five-nil, with a hat-trick for Dee Dee Dunne and two for one of the Igors.

The bad news is that Dee-Dee breaks his wrist when a big Armagh man with no teeth and an exceptional collection of misspelt tattoos smacks him from behind at a corner. But while Dee Dee will miss the next game or two, the Drumcree centre-half is out for the rest of the season, after two of the Igors snap his dirty Muscovite knees in the car park after the game.

Thus Derry Fianna are into the last sixteen, and their next tie is away to Third Division strugglers Swatragh Farm.

This proves to be even more of a cakewalk for the Chechens, even with Dee Dee on the bench.

And it's also a lot more fun. The territory is a lot less hostile, so around 500 Fianna fans make the trip up to North Derry.

Indeed, the only incident of note, other than the visitors' nine goals, is when the Swatragh and Fianna supporters join together to give Harry the Hurler a standing ovation after he comes on as sub with two minutes to go.

※

Across the city in Nelson Drive, Gigi McCormick's Londonderry Legion are also fighting their way through the early stages.

In the shock result of the first round, they put out top flight Glentoran one-nil, courtesy of a Red Rogan penalty. The referee's decision to award the spotkick to the home side, given that Red falls over eight yards outside the box, is curious to say the least. And he shows commendable bravery by sending off two Glens defenders for swearing at him in the aftermath.

A riot is averted, however, when Switchblade Vic announces through the PA that there will be free beer at the Sash & Drum for all Glens fans after the game. And the ref drives home with a bulge exactly the size of two grand in his pocket.

The Legion's second round game, against Division Two front-runners Bangor, goes to a replay. But when Gigi promises her lads she'll give them each a dance at the post-match party, they dig in their heels and win by the odd goal in three. Gigi keeps her side of the bargain too and cuts a rug with each and every one of her fourteen man squad, even if she does insist that the DJ plays nothing but *The Birdie Song* all night.

※

The Legion's third game, however, proves a little more contentious. A week before the match, their opponents, Lisburn Rangers, are thrown out for fielding an ineligible player in an earlier round. And it looks as though the Legion are going to get a bye direct into the quarter-finals.

But then, all of a sudden, Stranocum are back in the Cup after winning a High Court challenge against their earlier eviction, and they get to make the trip to Derry instead of Rangers.

On a very good day, Legion might fancy themselves to get a draw against Stranocum. But a new fish factory is after opening in the County Antrim town, and it is staffed almost entirely by Brazilian immigrants. And Stranocum are boasting that they'll be lining out three former stablemates of Ronaldo.

About an hour before kick off on match day, however, a call comes through to Legion's ground at Nelson Drive, to say that a cardboard box is sitting under the Stranocum team minibus, and they'll not be coming.

One witness reports seeing a remarkably ugly, ginger-headed bodybuilder in the area just before the box is discovered. But coincidentally, Red Rogan has thirteen men putting him at a training session fifty miles away in Derry at the exact same moment.

※

Gigi is pleased to avoid the Fianna in the quarters. Both sides pull home ties — the Legion getting a fighting chance against Cliftonville, who're doing no business at the bottom of the Premiership, while Harry's men are to face the league's real giants, Linfield.

The Fianna, of course, aren't allowed to host any more games on the west bank, and since the second Stranocum debacle, it appears that the Legion can't play on the east bank. So Gigi, being a practical sort, decides to call up Harry the Hurler and propose a temporary ground swap. She rings the Celtic Bar, gets the number for Derry Fianna, and who should pick up the phone but Dee Dee Dunne.

"Hiya, Monkey Boy," chirps Gigi who is well used to abusing the hirsute Dee Dee from the line at university matches. "Is your uncle the organ grinder about?"

"'Fraid not," answers Dee Dee. "Though I'll tell him the charming Grainne Gael McCormick is looking for him."

"How do you know my voice?" she demands, a little surprised.

"You're on the wireless after every game now. Surely you're never as stupid as your old man as well?"

"You know yourself, you can't escape the genes," laughs Gigi. "Though at least my family marry inside their species."

"The jury's still out, there, sister," shoots back Dee Dee. "The way I hear it, you're hoping to mate with the world's only red-haired yeti."

"At least they let him shower with all the other boys, sweetheart. I hear that they won't let you back into the changing room until you get yourself a lady friend. Indeed, the story in these parts is that the GAA is not the only other team you're batting for."

"Just saving myself for the right girl, Gigi. 'Fraid those wannabe models and football groupies do nothing for me. In fact, word over here is they might be more in your line, sister..."

"My, aren't we bitchy today? With a mouth like that, Monkey Boy, you're never going to land a girl. Unless maybe she runs out of legs to wax and fancies a challenge."

"This from a doll who hides the finest pair of legs in Derry under a pair of baggy tracksuit bottoms. What's wrong, are you scared you might turn some nice boy's head?"

"It'll take more than that to turn *you*. Anyway, how do you know what my legs look like?"

"Sure, they're the jewels in the crown of the Queens Cross-Country team. I remember many a Saturday morning standing at the finish line to watch you break the tape. It's Coach's way of firing up the GAA squad before their afternoon match. Nothing better, he says, for stirring the blood than the sight of McCormick's legs, damp and dirty. The number of nights, even yet, I go to bed and thank the Lord for the man who invented bikini shorts for women runners. Your jogging bottoms, Gigi, are a sin against God."

She giggles. "Enough! Any more of your charm and I might forget I'm a football manager. Look, we were thinking. Do you want to trade home grounds for the quarter-finals? Vic reckons the IFA will okay it, if only to stop Linfield getting a bye into the semis."

"Per-sactly what we're thinking too," says Dee Dee.

❦

The IFA, predictably, try to insist that both quarter-finals are held in Belfast. But Tommy Bowtie then ties them in knots in the courts and Stammering Stan makes them look so bad in the press that eventually they allow the ground-swap.

Legion get to play their game first at Swilly Stadium on Friday night.

The ground is only half-full as there are still quite a few Legion fans who won't travel west of the river. But Gigi's charges quickly hit top form regardless. It helps that

Cliftonville are so bad that their own supporters are throwing chips at them by half-time. There are no complaints when Legion run out two-nil winners.

The following afternoon at Nelson Drive, the cup-holders Linfield arrive in big numbers. At least nine-tenths of the two thousand strong crowd are Blues fans from Belfast — and they are expecting no less than a shootie-in. The other two hundred are Legion fans hoping to see the Fianna get a tanking.

As a gesture of respect, the home team vote not to wear their green and white hoops in the Waterside. And Harry the Hurler agrees to remain in the Celtic Bar and patch in his advice via mobile phone.

No one is giving the Fianna a prayer. Indeed, Gigi McCormick — who for once is wearing a pair of shorts — and her father are holding a big banner which reads, "See you in the final, Blues!".

No one, however, is reckoning on Dee Dee Dunne's determination to prove his host and hostess wrong. His team talk before the game is short and sweet. "When you get the ball," he tells the Chechens, "give it to me. And anyone who goes to hurt me, stop them. Anyone who does hurt me — well, you know the drill. Now let's go and teach these dirty Russian bastards a lesson they'll not forget."

Linfield, however, are a very different prospect to all the Fianna's other opponents so far — they're full-time professionals and are a lot fitter than the Chechens.

The visitors start with all guns blazing and within five minutes they are a goal to the good. Seamus Coyle, the traitor, rattles in a volley from twenty-five yards which hits the net before Big Vlad the keeper can even move.

Indeed, for the first forty minutes, it's all Linfield pressure and the Fianna are quite happy not to concede another. They have ten men behind the ball, and only Dee Dee up the field.

Just before half-time however, Dee Dee gets on the end of one of Big Vlad's kickouts and is so badly fouled in the box that even the ref can't ignore it. Dee Dee gets up and tucks away the penalty, while the two Igors quietly tell the Linfield centre-half they will be speaking to him in the tunnel after the game.

The second half is all Linfield, apart from the centre-back who doesn't reappear. Big Vlad is busier than last orders on Christmas Eve, but nothing gets past him.

Then, two minutes before the end, Derry Fianna break. Little Igor the Winger gets to the byline and crosses to Dee Dee in the box, who pretends to shoot and takes the full weight of a Linfield defender in his ribs. But just as the defender crashes into him, Dee Dee dummies the ball through to Igor the Striker who wallops it past the keeper from fifteen yards.

Two-one, the game finishes, and the Fianna are in the last four.

As the final whistle goes, Dee Dee is carried off on a stretcher, to catcalls from sulking Blues fans. Though at least this way he has a chance of getting out of the gate alive.

As the stretcher is passing Gigi, still resplendent in her Bermuda shorts, Dee Dee props himself up on his good side and points over at her discarded Linfield banner. "Guess you'll be needing a new one — for when you meet real men," he quips with a wince.

"A real man would get up and walk, Monkey Boy."

"Walk," he laughs, "I can barely breathe..."

"Maybe if you ask one of your nice Chechen boys they'll give you the kiss of life."

"Well, it looks as if it's the only offer I'm getting round here. If you don't start being a bit nicer to me, Gigi, I just might let that big yeti of yours score in the final."

"Do that, and I'll never wear shorts for you again." And

with that, Gigi and her lovely long Spanish legs turn on their heels and head for the clubhouse.

※

The draw for the last four is made that night and the romance of the cup strikes again. The Fianna are away to Omagh Town, while the Legion travel to Institute for an all-Derry derby at Riverside Stadium, Drumahoe.

Institute are the clear favourites to win their leg — but Paul Hegarty's injury-wracked squad is further weakened by the fact that two of his midfielders are nephews of Switchblade Vic and are refusing to line-out.

'Stute and Legion opt to play their match on the Friday night, while Omagh and the Fianna will go the following day.

The night-time kick-off, however is to prove another nightmare for 'Stute. All three of Hegarty's first-team strikers have day-jobs in Belfast, and are travelling down the M2 for the game together when an oil-tanker jack-knifes about a quarter-mile down the motorway in front of them. The spill causes one of the biggest ever traffic snare-ups in the North, and the three players, along with hundreds of others motorists, are trapped in their car for the night.

Police reports say that, just after the crash, a remarkably ugly, red-haired bodybuilder is seen sprinting out of the truck and into a red sports car a hundred yards the right side of the melee. But they later concede that Red Rogan is playing cards fifty miles away at the Sash & Drum in Derry at the exact same moment. Oh, and the barman is certain that Switchblade Vic's new Porsche never leaves the car park.

So, back at the Riverside Stadium in Derry, 'Stute are forced to start the semi with five reserves and, in truth, they never get going. Hegarty's men are resolute in defence, but have no creativity in midfield, and with three sixteen-year-olds for forwards, they eventually come unstuck.

FIRST TO SCORE

Red Rogan gets the winner for the Legion with a few minutes to go, heading in from a corner-kick.

Quite a party breaks out in the Legion's changing room after the game. It's the first time in forty years a Derry team is in the Irish Cup final. And a crate of champagne quickly appears, courtesy of the Sash & Drum. Gigi, however, is madder than hell and leaves the celebrations to hunt down her father in his office.

"You'd damn well better not be planning any stunts like that against Dee Dee and the Fianna tomorrow," she yells.

"Well, I can't hardly have Harry the H walking off with your inheritance now, can I?"

"Right, so," replies Gigi through gritted teeth. "I'm dropping Red Rogan from the team for the final."

"Chrissake, pet. I have a thousand pounds of my own on Legion to win the Cup at a hundred to one. I'm on since the first round."

"Tell you what then, in that case, I'm going to drop the entire squad and field the ladies instead."

"Okay, okay," says Vic, recognising his wife in Gigi's flashing eyes. He picks up the phone and dials a number. "Hello, is that Mr X? I need you to remove Object A from under Location B immediately — no arguments. That's right, immediately. I don't know...toss it into the river."

"Thank you, Daddy." Gigi nods as he puts the phone down. "Now, I'm going down to the Omagh game myself tomorrow to make sure there are no surprises."

Vic quickly picks up the phone again: "Mr X? Better call off Sniper C as well."

※

Dee Dee, with his four broken ribs, is quite understandably banjaxed for the semi-final. But Omagh are less of a threat than Linfield, and he is quite confident that the Chechens can handle them on their own. He's even planning to give Harry the Hurler a run-out for a bit of comic relief, if all goes well.

And sure enough it turns out to be very easy — with the Fianna running out five-one winners. But the headlines are reserved for Harry the H, who becomes the oldest, and undoubtedly most unfit man ever to score in a cup match. And you'd think his bet is up, the way he celebrates his last minute tap-in.

The only other point of interest is that Gigi McCormick turns up at the St Julian's Road ground for the game, and this time she has her civil tongue with her. She even comes over to congratulate Dee Dee as his side disappear into the changing rooms.

"So," Dee Dee asks her, "are you nervous about the final?"

"Only about one particular part of it, as you know very well. Vic is already writing his Father of the Bride speech, and Red is getting a special tattoo done as a surprise for me."

"Well, if it's any consolation," says Dee Dee, "we'll do all we can to kick your big ugly yeti out of the game."

"He's not my big ugly yeti yet, he's still my father's. Your Soviet hitmen don't do private contracts, by any chance, do they?"

Dee Dee laughs. "Wouldn't know. But on the other hand, if Harry scores first, it'll cost Vic 500K."

"Cheap at twice the price if it'll stop him meddling in my life for a while."

"Maybe that'll leave a bit more room for the rest of us," says Dee Dee shyly, and is rewarded by a smile that Gigi's saved up for him all day.

Both managers are suddenly out of small talk, so they amble silently across the byline and head towards the tunnel. Dee Dee then points towards the dressing room and says he must go.

"Anyone sees me talking to a pretty face like you," he says, "and it'll ruin my reputation with the left-footers. Besides, I'm sure the lads will all be waiting for their after-match rubdowns."

"I give a pretty mean rubdown of my own," says Gigi, fixing Dee Dee with a look that shoots a thrill right through him. "And I'll tell you what, soldier, when you join my team, the rest will have to wait in line."

"Ah, but I'll still have to share my card with fourteen other dancers."

"Who worries about dancing," asks Gigi, "when you have your own private key to the steam room?"

"I hate to repeat myself, but you still have a captain of your own."

"But," she counters, flicking up two impish eyebrows, "a good manager knows exactly when it's time to hit the transfer market."

"To be honest, Gigi," replies Dee Dee softly, "you can have me on a free, any time."

⚽

The cup final is to be played in Derry's Brandywell Stadium as a one-off, instead of Windsor Park, after Tommy Bowtie drags the IFA back into court.

The Fianna tell the judge that the Concerned Residents in South Belfast will only torch their bus again, while the Legion argue that Linfield, who own Windsor, are responsible for wrecking the Sash & Drum after losing their quarter-final.

A ten thousand strong crowd pack into the Brandywell for the game — a full half of them from the Waterside, after Gerry the Hurler and Jimmy Fidget agree to a securityprotocol with Switchblade Vic. The entire Foyle Road from the lower deck of the bridge, right up to the ground, is cordoned off and marshalled by stewards to let the Legion fans in and out.

Noel 'No Friends' Flynn, meanwhile, is the agreed ref on the grounds that he is the finest bouncer and late night negotiator in the city. And also because both Harry and Vic are afraid of him.

The anthems are both played, the final gets underway and the Fianna immediately lay siege to the Legion goal. It is clear from the off that the Chechens are much fitter and more experienced than Gigi's crew.

The Fianna are badly hampered, however, by the fact that Harry must start the game at centre-forward. And Harry is slower than his mother and a lot less deadly around goal. No one else on the Fianna side is allowed to shoot, of course, so at half-time it's still all square, and Harry is having about as much luck as Johnny the Dwarf in a police line-up. He is also exhausted, as nineteen stones is a considerable amount to haul about for 45 minutes. Indeed, the last time Harry ran for real was way back in the bad old days, when someone set the wrong time on a home-wrapped alarm clock.

About forty yards behind him, Dee Dee Dunne is still feeling the rib damage and thus playing in defence, where up 'til now things are pretty quiet.

Then, just after half-time, disaster.

Right from the restart, Igor the Winger puts Harry the Hurler clean through. But he blarges a sitter wide of an open goal from five yards and Legion get a kick-out.

Their goalie lamps the ball, hard, into the Fianna half. Red Rogan leaps high to head the ball down to his younger brother, Black Angus, who's about thirty yards from goal. Angus looks up and sees the Fianna keeper Vlad off his line and lobs the ball over the Chechen's head.

It looks a goal all the way, and the perfectly weighted chip is just dipping under the crossbar, when in rushes Dee Dee Dunne and punches the ball out over the byline.

There is uproar. First from the Fianna when No Friends the

Ref gives a penalty, and then from Gigi on the touchline when she sees who's taking it.

Despite protests from the bench, No Friends refuses to allow Gigi to substitute Red before he takes the penalty, which, of course, he drives home.

Red immediately rushes over to the celebrating Legion fans and pulls off his shirt to reveal a vest announcing, 'I love my Gigi'. But he is quickly knocked unconscious by a tyre-iron marked 'Porsche', which appears to come out of the Legion dugout.

Dee Dee, meanwhile, is sitting on the pitch with his head in his hands wondering if his uncle or Gigi is going to be the first to skin his stupid, hairy hide.

He is so distraught that he doesn't even see Harry, who taps him on the shoulder and tells him to get his chin up.

"Come on," says Harry, "we can take these boys, easy. Besides, we can't let Vic lift another hundred K. But first things first, I'm going off."

And then all of a sudden, it is men versus boys.

Dee Dee slots himself up front with Big Igor and starts banging in goals like there's no tomorrow. It's so one-sided, they even bring on Stammering Stan for the last three minutes — and he becomes the first man ever to score in a cup final he's reporting on. Seven-one it ends to the Fianna, with Dee Dee Dunne becoming the first man ever to net five goals in a final.

Of course, no one is really happy, except maybe Red Rogan — and, naturally enough, the Chechens who don't know a curse what's going on.

❧

The Fianna are holding their post-match party at the City Hotel and invite the Legion along for a consolation drink and to celebrate Red Rogan's engagement to Gigi.

Despite losing the game, Switchblade Vic is beaming and walking about with his arm around the new son-in-law. The lucky bride-to-be, meanwhile, is in the corner numbing the pain with a tumbler full of neat gin.

Dee Dee's future looks little better either. Jimmy Fidget, Gerry the Hurler, Get-em-up Gormley and Dumpy Doherty, all of whom are businessmen and none of whom are particularly sympathetic individuals, are blaming him for conceding the penalty. They claim that Black Angus' effort was set to go over the bar and are insisting that Dee Dee pay them the £10k each they were due when Harry the Hurler scored first.

Worse again, Dee Dee has no idea how much the seriously interested parties — Harry the H and Tommy Bowtie — are going to try and recover from his lousy £400 a week paycheque.

Doctor Death, however, who is a good soul, assures Dee Dee he'll not be looking for his cut, before going over to console Gigi McCormick in turn. Indeed, the Doc spends quite a while chatting to Gigi, and even presents her with a little gift-box which he says is on behalf of the Fianna.

As is tradition, the losers pay to fill the trophy with drink. So Gigi takes it upon herself to arrange this and the Irish Cup is passed round the room. Gigi even manages to make a speech toasting the victors and — after swallowing hard — her husband-to-be.

Gigi is almost on her ear with all the gin and so gives the cup a miss, as does Dee Dee in the corner who doesn't feel much like drinking. Instead, they toast one another sombrely across the room with coffee cups.

But then, a very strange thing happens. All of a sudden the Derry Fianna players start couping over. Mid-sentence. Heads are whacking off tables, and bodies are slipping off chairs.

As Dee Dee looks round, stupefied, the Legion squad starts to follow suit — then the top table of Vic, Red Rogan, Harry and the rest of the Fianna board members.

Within the space of a minute, the only people left standing in the room are Dee Dee, Gigi, Doc Death and the waiter. Everyone else is slumped in a heap.

"This is where we make our exit," says an all-of-a-sudden alert Gigi skipping across to take Dee Dee by the hand.

"We've four hours head start before the little tablets the Doc prescribed wears off them. Though I think for Red it'll be a bit longer as he's after pinning a double-dose."

"So what makes you think I'll run away with you? Unless maybe you're going to drug me too."

"Because," says Gigi, steering them towards the door, "the only thing hotter than me is the Porsche you'll be driving to Dublin. I don't know if you can handle the powerful engine, though. It's got one hell of a charge — and it needs just the lightest of touches."

"I love it already."

"I'm not talking about the car, Monkey Boy."

"Neither am I," says Dee Dee, as they scuttle out through the little wicket gate to the garage.

❧

Now, both you and I would be certain there are going to be ructions following the disappearance of Dee Dee and Gigi — but then again, we would both be wrong. The first inkling I get that things mightn't be as bad as they're painted is when I see Stammering Stan driving a brand new Volvo S80 into the Brooke Park car park about a month later. He is late for his Wednesday night indoor game at the centre, so I catch up with him over a pint of Coldflow in DaVinci's after the match and ask him for the latest.

"Strictly off the record," he explains, "we are just after

getting very substantial win bonuses — courtesy of Switchblade Vic. Vic, as you might imagine, is sweating the night before the final and rings Harry with a proposal. He offers to buy Harry out of the bet for £100k. But Harry hangs tough for a while, and eventually they agree on double that. Way Vic looks at it, he's still saving quite a bit of dough."

"Why then is Harry playing in the final like his life depends on it?" I ask.

"Simple," answers Stan, "he's having the time of his life. And he doesn't want anyone to know the bet's off in case they won't let him start. He also really wants to be the first to score — it's a matter of pride."

"So they're not angry at Dee Dee?"

"Not at all," says Stan, "apart maybe from Jimmy Fidget who's allergic to Valium, and is just out of intensive care. But even he'll be okay when he gets his cut."

"And what about Red Rogan?"

"Well," says Stan, "he's still very angry, and Dee Dee and Gigi may be forced to extend their honeymoon in Dublin for a couple more weeks 'til he cools down. But they're more than happy as Harry the H is after sending them on a twenty thou of an elopement present. In truth, though, Red's stock is running pretty low at the moment. I don't think he'll be playing for Legion much longer. Switchblade Vic was most distressed when we showed him the CCTV footage of this ginger-haired yeti putting a metal box underneath Harry the Hurler's car. Strange thing is, though, Red comes back and removes the same box about an hour later. Anyhow, any thoughts that Vic would have him for a son-in-law are now well and truly kyboshed.

"I mean, you can't be inviting criminals into your family, now, can you?"

FISHERMAN'S BLUES
AN INSPECTOR DEVLIN STORY
WRITTEN BY BRIAN MCGILLOWAY

The myth of Finneagas is one that has always stuck with me and, as may be evident from the story I wrote using it, it is the one key incident that really stood out; the blistering of the fish skin and the nature of accident. I also liked the idea that the fish confers knowledge, as this is what a policeman is constantly seeking. In this case, it's not so much the fish as the character of Finneagas who has the knowledge, of the river and those who fish it. And the pressing of the blister struck me as something that a man who means well but often makes mistakes would do — perfect for Devlin then. As for the nature of accident in crime? Not all killings are planned, nor are they motivated by the promise of millions.

—

The morning mists still clung low to the ground despite the fact the sun had already crested the Blue Stack Mountains to the east. Cattle moved spectrally across the fields behind us, while, in the expectation of food, three or four had gathered against the barbed wire fence near where we stood, silent witnesses to our work, their large, frightened eyes lolling in our direction.

I stood with the doctor I had called to the scene. To our left, sitting on the grass a few feet from the river bank, an ashen faced man, Sean Killian, was still trying to reconcile himself to the sight he had discovered thirty minutes earlier.

A man's corpse lay face down, his body caught in a shelf of tangled roots near the edge of the riverbank, his left arm suspended in the water. The man's head was partially submerged, loose strands of his hair drifting in the surface current of the river. The body was dressed in the combat fatigues popular among fishermen. On the bank a large net was discarded amongst an area of flattened grass.

"He's dead all right," the ME stated, fulfilling his legal obligation. "Crack to the head by the look of it." He leaned over the body, extending his leg to stabilise himself on the bank. He used a thick tongue depressor to brush back the black hair above the man's neck line.

I slid down the bank and squatted beside the body, one foot in the shallows of the river. The lazy drone of insects built around us closer to the water. A lone water boatman, skimming the river surface close to the dead man's head, drifted inquisitively near then shifted at a tangent away from us again.

I peered closely at the area the ME, John Mulronney, was exposing. I could see a rounded wound on the scalp, a few centimetres wide, the skin livid red.

"There's no blood," I said.

"Not externally," Mulronney agreed. "But look closely and you can see the dent in the bone. It looks like a single blow, small implement. Might not have meant to kill him." He glanced along the bank. "You might find in the post mortem that he drowned; knocked on the head, rolled down the bank, face in the water." He straightened up and nodded, though I had not spoken. "That's it, I'd say. You'll be looking for a fisherman's priest perhaps."

"Not in the clerical sense, I take it?"

"You know what I mean," he said, smirking. "It's a small

wound, inflicted on someone along a river bank; hardly Holmesian deduction."

"Check his pockets when you're down there too, would you?" I said.

Mulronney glanced at me askance. "Haven't you Scene of Crime people to do that?"

"Not today," I said. "Skeleton staff. There's a big luncheon in Letterkenny for the new Commissioner."

"And you're not there because?"

"I'm *persona non gratis* apparently," I said, shrugging.

Mulronney looked at me steadily. "You shock me," he managed finally, then bent again to frisk the lower half of the corpse. He located a wallet in the back pocket, which he handed to me after I pulled on my own latex gloves.

"Robert Price," I read from the bank card inside. I flicked through the contents. "Fifty quid in here too. Which suggests this wasn't a robbery."

Behind the bank card was a card for a local taxi service, an insurance claim helpline number and a laminated fishing licence with the dead man's name and date of birth, but no address.

"Ever see a fishing licence like this before?" I asked holding it up to Mulronney.

He shrugged, shook his head. "Finneagas'll know."

※

Finn 'Finneagas' Duffy was the bailiff who worked the river at night on the lookout for poachers. I knew he had his own prefab hut a few miles downstream from which he worked and in which he slept when he was doing nights. When Paul Black, one of our uniforms, finally made it to the scene, I left him on duty and, taking Robert Price's fishing card with me, drove down to Finneagas' hut.

I had to knock several times on the flimsy door before

Finneagas finally answered. Despite being dressed in a checked shirt, jeans and heavy woollen socks pulled halfway up his calves, he still looked as if he was only out of bed. In fact, he had yet to get to bed; the camp bed he kept in the hut sat in the corner, the blankets straight and undisturbed.

"How's things?" I asked, taking out my cigarettes and offering him one. He shook his head in response though gestured that I should go ahead myself.

"Just having breakfast," he grunted, rubbing at the ginger stubble of his jaw line as he moved over to the workbench by a small gas stove.

He lifted a small salmon from a plastic bag lying on the counter. "Confiscated goods," he explained.

"Poachers?"

He nodded. "Guy named Paul Carlin. Lifford man. Killeen's Restaurant are looking for fresh salmon for some dinner they have on this week; half the town's been on the river. They're paying top dollar. Carlin had caught a load."

As he spoke, he lifted a filleting knife from amongst a number of varying sized knives in a jar on his window sill and slit a line up the soft belly of the fish. He angled the body, began to saw lightly above the gills, removing the head, then shifted his position slightly and removed the tail.

I glanced away as he began to gut the creature, stood at the doorway of the hut and flicked my ash out into the morning breeze.

"Robert Price," I said. "Do you know him?"

"I do indeed," he replied. I glanced round to see him use the knife to scrape up the fish innards into the cupped palm of his hand and drop them into the plastic bag from which he had removed the fish. Wiping his hands on his shirttail he moved to his small stove and clicked the gas ring alight. As he twisted a knob of butter from a dish to his left into a small pan, he glanced over his shoulder at me.

"What about him?"

"He's dead. The ME reckons he was smacked on the head with a priest."

Finneagas lifted the two fillets of salmon he had cut and laid them both, meat down, into the pan.

"Maybe you'd come up and identify him, if you don't mind. I'll need an address for him," I said. "Has he family?"

Finneagas scratched at his chin. "I don't think so." He nodded at the pan; "Watch these," he said, then moved into the small office at the back of the hut to a filing cabinet.

I flicked my cigarette onto the ground and went over to the stove. The salmon was sizzling in the pan already, the silver skin greying as it heated, a rainbow glint rippling across the scales. A large heat blister was ballooning on the skin of one of the pieces and instinctively I pressed it with my thumb, bursting it and scalding myself in the process. I was sucking my thumb when Finneagas reappeared at my side with a sheet with Price's home address in Porthall.

"Don't let it burn," he scolded, taking the spatula and flipping the two cooking pieces of meat.

He bent and took a plate from the cupboard beneath the counter.

"Sure you won't eat? You're waiting for me anyway."

"I'm good," I declined. "But you take your time. He's not going anywhere up there."

🐟

Twenty minutes later we were back up at the scene. Finneagas leant over the corpse, seemingly undisturbed by his proximity to a dead body. Perhaps he realised my thoughts for he said, "I've helped pull enough floaters out of the river to not be shocked by a dead man, Inspector."

"*I* still find it kind of shocking," I said. "Thinking that that man stopped being last night and someone made it happen. Is it Robert Price?"

Finneagas nodded. "It's him."

"Any reason anyone would want to kill him?"

"Not that I can think." He glanced around us, taking in the net, the area of flattened grass. "His tray's missing," he said finally.

"So is his rod," I suggested, assuming this would have been the more obvious absence.

"He wasn't using a rod," Finneagas said. "He was using that net and he would have had a large plastic tray, a bit like a bread-man's tray."

"About the size of that?" I said, pointing to the area of grass.

"That's it. Looks like someone has stolen his catch."

"You don't think someone would kill him for a fish?" I asked incredulously.

"Not quite." Finneagas seemed distracted now, dropping to his knees and beginning to comb through the grass around where the net lay. Eventually, with a triumphant cry, he knelt up, holding in his hand a small, glass black creature slightly larger than a worm.

"That's what he was catching," he explained. "Elvers. Baby eels."

"You think someone killed him for baby eels?" I said, even less convinced than I had been when he suggested the cause was fish.

"These are rare," Finneagas said, his tone warming with enthusiasm. "They're born in the Sargasso Sea and come here to mature. Wild fresh water elvers have dropped in numbers over the past few years by a huge amount. You need a special licence to fish them. We only have a few people on the whole river here who have one."

I hunted through my pocket until I found the laminated card I had taken from Price's wallet and held it out.

Finneagas looked at it, nodded. "That's it. Bob could make £500 per kilo easily. If he had a good night, he could have netted a couple of grand."

"More than enough to smack someone on the back of the head for," I agreed.

By noon, I had searched through Bob Price's small flat in the centre of Porthall. He had no immediate relatives that I could trace. His neighbours claimed he was unmarried. He had been dating someone in Strabane, though they didn't know her name. He was a quiet, unassuming man, never got in trouble. Never held late-night parties — quite the opposite in fact; he was more likely to be up before dawn to go fishing.

His flat seemed to bear out this, the only pictures on the walls were of Price himself, holding aloft various fish he had caught. One wall of the living room held two shelves of trophies and small cups. One or two of the awards were fashioned in the shape of an angler. There was nothing to throw any further light on who might have killed him.

Despite being warned by my superintendent, Harry Patterson, not to disturb the luncheon under any circumstances, I knew I would need to go back to the station and call in some more uniforms to canvass the river for witnesses.

When I got there, our desk sergeant, Burgess, had spread his considerable girth on a chair at the front door. He was studying a large laminated card intently, his face flushed and angry.

"Have you seen this?" he snapped at me.

"What is it?"

"What we're missing — the bloody lunch that crowd are getting in Letterkenny while we're stuck here."

"If it's any consolation, a free meal's rarely worth all the bullshit you'd have to listen to at those events."

"Salmon steaks," Burgess continued regardless. "With ginger, red chilli, coconut milk and lime."

"I've seen enough fish to do me for the day," I said, taking off my jacket and throwing it onto the front desk.

I walked down towards my office but Burgess wasn't finished. He waddled after me, reading from the menu.

"And what the hell're elvers on toast?"

"What?"

"Elvers on toast. Aren't those baby rabbits?"

"Those are leverets. Elvers are much more interesting."

I pushed past him, grabbing my jacket again.

"Where are you going now?"

"To lunch."

The kitchen in Killeen's restaurant was heaving with figures in white catering suits, bustling about carrying pots and pans. The cacophony of pans clattering made it almost impossible for me to hear the Chef, Tom Magill. Finally, despite his protests, I pulled him over to the back door of the kitchen, as much to have a smoke as to escape the noise.

"You're cooking elvers today, is that right?"

Magill tutted, rolled up the sleeve of his jacket, though it immediately slid down his arm again.

"I haven't time for this," he said. "I'll be done in an hour."

"I can't wait an hour. Who's your supplier?"

"Different people — whoever catches whatever we need."

"What about today? Who were your suppliers today?"

"Just the one for the elvers. He brought in a haul — enough for the whole lunch."

He gestured towards a large bread-man's plastic tray which lay discarded near the door, its interior surface slick under the reflected lights. I suspected, if we dusted it, we would find Bob Price's prints all over it.

"Who was he?"

"Carlin. Some guy Carlin from Lifford."

I checked the name of the poacher Finneagas had given me. "Paul Carlin?"

He nodded. "That's it. He got over a grand. Are we done?"

"One thing more — where are the elvers now?"

My superintendent, Harry Patterson, stood up when he saw me enter the dining room, picked up the last mouthful of food from his plate and, jamming it in his mouth, pushed back his seat and hurried over.

"You're meant to be keeping watch in the station," he said. "You better have a good reason for being here."

"A murder. How's your lunch?"

"Shit. They served my bloody table last. The Commissioner's on his dessert and we're only on the starter. What's the deal with the murder?"

"Don't worry. It's solved already," I said. "I'll be wanting to get forensics to check out the fishing equipment of a Lifford poacher named Carlin. I'm betting they find human blood on his priest."

He grunted approval as he swallowed the last mouthful of food. "You can organise that yourself. What are you doing here?"

"Looking for evidence," I explained. "And you've just eaten it."

THE LIFE BUSINESS
WRITTEN BY JOHN GRANT

I can't remember how small I was when I first came across the legend of St Patrick having rid Ireland of its snakes, nor the book in which I read it — although I can almost make out, in my mind's eye, the open spread of text and the black-and-white illustration that filled the upper half of the left-hand page. My guess is I must have been seven or eight. What fascinated me about the legend at the time was not so much the mere banishment of the snakes — that seemed to my youthful mind the kind of feat any self-respecting saint could knock off before breakfast — but the fact that Patrick was supposed to have gotten rid of them **all***. This still seems to me the crux of the miracle. Surely snakes are like lice and fruit flies and memories of old embarrassments: try as you might, you can never quite eliminate the last of them.*

Half a century later and an ocean away, that childhood fascination has given rise to the story **The Life Business***. I don't think any other story of mine has taken quite so long in the nurturing.*

Other elements from my youth play their part in the story. At the time in which **The Life Business** *is set, Magilligan Point — later to be the site of a high-security internment camp for terrorist suspects during the troubles and now, I gather, a low-security prison with a focus on (and reportedly impressive reputation for) rehabilitation — was a run-down British Army camp. I have no* idea what other purposes it might have been put to, but one of its uses was as a training base where, during the holidays, school Army cadet forces could send contingents of teenaged boys like Peter Greenham.

And, in fact, like me. Although all the people and situations in the story are born from my imagination, as is the story itself (and most emphatically, Peter bears no resemblance to the teenaged me), the described layout of the camp is as close as my memory will permit to the real thing. Certainly the details of the lavatory building are seared into my brain: that intimidating outhouse really existed, and rather than use it we cadets did indeed pepper the surrounding landscape with unpleasant surprises for future foot-travellers.

One other vividly recalled element of my fortnight at Magilligan I was unfortunately unable to work in. This was an Army-issue mechanical potato peeler, a device that weighed about a tonne and in which I foolishly displayed interest the first night we were there, thereby defining my kitchen duty for the next two weeks. Imagine if you will, a hand-operated tumble dryer, the metal inner surfaces of which have corrugations like those on a file, although larger. You tipped in a bucket of potatoes, cranked like a mad thing for twenty minutes, and were rewarded with...well, you couldn't exactly say the potatoes had been peeled, but much of the skin was off them. Then you had to empty the device of all the scrapings. I think I was still finding the occasional tiny fleck of potato skin in my hair a week after I'd got home.

I visited Ireland, both north and south, a number of times during my teens, and developed a great fondness for the land and for almost all of the people I met there. Eventually, alas, it became too dangerous for a mainlander to visit, so I acquired myself an Irish girlfriend instead. But that really is a completely different story.

—

"I live in a world made entirely of memories now," the ageing man says, adopting a solemn oratorical tone, regarding us earnestly from the other side of the grey plastic tabletop, a lunar terrain of coffee rings and carved initials and obscenities. "They're the landscapes and gardens among which I walk. They're my companions. I can throw sticks for them and call them to heel."

One of his pale blue eyes seems slightly larger, slightly looser than the other, and reacts more slowly to movements in the room. Its outer corner is full of tears, and I suspect is always that way. He must have had a stroke at some stage, although he walked normally enough when he came in. He's drooling a little, like an over-eager cat. Perhaps these signs aren't the aftermath of stroke but merely side-effects of his medications.

As I watch, a dribble of tear makes its jerky way down his grey-stubbled cheek to join the well of drool at the corner of his mouth.

It's the way we'll all be, eventually. He just got there sooner than most of us.

Martinmas told me I'd find the old man an interesting case. So far there's been little evidence to support that assessment.

"Tell us a memory," says Martinmas now, seated alongside me.

The older man shifts his gaze slightly to focus on Martinmas' face. "With a lady present?" He gives a slight inclination of his head to indicate me. His accent is hard to place, like a stage actor's.

"She'll have heard worse," says Martinmas.

I join him in a small, professional chuckle.

"Even so. Even so. It wasn't her embarrassment I was thinking of. I'll not be telling you anything too juicy, then. Which is hard for me," he clumsily parodies the apologetic, "because so much of my younger life was filled with juicy bits. I was a lad whose arse the ladies couldn't help but want to get their hands on, if you'll take my meaning."

I smile, again professionally. "There's nothing you can say that'll shock me." As soon as the words are out I hate the way I sound so prissy.

He holds my gaze in a long stare, then looks down at his knotty hands on the table in front of him. They're big hands. He was once a big man.

"Even so..." he repeats.

❦

The first thing I noticed when the old, khaki Army bus stopped at Magilligan Point was how the grass covering the uneven ground between here and the steely grey water of Lough Foyle was the same colour as the rusted, corrugated iron of the roofs of the three long Nissen huts. Sixty teenaged boys, me one of them, would be spending the next two weeks in those huts, pretending to be soldiers by day and at night thinking about how maybe being at home wasn't that bad after all.

This was back in the mid-'sixties — must have been 'sixty-four or 'sixty-five, I'd be thinking. It was around the time my mum and my dad were having all the fights about the divorce they were planning to get. They'd separated a few months before; now they were wading into the legal stuff about who'd get the house and who'd get the car.

When the school cadet force put out the announcement that there'd be a field trip to the far side of the Irish Sea this summer, Mum had been one of the first parents to sign the forms.

My parents had already got me out from under their feet most of the time by sending me off to public school in Edinburgh — too far away for weekends home in Chelmsford. Now yet another sixteen days of uncomplication was theirs thanks to the good graces of the British Army.

And it was free.

Me? It was no skin off my nose to miss a few of their screaming matches. I was as glad to see less of my parents as they were to see less of me.

Once I got off the bus I noticed the second thing, other than the alien landscape, that was strange about this place whose name had had everybody on the bus doing Eccles and Bluebottle impressions ever since the ferry landed in Belfast.

It was the smell.

The air in the bus had been pretty full of the concentrated aroma of underwashed boys and incredibly hilarious farts, so I knew I shouldn't be complaining about the change to what now hit me in the face — and that was exactly what it felt like: being slapped across the face, not too hard, by a hand that was soft and quite small. A girl's hand. The shock came not from the strength of the blow but from its determination.

I was brought up by the sea, so I'm no stranger to what salty water and decaying seaweed and the occasional carcase of fish can conjure up between them, but this was something different. Away in the distance was the smooth surface of the lough, and beyond that the hills of Donegal loomed, an ancient purple against the sky's grey readiness to rain. The scorched-looking grass, kept tuftily short by as yet unseen wildlife, or just by the hostility of the soil so close to the water, added to the sudden sensation I had that I could have stood here a thousand years ago or even a million and not very much would be different except the lack of the Nissen huts and the pings and pops of the cooling bus and the yells of my schoolfellows and the masochistic masters — or cadet-force officers, should I say — who'd come with us to try to keep us under control.

There's a low-security prison at Magilligan Point now. Years before the prison came, those three dreary Nissen huts were replaced by H-blocks where the Brits kept suspects during the Troubles, but I imagine everyone who's ever had to be there, for however long, has breathed that same strong, unsettling air.

The place smells of time, and antiquity, and of people who walked here long before our kind.

"Are you just going to stand there dreaming, Greenham?" said Drac Johnson, the maths master, only he was Sergeant-Major Johnson for the next two weeks and I'd better not forget it. "There's supplies to be stowed before we can get our supper tonight. Get a move on! Chop, chop!"

He shoved my kit bag into my midriff and pushed me away in the general direction of the nearest hut.

༄

We stowed. We squabbled over bunks. We cooked. We ate. Darkness fell.

We discovered the latrines.

Even the timeless odours of Magilligan Point couldn't disguise those latrines from us — which was strange, because whoever had designed them had had a clever idea. The shed containing them was built straddling a biggish, busily flowing stream. Inside the shed were two long wooden benches with rows of standard lavatory-seat ovals cut out of them. There weren't any partitions or anything, no fear. To the British Army, crapping among the enlisted men was a spectator sport, with everyone being both performer and audience.

I'd been off the idea of public crapping since toddlerhood, and saw no reason to rethink my attitude now. I resolved to steal some bog roll and make do as best I could for the next fortnight out in the surrounding tundra.

I could see everyone else making the same decision.

༄

The days passed. Although it was part of my self-image at the grand age of fifteen to distance myself from my contemporaries — I hadn't managed to get as far as page fifty-two in *L'Étranger* for nothing, you know — I had a pretty good time. We were up every morning before the sun, of course, but I quickly got used to that. Although there was a certain amount of drilling and polishing of boots and brasses forced upon us, most of the time we were doing stuff like map-reading and hiking; a bunch of us even went up one of the local mountains, which was no Everest but offered from its summit a view of a satisfyingly large slab of Irish countryside.

We all peed on a cairn up there, watched by only clouds and birds.

※

From the bus window, as we'd been arriving, we'd seen a black corrugated-iron shanty in the middle of a rape field with the word PUB stencilled in enormous white capitals on its roof.

Chickenhearted that we were, none of us dared go there. It took us most of the first week to work out that the masters — officers — were sloping off to PUB at nights after they'd bedded the rest of us down. They probably went not so much for the drink as to use the pub's lavs.

They tried to get the school chaplain, a.k.a. Commander Sparrow, to stay behind, but he was having none of it.

After this discovery, you'd have expected we boys to be more relaxed about the after-dark curfew the officers had imposed upon us, but no. Except for essential excretory excursions, our curious schoolboy sense of honour kept us inside the huts at night — oh, and except for the occasional brave soul who dared slip out for a ciggy; for some reason that was allowable within our code of ethics.

I think it was the Monday after our first weekend at Magilligan that I woke in the middle of the night and realised I was going to have to go out. No question of using the latrines, of course — not even at three in the morning when the place was deserted. Think how much worse it would be if someone else *did* stumble in upon you. You'd be like the last two people left alive in all the world, with nowhere else to look.

Guts wrestling, I slid off my bunk and groped through my kit bag for the embarrassingly girlie flashlight my mother had given me for the trip. There was enough moonlight coming in through the grimy windows for me to see my way to the door, but I'd need the torch once I was outside because otherwise I'd be risking a sprained ankle among the treacherous half-swamps of the point.

"What the fuck're you—?" said a voice.

"Sssh."

"Piss off, then, Greenham."

Springs creaked as whoever it was turned over and went back to sleep.

I crept outside and leaned against the hut wall as I got my feet into the gymshoes I'd brought with me from my kit bag. Away in the distance I could hear the waters of Lough Foyle dallying with the beach and, closer by, the stream was holding a whispered argument with itself as it negotiated the rocks in its bed. Other than that, there was a sort of claustrophobic emptiness pressing in upon me from all sides. Above, there was a three-quarter moon and more stars than God ever knew to count.

Shoes on, I moved swiftly across the little misshapen square compound formed by the sides of the huts and the bus, which was occasionally used to take us out for longer expeditions but most of the time just sat there looking as if it were reading its newspaper and smoking its cigarette and hoping no one would ask it to do anything.

Sometimes at nights we'd hear sounds through the metal walls of the hut and tell each other there were wolves and bears still at large in Ireland.

This didn't seem so very funny now.

Once I was outside the compound I clicked on my torch. The latrine shed was off to my left and I had to make at least some pantomime of heading in its direction in case a master stuck his head out of a window behind me and asked me where the hell I thought I was going. After a few tens of yards I abandoned the pretence and turned instead towards the coast. The nearer you got to the water the softer and sandier the ground got, and the easier it was to scoop out a hole to crap into, then cover up your poop afterwards.

Away from the buildings, I felt like I was moving through a tunnel, the two concentric ellipses of the torch's light bouncing along the rough ground in front of me. The clamour in my guts was growing (*Those damned liquorice allsorts...!*) and I broke into a jog, whatever the dangers of potholes underfoot.

When I reckoned I was far enough from base camp, I bent over, checked quickly that I hadn't chosen a spot someone else had used before me, and scrabbled at the ground. Soon I was able to pull back a divot of grass and toss it to one side. I was standing in what I think is called a sinkhole, a place where a circle of ground seems to have dropped a few feet below the level of the rest. The terrain around Magilligan Point was full of them.

I tugged down my pyjama trousers, then on second thoughts pulled them right off and tossed them aside.

Moments later I was feeling much easier about life.

I wiped myself thoroughly using the bog roll I'd brought, covered up the evidence, and readied myself for the trek back to my warm bunk.

It was then I heard the voices.

"D'ye have him?"

"Sure I have him. D'ye want me to hit him again?"

"Just make sure he doesn't wake up. Not yet."

I froze where I was, halfway through picking up my pyjamas. Gradually, gradually, as if moving quickly would be noisier than moving slowly, I leaned down and switched off my torch, which I'd left lying on the crude grass. The shaft of light that had been bathing my gymshoed feet disappeared.

It didn't occur to me in the slightest that I might be in any danger. At the same time, I was terrified of being caught out here. Though none of the masters had said in so many words that crapping alfresco was forbidden, we were all of us aware that it almost certainly was.

With the same exaggerated slowness as I'd bent down, I straightened up again, still holding my mother's blasted Rupert Bear flashlight. I grabbed my pyjama trousers and began getting into them.

"He's a heavy fucker, isn't he?"

"And fat."

"Yes, fat. Fat as well as heavy. The fucker."

"Just hold on to his feet and stop talking, Lar."

They were coming closer.

Still I didn't move.

The fringed edge of a cloud began to slide across the moon.

The moon? Oh, *Jesus!*

Obviously the strangers in the dark hadn't seen me, but they had only to look in this direction and they'd be bound to notice the torso of a boy sticking up above the surface of the ground.

I dropped into a crouch, thankful for the sinkhole I was in.

"Funny thing, him being so fat, the way his wife's such a

pretty little thing."

"Shut up, Lar, you daft gobshite."

"I was just saying, Billy."

"I *know* what you were saying."

"It's just, that Maire, I've seen the way you look at her sometimes."

"I don't look at her. I mean, I *don't* look at her."

"Get the knickers off her and I'll bet she—"

"I said, shut *up.*"

They were dragging a heavy weight between them. I could hear it scratching along the coarse grass. I knew only too clearly what that weight was.

I wished I didn't.

The other thing I could hear far too clearly, curled as I was almost into a ball at the bottom of that shit-smelling sinkhole, was the way my heart was thumping.

Before I'd just been worried about being caught and getting hell for being out of bounds. Now it had finally penetrated my thick adolescent skull that very much worse might happen to me if I were found.

Hitchcock should have filmed this, I thought, hoping to use my trick of distancing myself from the situation to calm myself down, *and Erskine Childers should have written about it.*

What had Childers' hero been doing when he'd heard the whispering that led to his great adventure?

Not standing there trying to work out how to finish tying his pyjama cord while he'd got a Rupert Bear flashlight in one hand, that was for sure.

I risked a peek over the edge of the crater in which I was sheltering.

"Oh, hello, Billy," said one of the voices. "We've got a friend."

"Sixty of you?" said Billy. He was a big man but nonetheless by some margin the smaller of the two. His face was wizened like a gnome's, though otherwise he didn't seem old.

"About that number, yes," I said, my teeth chattering.

They didn't seem to have any weapons. And they hadn't threatened me in any way. They didn't need to. Lar, who'd picked me up out of my hiding place, was half the height of a house and almost as wide. He looked to be hardly out of his teens, with a wispy stubble of blonde beard clinging to his broad, shiny face. He stood behind me as I sat on a tussock of sharp-bladed grass facing Billy. Swarms of alcohol fumes hung around both men; Billy had offered me a swig from his flask but I'd refused, telling him primly that I was underage for that. The truth was I didn't want to swallow his spit.

Behind Billy, lying flat out and motionless on the ground, was the man they'd been carrying. Once, when the light from Billy's torch had strayed in that direction, I'd seen that the dead man's mouth — he had to be dead, surely? — was a mass of black, sticky blood where someone had been pulling out or breaking off his teeth.

That was why Billy and Lar didn't need to threaten me.

"And they're all as big and tough as you?" said Billy.

Lar chuckled.

"Most of them bigger," I said. "And we have some mast...some teachers with us."

An image of the Reverend Sparrow came into my mind, smoking his perfumed Dutch pipe tobacco and with the leather patches always looking as if they were just about to pop off his elbows. In case these two Irishmen were telepathic, I hurriedly thought of Grizzly Bradshaw, the gym teacher, instead.

"So we'd better not waken them, had we, Peter?"

My name was one of the first bits of information they'd got out of me. I knew from the war comics I never read that it was standard practice to give out your name, rank and serial number when captured by the enemy, so I assumed it was okay to give them just the name.

I shook my head. No, we'd better not waken them. If we did, some of them might see my Rupert Bear flashlight, sitting on the ground between me and Billy. I could try to pretend it was Billy's, but no one would believe me.

"Be like poking a wasps' nest," observed Lar from behind me.

"Which we don't do," agreed Billy, "for fear we might get our bottoms stung."

Lar laughed.

Billy took another glug from his flask. It seemed to be bottomless. I was sure he'd already drunk its contents three times over.

"Which leaves us," said Billy, wiping the back of his hand across his mouth, "with the small problem of what we're going to do about you, eh, Petey boy?"

From somewhere I found the courage — or perhaps it was just that I didn't want to think about any of the possible answers to that question — to ask a question of my own.

I pointed at the body behind Billy. The man was fat, just like Lar had been complaining.

"Who's that?"

Billy half turned his head, as if he needed to check.

"That, Petey, is Dennis McLeary. Dennis has been a bad boy, and has had to be spanked."

"His wife is—" began Lar.

"His wife is neither here nor there, Lar, no matter how much her smiling face might fill many a man's dreams."

"I wasn't thinking of her—"

"Enough, Lar." Where just a moment before Billy's voice had been mellow and slightly slurred, now there was an edge of steel to it. "That's enough. Now, where was I?" His shoulders relaxed again. "Ah, yes, I was telling our young friend about Dennis McLeary. You, see, Petey boy, until quite recently I could have sworn that Dennis McLeary was a friend of mine too, just the same way as you are yourself. Only then there was evidence came to light that he wasn't a friend to me at all, that he was blabbing away about all the things I'd thought were secrets between us, babbling to people who're *definitely* not my friends. Do you understand how much that discovery pained my trusting heart, Petey boy?"

I shrugged, and shuddered. Maybe the blood around Dennis' mouth hadn't come from just his teeth being extracted.

"He's put me in a position that I can only describe as being one of great embarrassment," Billy was continuing. "If it hadn't been for the fact that I have ears of my own in the places where Dennis was doing his whispering, I might never have known what was going on until I was looking at the world through a barred window, if you'll be understanding my meaning."

A police informer. That was what Billy was telling me Dennis McLeary was — or had been. Which meant Billy was some kind of a criminal. There'd been talk that the resentment between Ulster's two communities, Catholic and Protestant, was beginning to boil up again, but there'd not been enough trouble for the school to think twice about sending three score of its precious pupils here to Magilligan Point. And clearly the Army hadn't been worried either — aside from a corporal who'd said a few words of hello to the masters on our arrival and then driven away in a Jeep, we'd seen not a sign of a regular soldier.

It occurred to me I hadn't the faintest idea if Billy was a Catholic or a Protestant militant, or even a militant at all. Maybe this had nothing to do with the sectarian unrest and he was just someone who'd been handling hot tellies.

I didn't really think that, though.

There was something in his eyes, glinting in the torchlight, that told me Billy was being driven by a cause.

"Do you know why there aren't any snakes in Ireland, Petey boy?" said Billy, seemingly apropos of nothing.

"Saint Patrick," I said. "He's supposed to have driven them all out of the island, with God at his shoulder to help him do it."

"They teach you better than I'd have thought they would, in that fancy mainland school of yours. Well, I'm a bit like Saint Patrick, you see, Petey. I'm driving a snake out of Ireland. A big fat snake with a big fat mouth — a big fat snake called Dennis McLeary. Are you taking my meaning?"

I ignored the question. "Except," I said, "the trouble with the story about Saint Patrick and the snakes is that it's complete bollocks."

Billy's eyes narrowed. "What'd be making you think that?"

"There's no way you can ever get rid of the snakes entirely from somewhere, not once they're fully in occupation. The only way you can drive out all the snakes is if there weren't any snakes there to begin with."

"And is that the gospel truth?"

I nodded.

"You're a scientist, are you?"

"I've got an O-level in Biology," I answered weakly.

Lar shifted on his feet behind me, becoming impatient.

"Someone's going to start wondering where I am," I said, my voice sounding frail in the cold dark air.

"I don't hear any sound of upheaval, do you, Lar? No din of people being turned out of their beds to form a search party."

Even though I couldn't see him and wasn't about to turn my head to look, I could sense Lar pantomiming, raising a cupped hand to his ear. "Just the waves lapping gently against the shore, Billy. And the moonlight caressing the—"

Billy giggled, a surprisingly girlish sound. "Quite the poet, aren't we, Lar, my boy? Quite the poet."

Lar nudged my rear end with the side of his foot. "We can't stay here forever, Billy. We need to decide—"

"I know, I know." Billy raised his hand as if beating back a fusillade of questions. "But we owe it to him not to rush the judgement too much."

"And there's Dennis as well."

"There truly is." Once more Billy turned to look at the big carcase. Dennis hadn't moved since they'd dumped him down and Lar had pulled me from my concealment. I was pretty sure Dennis was dead. Although it was difficult to tell in the uncertain light, there seemed to be no rising and falling of his chest. I'd never seen a dead body before, not even at Gran's funeral. I felt I was lacking in expertise. I also felt that, if through some miracle I managed to survive this night, I'd have changed from a boy into a grown man just because of having seen a dead body.

God had never listened to me before, and especially He hadn't listened when I'd explained to him how good it would be if He could do something about the way things were worsening between Mum and Dad, but now I sent Him up an urgent little bundle of pleading anyway.

"Do you know what this is, Petey boy?"

My attention had wandered. Billy's words drew it back again. From somewhere he'd produced a gun, and now he was holding it out, flat on his open palm, in my general direction.

"If you were about to say 'water pistol', Petey, that's the wrong answer," said Lar from above me.

Curiously, it was Lar more than Billy I was frightened of, out there in the night. I'd met his kind before — big boys who seemed affable and jovial until the very moment something made them decide they needed to beat the shit out of you. And, all the while they were punching and kicking you, you could see through the haze of your blood and your tears and your pain that they were still smiling that same cheerful, appealing smile. Billy was at least pretending to think of a way they could leave me alive while still protecting their own backs. If Lar had been the one in charge I'd have been dead already. And he might have enjoyed himself a bit while making me that way.

I tried not to think of what could be in store for Dennis McLeary's widow, when Lar came to call on her. And it *would* be Lar who came to call on her, not Billy, whatever either of them might think now.

"It's a gun," I said, making as if to push his hand away. "Of course I know that. What do you think we've been lugging around on our parades all week long?"

Billy had a sudden thought. "They loaded, those guns of yours?"

"You mean, do we have ammunition for them? Yes. Obviously we do."

"What kind of guns are they?"

"Three-o-threes, mainly. A scattering of two-twos."

He smiled slowly. "Ancient rubbish."

"Ancient rubbish," I agreed. "But they're guns, still."

I could see he'd been wondering if our armoury was worth raiding, and had now decided it wasn't.

"Are you going to shoot me?"

"I'm hoping not, Petey boy."

"You know, there must be a million people called Billy in Ireland."

"True."

"And plenty of people called Lar."

"Likewise true. And who's to say those are even our real

names?"

Silence lay between us. All three of us knew that particular notion of his wasn't going anywhere. I'd heard them use the names before they'd known I was listening.

"But—" Billy broke the quiet, shaking his head sorrowfully "—there aren't a million people in the *whole wide world* who're called Dennis McLeary, now are there? And who'll be being looked for high and low come tomorrow? Whichever way I examine these matters, Petey boy, there just seems to be no way we can let you go, free to sing like a lark."

"What are you going to do to him?" I said, stalling for time.

"To Dennis? Oh, Dennis is going for a long, long swim at the bottom of the lough, is where he's going. Which reminds me — Lar, could you go and be gathering us some rocks and stones? We need to fill the fat man's pockets so he'll not be floating out to sea. Petey will be safe enough here with me to look after him."

Lar lumbered off, leaving the two of us on our own.

"But what if Mr McLeary's not dead yet?" I said.

"What does that matter?"

It was a cold answer.

"You need to be thinking a bit less about McLeary's fate, Petey boy, and a bit more about your own."

Was this going to be it? A bullet in the brain and then an eternity bobbing alongside fat Dennis in the darkness at the bottom of Lough Foyle?

I sent off another package of requests for mercy in the general direction of God, not that I expected Him to notice. The fault was my own. I'd never been entirely convinced of His existence and the events of tonight, rather than causing me to cling to the hope of Him as a drowning man to a straw, the way all the clichés say should happen, had made me increasingly of the mind that he was just a myth.

A nasty, dangerous myth, if Billy and Lar here were two of His foot-soldiers.

And if there wasn't a God then there almost certainly wasn't a life after death, either. To be honest, I'd always relied even less on the possibility of the afterlife than I had upon that of God, but it was nice to feel everything interlocking so neatly.

Either I was thinking more logically, more dispassionately than ever before or I was in a complete blind funk and filling my head with rubbish thoughts so I wouldn't have to face the immediate future.

Or lack thereof.

Because if there *wasn't* an afterlife, if there was no judgement awaiting me, then death didn't seem so very frightening after all. Assuming it was a painless death. In this context it was reassuring that Billy had a gun — he wouldn't have to rely on Lar pounding my skull to mush with a rock. Death itself could surely be no worse than having to watch powerless as the pillars of my existence were being pulled apart and tumbled down in wreckage, of knowing that the only part anyone wanted me to play in the unfolding tragedy was to stay out of the way as much as much as possible — to be out of sight, out of mind, so that any tears I shed weren't seen and therefore didn't exist.

I decided to make one final attempt at the life business, just for the sake of appearances if nothing else. I'd go into oblivion more fulfilled if I knew that at least at the last I'd given it my best shot.

"I could promise I'd never tell anyone," I said.

"You could, could you? And what makes you think I'd believe in your promise?"

"I'd give you my word."

"And what would that be worth?"

"Plenty. I'm good at keeping secrets. I have to do it a lot."

"What kind of secrets?"

I started to speak, then bit back the words. I wasn't going to start telling him the things about Mum I didn't tell Dad or the things about Dad I didn't tell Mum.

Or the things about me I didn't tell either of them.

"They'd not be secrets if I told you," I said at last. "We've only just met."

Billy laughed aloud and slapped my knee with his free hand, the hand that wasn't still holding the pistol. "I like you, Petey. Oh, I do surely like you. But—"

"Even if I broke my word, and I wouldn't, what would I have to tell anyone? They're going to be pretty certain Mr McLeary's dead when no one can find him, aren't they? And I'll bet they'll have a fairly clear idea who did it. If he's been grassing on you" — I liked the professional way I used the term "grassing on you", so I repeated it — "If he's been grassing on you, you're the first person they're going to be looking for. And Lar? Well, he's not so very difficult to notice, is he? So tomorrow everyone's going to be hunting for you and Lar *anyway*, and the most I'd be able to tell them — even if I broke my promise, which I wouldn't — is what you've done with the body. Which piece of information wouldn't be of much use to anyone because how're they going to find him at the bottom of Lough Foyle?"

"But what about tonight? What's to stop you running back to your barracks as fast as your legs will carry you and rousting out those three-score fierce wee warriors of yours?"

I'd been right. He didn't want to kill me if he could help it. He was looking around for some excuse not to have to.

"You could tie me up, gag me," I said, pressing home what I was beginning to hope was my advantage. "By the time anyone found me in the morning the two of you would be long gone. And Dennis McLeary too."

"Uhuh, uhuh." Billy took the gun in his other hand and

began slapping it gently on the palm where it had lain. "You're not daft, are you, Petey boy?"

"And I'd even have a reason to keep my mouth shut."

He raised an eyebrow. "And what would that be?"

Very deliberately I answered him. "I'll help you fill up Dennis McLeary's pockets with rocks and stones. I'll make myself an accessory. That way I'll have as much cause as you and Lar to keep quiet."

"I'm not sure that exactly makes sense," said Billy after a long pause, "but I'll give you credit for making a good argument. And I'll not say no to the offer of helping load up our Dennis with rocks. Afterwards? Well, afterwards we'll see."

I forced myself not to say anything more, not to risk ruining the good work I'd done. Billy was already halfway convinced there was a way out of this that didn't involve killing me, and by the time we'd finished giving poor Dennis his ballast the other half would have taken care of itself, I was certain. Then my thoughts sobered. There was always Lar to consider. Maybe Lar would change Billy's mind, once he got back here...

Which he did, right then, bearing an armload of big, water-rounded boulders. It was a good thing he was such a giant. I don't think I could have carried all of those even if you'd put them in a rucksack for my back.

Lar let the rocks crash to the ground beside Dennis McLeary's feet. One of them bounced with a crack off the rest and landed with a soft, sickening thump smack in the middle of McLeary's groin.

There wasn't any reaction from the fat man.

Billy snickered. "I'd say that answers your question, Petey boy, as to whether Dennis is dead or not."

My stomach tried to rebel, but I refused to let it.

"Shall we set to work?" I said.

Once we'd got started, once I'd learnt to stop thinking about Dennis McLeary as a human being from whom the life had fled — from whom it had been expelled — and started just treating his carcase like an inanimate, irksomely unwieldy object that we had to drag between us down to the water's edge where we located, bobbing in the shallows, a little rowing boat some confederates of Billy's had left there earlier...

Once Dennis McLeary's corpse was just a fucking *nuisance*, then I found it all very much easier. He was a side of beef, or a slaughtered pig in the butcher's window.

Billy and I did the hauling. Lar had been told — *you stupid gobshite!* — to pick up the stones from where he'd dropped them and carry them down to the shore alongside us. We'd load up Dennis McLeary with the stones once we were out on the water, not before.

I lost my Rupert Bear flashlight at some stage while we were heaving the dead weight of McLeary into the boat.

I couldn't see how we were going to get the three of us — and the stones — in beside it, but we managed.

One foot planted firmly on McLeary's chest, the other between Billy and me where we sat on the boat's second seat, Lar rowed us out from the shore until we could see nothing at all of the land. We might have been floating in some distant limbo, with the stars and the reluctant moon above and a restless obscurity below.

"Here'll do," said Billy.

"Will I be rowing back two of us or three?" said Lar pointedly.

"I've still not decided."

"Ah."

I knew, I knew — surely it was definitely a matter of my *knowing*, not just of my hoping — I knew that Billy had already decided all three of us were returning to shore once the object called Dennis McLeary had been disposed of.

"I was just asking, like," said Lar cheerfully. He winked at me. "Nothing personal."

"Here's far enough," said Billy, ignoring Lar's remark.

As soon as we'd got to the water's edge, Billy had pocketed his own torch. He hadn't needed to tell me why. There was no gain in sending reflections dancing across the water all the way to Donegal, or back behind us to anyone who might have wakened at Magilligan. In the gloomy moonlight I couldn't know what it was Billy was doing except that he was making a great rustling about it.

He must have sensed my incomprehension.

"Plastic carrier bags," he said. "Fat Dennis has only got so many pockets. The bigger stones we'll put into the bags and tie them on to him. It takes longer than a dozen lifetimes for plastic to rot. By the time it does, he'll be just bones — and so will we."

"Ah," I said, as if I'd already known all this.

Ten or twenty minutes later, at grave risk of capsizing the boat, we managed to roll the uncooperative mass over the edge. I'd have liked to think that the dead eyes of Dennis McLeary gave the sky one last nostalgic glance before the water covered them, but that wasn't so. He — he and the anchors we'd tied around his wrists and ankles and neck — sank beneath the surface instantly, leaving hardly a ripple on the lough's face.

"And?" said Lar, nodding his head towards me, once McLeary had gone.

"I've become very fond of Petey boy," said Billy.

"Haven't we all?"

"He'll say nothing."

"I'm sure that's what he'd want you to believe. You're not growing soft in your old age, are you, Billy, my one true friend?"

"I'll never grow soft, Lar. You know that."

"Then...?"

Billy had the gun in his hand. He looked at me, then at Lar, then at me again. The oily metal of the gun glistened like a slug's trail in the moonlight.

"I trust him as much as I do you, Lar. He's given me his promise as a fine young English gentleman and probably a Boy Scout, although he didn't mention that...Are you a Boy Scout, Petey?"

I nodded. I knew what was about to happen as if I'd scripted it myself.

"That's a promise not to be ignored lightly, Lar. Whereas you? All you want to do is fuck Maire. Isn't that it?"

"I never—"

The sound of the gunshot was far quieter than I thought it would be.

And weighing down Lar with the remaining stones and plastic carrier bags was far worse than I thought it would be — far worse than doing the same to Dennis McLeary had been.

McLeary hadn't still been warm.

But I got through all of this somehow. And then, with Billy's gun pointing at my face, I rowed us back to shore.

It was Drac Johnson who found me in the morning. I can't have been lying there longer than a couple of hours. Billy had pulled off my pyjama trousers and stuffed them into my mouth as a gag, which was a rotten thing to do because they tasted the way shit smells and because it meant Drac and all the others who came after him could stare at my shrimp-like penis and my walnut balls in the freezing air of morning. Still, as Drac said while untying me and carrying me off to put me under a hot shower, just about anything was better than being dead from exposure, wasn't it?

I remembered how, in the middle of the night, I'd begun to see death as a warm and welcome harbour, and I said nothing to him.

In the years that followed, I said nothing to anyone else, either — I kept my promise to Billy. Why not?

Life, on the other hand, didn't keep its promise to me. Mum and Dad both did just exactly what they wanted to do, which meant I became an orphan even though my parents were still alive, with me shuttling between them and irritatingly reminding them of my existence. They practically shouldered each other aside when it came to paying for the various therapists I saw, because coughing up mere money was far easier than accepting they had a son.

I had far more urgent things on my mind for the next few years than telling anyone about what had happened to Dennis McLeary.

And to Lar. Although, to tell you the truth, I was rather glad about what had happened to Lar.

If he'd have stayed alive, he'd have grassed on me and Billy.

The old man keeps on speaking. I suspect that sometime soon he's going to begin repeating himself, but what do I care, that's part of the job, et cetera, et cetera, et bloody cetera.

Martinmas tugs on my sleeve, nods towards the door.

"Call me by my name," says the old man. "I don't ask you for forgiveness, I'd not ever do that, but I do ask you to know me for who I am."

It seems to me we're just getting to the point where therapy can start. I look quizzically at Martinmas. The patient notices nothing.

"I'm Patrick," says the old man. "I'm the driver out of snakes. I'm the saviour of the Emerald Isle, whatever anyone else might say. I drove out all the serpents who—"

Martinmas' tug on my elbow grows more urgent.

I give in, assuming he must know what he's doing. We stand up, pushing our chairs back on the marbled green vinyl tiles that must have seemed like a concession to luxury when they were first laid in this institution. Now, of course, they're curling up at the corners. This is not the Ritz.

It's my first day here. I don't have the option of disagreeing with Martinmas. I follow him out into the corridor.

"So Peter's been haunted all this time by the decisions he made that night?" I say. "Yet who could condemn him? He saved his own life. He crept out from under the shadow of a psychopath. He—"

"That's not altogether what happened," says Martinmas. He stops, making me stop with him, outside the little rectangular observation glass that looks from the corridor back into the room we've just left. The old man has put his head down on the table but I can see, even though I cannot hear, that he's still talking.

Still confessing, I suppose.

It must be hell, being Peter, knowing what you should have done but didn't.

"We think Peter Greenham was shot through the head on Lough Foyle in 1964 and dumped in the water alongside Dennis McLeary," says Martinmas, interrupting my thoughts.

For a moment I can't think of any way to reply.

Inside the silent bubble of his cell, the old man's still talking. He's raised his head now, and he's looking in our direction as if he can see through the one-way mirror. Leaning against the room's far wall there's an orderly watching everything with her arms crossed on her chest.

"So that isn't Peter?" As soon as I've uttered it, the question seems monumentally stupid.

"No," says Martinmas. "He's very convincing, isn't he? But he's not Peter. That's Billy Flanagan in there. You'll soon grow used to how many other people he is as well. Every day of the year, it seems like, Billy digs out a memory he thinks is his own. But it's someone else's, really — if it's a memory at all, and not just Billy's way of attempting to rationalise to himself the things he's done. To justify them, or maybe even to try to undo them, in a sense, by bringing his victims back to life. I'm certain, for example, that he genuinely did like Peter, the unfortunate kid he and Lar Meekin found that night at Magilligan Point. It didn't stop him getting rid of the evidence, though."

I swallow.

"Which side was he on?" I say.

"Who knows?" says Martinmas. "Not the side of Peter Greenham."

A nurse bustles past us, on her way to somewhere in a cloud of antiseptic.

I look at the floor, back up at the window. "How many people did Billy kill?"

Martinmas shrugs. "Who knows?" he says again. "Enough. Too many. Who can judge? That's not what we're here for. Our job is to try to understand him so we know better how to cope with others like him."

"That's what we should be doing, is it?" I say, still staring through the window.

"Yes," says Martinmas.

He's right, of course, however much I'd like him to be wrong.

For a few more moments Martinmas and I stand side by side watching as a mumbling, broken-down old man tries to rid himself of all his serpents.

Then we go off to the canteen, where Martinmas buys me a coffee.

ABOUT THE AUTHORS

TONY BAILIE

Tony Bailie's first novel, *The Lost Chord*, was published in 2006 (Lagan Press, Belfast). His new novel, *ecopunks*, will be published by Lagan Press in 2010. *Coill*, a collection of poems, was published by Lapwing Publications in 2005 and a second collection, *The Tranquility of Stone*, is due out soon under the same imprint. He lives in Co Down and works as a journalist in Belfast. His web site is www.tonybailie.com

TONY BLACK

Tony Black was born in New South Wales, Australia and grew up in Ireland and Scotland. An award-winning journalist he is the author of the *Gus Dury* series of novels — *Paying for It*, *Gutted*, *Loss*, and *Long Time Dead*. He lives in Edinburgh. Visit his website at www.tonyblack.net

KEN BRUEN

Ken Bruen was born in Galway in 1951, and is the author of *The Guards* (2001), the first of the *Jack Taylor* novels which have, to date, won ten awards.

Ken has a PhD in Metaphysics and spent twenty-five years as an English teacher in Africa, Japan, S.E. Asia and South America. His novel, *Her Last Call to Louis Mac Niece* (1997), is in production for Pilgrim Pictures. *Blitz*, *London Boulevard* and *The Guards* have been filmed and will premiere in 2010. *The Killing of the Tinkers* begins shooting in April and the new Taylor book, *The Devil*, comes out in June 2010.

GARBHAN DOWNEY

Garbhan Downey has worked as a journalist, broadcaster, newspaper editor and literary editor. He spent two years as a full-time student politician after graduating from University College Galway in 1987 and was Deputy-President of the Union of Students in Ireland. His debut fiction, *Private Diary of a Suspended MLA* (2004), was described in the Sunday Times as "the best Northern Ireland political novel of the century".

He has released six novels, the latest of which, *The American Envoy* (2010), was the first to be issued simultaneously as an e-book by an Irish publishing house. Downey lives in Derry with his wife Una and children Fiachra and Bronagh. www.garbhandowney.com

JOHN GRANT

John Grant is author of some seventy books, of which about twenty-five are fiction, including novels like *The World*, *The Hundredfold Problem*, *The Far-Enough Window* and most recently (2008) *The Dragons of Manhattan* and *Leaving Fortusa*. His "book-length fiction" *Dragonhenge*, illustrated by Bob Eggleton, was shortlisted for a Hugo Award in 2003; its successor was *The Stardragons*. His first story collection, *Take No Prisoners*, appeared in 2004. He is editor of the recent anthology, *New Writings in the Fantastic*, which was shortlisted for a British Fantasy Award. His novella, *The City in These Pages*, appeared from PS Publishing at the start of 2009.

In nonfiction, he co-edited with John Clute *The Encyclopedia of Fantasy* and wrote in their entirety all three editions of *The Encyclopedia of Walt Disney's Animated Characters*; both encyclopaedias are standard reference works in their field.

Among his latest nonfictions have been *Discarded Science*, *Corrupted Science* and *Bogus Science*; their successor, *Denying Science*, is subject to appear in summer 2011 from Prometheus. He is currently working on a book about *film noir*, on an investigation of Fundamentalist US hate groups, on a survey of end-of-the-world predictions, and on "a cute little rhyming book for kids about a velociraptor".

As John Grant, he has received two Hugo Awards, the World Fantasy Award, the Locus Award, and various other international literary awards. Under his real name, Paul Barnett, he has written a few books (like the space operas *Strider's Galaxy* and *Strider's Universe*) and for a number of years ran the world-famous fantasy-artbook imprint Paper Tiger, for this work, earning a Chesley Award and a nomination for the World Fantasy Award.

ARLENE HUNT

Arlene Hunt is 37 and the author of six crime novels, five of which are based on her creation, the *QuicK* investigation team of *John Quigley* and *Sarah Kenny*. Her latest book, *Blood Money*, will be published in March 2010. Arlene lives in Dublin with her husband, daughter, three annoying cats and her faithful basset hound, Opus. She is currently working on a new novel, a standalone which is based in the USA. When not writing, she likes to run long distance and kick/punch the hell out of a heavy bag in the gym.

DAVE HUTCHINSON

Dave Hutchinson was born in Sheffield in 1960. He's the author of one novel and five collections of short stories and the editor (with John Grant) of *Strange Pleasures 2* and (on his own) of *Strange Pleasures 3*. His stories have appeared in

Interzone, SciFiction, Revolution SF, Infinity Plus, DayBreak Magazine, the Lou Anders-edited anthology *Live Without A Net*, and the Ian Whates-edited anthologies *Celebration* and *Subterfuge*. His most recent publication is *The Push*, published by Newcon Press. He lives in North London with his wife, Bogna, and their cats, and he works as a journalist.

MAXIM JAKUBOWSKI

Maxim Jakubowski has toiled in the erotica and crime galleys for many years as writer, publisher, editor, reviewer (for Time Out and the Guardian), lecturer and bookseller. He edits the annual *Mammoth Book of Best British Crime*, now in its 7th year, and has also published *Paris Noir*, *London Noir* and *Rome Noir*, as well as 60 other anthologies. His last published novel was *Confessions of a Romantic Pornographer*, and his last collection of short stories was *Fools for Lust*. His next novel, *I Was Waiting for You*, will appear later in 2010. He also runs London's annual film and literature festival Crime Scene. He lives in London with his wife, the children having now flown the nest...

GARRY KILWORTH

Garry Kilworth was a service brat, born in York, 1941. He began writing at the age of 12 and hasn't stopped since. He delves in a variety of genres, from science fiction to historical novels, but his overriding love is the short story. His latest novel is *Scarlet Sash*, a detective-military novel set during the Anglo-Zulu wars of 1879, due out soon. Also coming shortly is a book of short stories set in Hong Kong, *Tales from the Fragrant Harbour*.

JOHN MCALLISTER

John McAllister holds an M.Phil. in creative writing from Trinity College, Dublin and has being doing readings and giving lectures in creative writing for some years.

John has published poems and stories worldwide, and has read in places as far apart as Cork, Ireland and Boston, Mass.

Major Publications include *The Fly Pool and other stories* (Black Mountain Press, 2003) and *Line of Flight*, a novel (Bluechrome Publishers, 2006). He was also joint editor for: *Breaking the Skin*, twenty-first century Irish writing, (Black Mountain Press, 2002), and *Hometown* (ABC Writers Network, 2003).

UNA MCCORMACK

Una McCormack is the author of three Star Trek: Deep Space Nine novels, published by Simon and Schuster: *Cardassia: The Lotus Flower* (2004), *Hollow Men* (2005), and *The Never-Ending Sacrifice* (2009). Her short fiction has appeared in various publications including *Glorifying Terrorism* (ed. Farah Mendlesohn), *Subterfuge* (ed. Ian Whates), *The Year's Best Science Fiction Vol. 25* (ed. Gardner Dozois), and Doctor Who Magazine. A Doctor Who novel, *The King's Dragon*, featuring the Eleventh Doctor, will be published by BBC Books in 2010.

She lives in Cambridge, UK, where she reads, writes, and teaches. Her ancestors came from the west of Ireland and, as far as she knows, never had any trouble with the Romans. Her website is www.unamccormack.com

BRIAN MCGILLOWAY

Brian McGilloway is author of the critically acclaimed *Inspector Devlin* series of novels. He was born in Derry, in 1974 and is currently Head of English in St Columb's College in the city. The Devlin novels have been shortlisted for both the CWA New Blood Dagger and the Irish Book Awards Crime Novel of the Year. The new Devlin novel, *The Rising*, will be published this year in hardback, alongside the paperback of the third novel, *Bleed A River Deep*. Brian lives near the Irish borderlands with his wife and their three sons.

ADRIAN MCKINTY

Adrian McKinty was born and grew up in Carrickfergus, Northern Ireland. He studied law and then philosophy at university in England. In the early 1990s he moved to New York City where he worked in bars and building sites illegally for three years before getting his green card and becoming a school teacher. In 2004, his first full length novel *Dead I Well May Be,* was shortlisted for the Ian Fleming Steel Dagger Award. He has published both crime fiction and young adult novels since then. In 2009, he moved to Melbourne, Australia.

SAM MILLAR

Winner of the Aisling Award for Art and Culture; Martin Healy Short Story Award; Brian Moore Award for Short Stories and the Cork Literary Review Writer's Competition. Work performed by the BBC. Author of best-selling memoir, *On The Brinks*, and crime novels *Dark Souls, The Redemption Factory, Darkness of Bones*, and the *Karl Kane* series of books, *Bloodstorm, The Dark Place and The Dead of Winter*, due October 2010.

T.A. MOORE

T.A. Moore is an arts professional with a background in documentary research and the community arts. Recipient of three Arts Council Awards, T.A. Moore is an active member of the vibrant Belfast Arts scene and a post-graduate researcher at the highly respected Seamus Heaney Centre for Poetry at Queen's University, Belfast. Currently content developer for CultureNorthernIreland, T.A. Moore has also edited Three Crow Press, the CWN Magazine and the literary magazine Ulla's Nib.

Her first novel, *The Even*, was published by Morrigan Books in 2008. The second, *Shadows Bloom*, will be published in 2010. Her short stories have been accepted for the *Barefoot Nuns in Barcelona, The Phantom Queen Awakes, Dead Souls* and *Blood Fruit* anthologies and to the FlashScribe, Three Crow Press, Weird Tales and Drops of Crimson ezines. T.A. Moore also won the Northern Woman Short Story Competition with *Island Life*, a merry tale of incest and death.

STUART NEVILLE

Stuart Neville's first novel, *The Twelve*, was one of the most critically acclaimed crime debuts of recent years with rave reviews in newspapers like the Observer and Daily Mail, as well as garnering praise from such authors as James Ellroy, John Connolly, Ken Bruen and Jeff Abbott. Its American edition, titled *The Ghosts of Belfast*, was selected as one of the top crime novels of the year by both the New York Times and the LA Times. The sequel, *Collusion*, will be published in summer 2010.

NEVILLE THOMPSON

Neville Thompson is the Dublin-born author of five bestselling novels. His work has been translated into French, German and Greek. His first novel, *Jackie Loves Johnser Ok?*, is being made into a film produced by famous French producer, Alain Attal.

Neville has also edited two books of prison stories, *Streetwise* and *More Streetwise*, as well as editing a book of short stories entitled *By The Blue Gate*.

Neville has written and directed over seven professional plays and produced three short films. When not writing he does workshops for adults and teenagers. He is the chairman of The Castlecomer Writers Festival, a yearly event in Kilkenny.

Currently Neville is writing another play. He also writes a weekly blog www.nevthompson.blogspot.com

ABOUT THE EDITORS

GERARD BRENNAN

Gerard Brennan is a Northern Irish writer with an increasing number of mouths to feed. When he is not tinkering with a novel, screenplay, stage play or short story he runs Crime Scene NI, a blog devoted primarily to Irish crime fiction. His short fiction has appeared in such anthologies as *Badass Horror*, *In Bad Dreams 2*, and will appear in Maxim Jakubowski's *Sex In The City: Dublin* anthology in 2010. Brennan's work has also been published in popular crime fiction 'zines such as ThugLit, Pulp Pusher, A Twist of Noir and Crime Factory. He is represented by Allan Guthrie of Jenny Brown Associates who is currently flogging his first novel, *The Wee Rockets*.

MIKE STONE

Mike Stone was born in 1966 in Stoke-on-Trent, England. Since losing most of his eyesight he has retreated from your world to travel the dark corners of inner space — or to put it more prosaically, he thinks "What if?" a lot. The signs are clear to those that know him well, for his one not-so-bad eye glazes over and he is rendered deaf to all English except for "Would you like a cup of tea, Mike?" He will then engage with reality long enough to ask if there are any biscuits before drifting off again. He supposes this can be very trying for those around him, but remains unrepentant.

He is the author of over fifty published short stories and the novella collection, *Fourtold*.

His vanity has a name: www.mylefteye.net

ABOUT THE COVER ARTIST

REECE NOTLEY

Reece Notley was born and lived in Hawai'i until her late teens when her feet grew itchy, and she wandered off to see the world. After chewing through a pile of books, a lot of odd food and a stray boyfriend or two, she eventually landed in Southern California which she believes to be a very nice place but seriously needs more rain.

She has a day job herding pixels for the marketing department of a nice company with a fantastic view of the San Diego seashore and fits in editing Three Crow Press, a sci-fi, horror, fantasy, and speculative fiction ezine (www.threecrowpress.com) in her not-so-spare time.

As of this moment, she admits to sharing the house with three cats, a black Pomeranian puffball, a bonsai Wolfhound and a ginger Cairn terrorist and is enslaved to the upkeep of a 1969 Ford Mustang Grand Coupe, a 1979 Pontiac Firebird and a Toshiba laptop.

AVAILABLE NOW

"In this grim fable, the stakes are suicide by Apocalypse, and the question is what can endure, and what refuses to end."

— *Elaine Cunningham*

THE EVEN WRITTEN BY T.A. MOORE

In the Even — a city built in the intersection between the real and the not — is ruled by the iron whim of the demon Yekum. Treachery is brewed amidst the ever-changing streets and ancients dwell there who have out-lived their purpose and grown jaded with their immortality. They want only to die and will take the whole world with them if they have to: suicide by Apocalypse.

Only Faceless Lenith, goddess, cynic and gambler, stands in their way. The fate of the world rests on her shoulders, and mankind didn't conceive her to be wise.

www.morriganbooks.com

AVAILABLE NOW

"These tales are sharp and uncompromising, bitter and moving."
— Paul Campbell, Prism Magazine

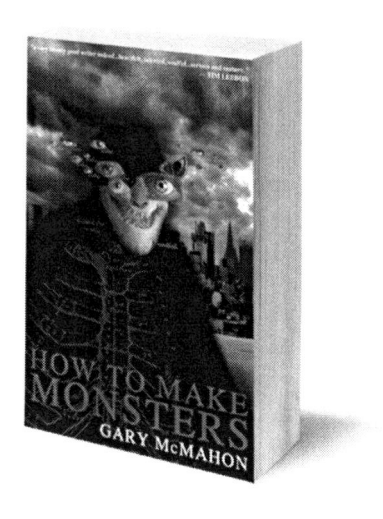

HOW TO MAKE MONSTERS WRITTEN BY GARY McMAHON

Since the dawn of mankind, we have always made our own monsters: the terrors of capitalism and corruption, the things between the cracks, the ghosts of self...terrible beasts of desire, debt, regret, racism...of family ties, and the things that get in the way of our aspirations...the familiar monsters of our own faces, of tradition, rejection, and the darkness that lives deep inside our own hearts...

Can you identify the component parts of your own monster?
Can you afford to pay the dreadful price of its construction?

www.morriganbooks.com

AVAILABLE NOW

"A brilliant premise of horror confined in twelve hotel rooms."
- *Australian Horror Writers' Association*

VOICES
EDITED BY MARK S. DENIZ & AMANDA PILLAR

In every room, there is a story.

In this hotel, the stories run to the wicked and macabre.

Well crafted psychological and supernatural horror offerings await you, each written by a master storyteller. Whether you are looking to be shocked, disturbed or out-right frightened, *Voices* will have something to titillate your nerves and make your hair stand on end.

Leave the lights on and brew a strong cup of tea, the voices in this room plan on keeping you up all night.

www.morriganbooks.com

AVAILABLE NOW

DEAD SOULS
EDITED BY MARK S. DENIZ

Before God created light, there was darkness. Even after He illuminated the world, there were shadows — shadows that allowed the darkness to fester and infect the unwary.

The tales found within *Dead Souls* explore the recesses of the soul; those people and creatures that could not escape the shadows. From the inherent cruelness of humanity to external malevolent forces, *Dead Souls* explores the depths of humanity as a lesson to the ignorant, the naive and the unsuspecting.

God created light, but it is a temporary grace that will ultimately fail us, for the darkness is stronger and our souls are truly dead.

www.morriganbooks.com

AVAILABLE NOW

GRANTS PASS
EDITED BY JENNIFER BROZEK & AMANDA PILLAR

Humanity was decimated by bio-terrorism; three engineered plagues were let loose on the world. Barely anyone has survived.

Just a year before the collapse, Grants Pass, Oregon, USA, was publicly labelled as a place of sanctuary in a whimsical online, "what if" post. Now, it has become one of the last known refuges, and the hope, of mankind.

Would you go to Grants Pass based on the words of someone you've never met?

www.morriganbooks.com

AVAILABLE NOW

THE PHANTOM QUEEN AWAKES
EDITED BY MARK S. DENIZ & AMANDA PILLAR

Love. Death. War.

The Morrigan goddess represented all three to the ancient Celts. Journey with our authors as they tell stories of love, war, hatred, revenge and mortality — each featuring the Morrigan in her many guises.

Re-visit the world of Deverry, and of Nevyn, with a previously unpublished tale by Katharine Kerr, watch the Norse gods meet their Celtic counterparts with Elaine Cunningham, meet a druid who dances for the dead with C.E. Murphy and follow the path of a Roman centurion with Anya Bast.

www.morriganbooks.com

COMING SOON

SCENES FROM THE SECOND STOREY
EDITED BY AMANDA PILLAR & PETE KEMPSHALL

Scenes from the Second Storey is an anthology that pays homage to an album that Morrigan Books' publisher, Mark S. Deniz, believes is one of the greatest of all time; Scenes from the Second Storey, by The God Machine.

Each story in this collection has been inspired by a track from the album. Quirky, dark, insightful and sometimes downright disturbing, these tales reflect the emotions and images our authors experienced when they heard 'their' song from *Scenes from the Second Storey*.

www.morriganbooks.com

THREE CROW PRESS

EDITED BY
J. LEE. MOFFATT, T.A. MOORE & REECE NOTLEY

Three Crow Press is an online magazine specializing in quality speculative fiction, fantasy (urban, dark and gothic), horror and steampunk, as well as non-fiction pieces and articles.

Well written young adult will be considered if the piece is within the 16+ market.

We are prepared to consider all forms of dark fiction works and are looking for stories that capture the imagination of the *Three Crow* staff. Please check submissions guides prior to submitting.

www.threecrowpress.com
www.morriganezine.com